P9-CCO-868

WHISPER THE DEAD

Recent Titles by Stella Cameron from Severn House

The Alex Duggins series

FOLLY
OUT COMES THE EVIL
MELODY OF MURDER
LIES THAT BIND
WHISPER THE DEAD

Other Titles

SECOND TO NONE
NO STRANGER
ALL SMILES
SHADOWS

WHISPER THE DEAD

An Alex Duggins Mystery

Stella Cameron

This first world edition published 2017
in Great Britain and the USA by
Crème de la Crime, an imprint of
SEVERN HOUSE PUBLISHERS LTD of
Severn House Publishers Ltd, Eardley House, 4 Uxbridge Street, London W8 7SY
Trade paperback edition first published
in Great Britain and the USA 2018 by
SEVERN HOUSE PUBLISHERS LTD

British Library Cataloguing in Publication Data
A CIP catalogue record for this title is available from the British Library.

ISBN-13: 978-1-78029-099-7 (cased)
ISBN-13: 978-1-78029-584-8 (trade paper)
ISBN-13: 978-1-78010-941-1 (e-book)

All Severn House titles are printed on acid-free paper.

Severn House Publishers support the Forest Stewardship Council™ [FSC™],
the leading international forest certification organisation.
All our titles that are printed on FSC certified paper carry the FSC logo.

FSC www.fsc.org
MIX
Paper from
responsible sources
FSC® C013056

Typeset by Palimpsest Book Production Ltd.,
Falkirk, Stirlingshire, Scotland.
Printed and bound in Great Britain by
TJ International, Padstow, Cornwall.

For Zipper, Boy, Maynard and Katie with love and gratitude

ONE

He seized the neck of the open bottle and slid it to rest on his chest, cradled the cool glass, closed his eyes to the lullaby sound of the whisky inside the bottle gurgling to the top.

A few drops hit his face and he reached for them with his tongue. 'Got you,' he whispered, sniggering, feeling the aromatic trickle on his lips. 'Waste not, want not.' And there it was within the subtle floral burst of scent, the soft, wood-smoke bite of eighteen-years-old Glenmorangie.

Sweet, sweet oblivion come to me.

He upended the bottle, used both hands to steady it. When his eyes slid open he couldn't see much. The lamp was off . . . wasn't it? Glass scraped between his teeth, chuddered, screeched. He choked, scrunched backward onto the pillows, heard the door to the sleeping compartment slam, closing him inside. The door. It closed, yeah. Being alone now was what he needed. Alone to fly.

Not enough room.

Couldn't cough.

Gagging – couldn't breathe.

The bottle was too heavy for him to lift. It crammed down into his mouth, his throat. Too heavy to push away.

He struggled to grab the bottle and found someone else's hands there. That hand – two hands – slapped his away.

Cracking under his teeth. *Let me go. Blood. It tastes sharp, sharp like the glass feels. Blood and glass.*

There was nothing to hold.

Alex Duggins sniffed, and blinked at an acrid stench coming to her in the waning afternoon light. That was not smoke from the chimney of some isolated cottage or farm.

The wipers pushed snow across the windshield of her Range Rover, packed in into a blinding sheet. Alex leaned forward, flinched away from flying mud.

Hurtling at her, bouncing over ruts in the frozen ground, a small filth-covered utility vehicle didn't slow down. If the driver saw her Rover, he ignored it, speeded up even, shot forward as if he wanted a collision. She didn't see the driver, only got the impression of a camouflage paint job that might be used in a war.

Alex yanked the wheel, steered onto the verge and pumped her brakes. Her tires were the best. They dug in and shuddered to a stop. She bowed her head and pressed a hand to her chest. Her heart thundered.

Still shaken, she searched the heavy, grey skyline for a source of the filthy smell of burning. She parked and got out. Her boots crunched into frosty grass and bracken beside a wide track leading up a gentle incline. If there weren't mature, leafless trees lining the way, anyone standing beside the rutted construction access might have concluded the developers had cut out a path for convenience. But they had used a lane that had been there a long time.

Perhaps she was getting a sign that she should have gone straight home from Stanton to Folly-on-Weir rather than deliberately taking a longer route.

Darkness began to gather but Alex didn't want to go back yet.

She carried on walking and watching. Ahead, wide utility gates stood open beneath a sign that stretched across the width of the track: *Robert Hill*. Just the name of the developer turning acres of perfect Cotswold land into a purportedly 'attractive' village. 'Luxury living at affordable prices.'

That wasn't the scuttlebutt throughout the surrounding villages and towns. 'One more cover-up to get damn good Cotswold farmland gobbled up by the elite incomers who can afford it,' was the way Alex had heard it described, far too many times. On a whim, today she had decided to see the new village for herself.

The final stretch was steeper, climbing to the top of a rise, and Alex leaned into the incline. It was Sunday, and that must account for the lack of traffic or the sound of any activity. This development was the talk of the Black Dog, the pub and inn she owned in Folly. People in these parts didn't welcome, or even in many cases, accept change, even if that change involved a large swathe of land already owned by the developer. According to Doc James, the local GP in Folly who remembered the Hill family from years earlier when they lived in the area, Robert Hill was building on his own property and it had never been farmed.

The oily smell grew stronger. Alex's eyes stung and she squeezed them shut repeatedly. Were they burning old tires? She didn't know what you could legally burn outdoors. If she hadn't seen the 'Robert Hill' sign at the junction of the B4632 toward Cheltenham and the B4077 which she would normally have taken on her way toward Folly from a small book auction in Stanton, she wouldn't have thought of stopping.

She wanted to see what all the fuss was about. And she wanted to delay getting back to Folly and to her mum's out-of-character and increasingly grim mood – not a welcome or pleasant feeling when it meant she didn't like the idea of going home.

Alex walked through the open gate. There was no sign ordering her not to come in. The nearest proposed buildings were little more than corner stakes with orange plastic ribbons that snapped in a brisk wind. Beyond this were houses in various stages of completion. The lots weren't huge but each building was very individual in design and cleverly sited to allow for privacy.

The outlook over valley and forest, and what she could see of the houses, gave credence to comments that this was no 'affordable' project. But whose business was that except the construction company, the Cotswold District Council, the surveyors and all the other official departments that got their hands into the building business? Leave it to them.

The roads were in place and Alex followed the first one branching to the right.

Something exploded.

The noise came from the west, over her right shoulder, and continued in spurts. She stopped walking and turned to watch, open mouthed, as a plume of black smoke rose from the visible end of a construction trailer surrounded by muddy equipment.

Run! No, someone could need help – desperately. Alex sprinted in the direction of the smoke, her gut clenching and the blast of rubbery smoke attacking her throat. And as she ran, she wrenched out her mobile and punched in the number for the emergency services. She was no shrinking violet. The worst that could happen would be that she had been too hasty in raising the alarm – or she hoped that would be the worst.

She didn't have far to go. The end of a large trailer jutted out just beyond two framed houses. The sound of crackling fire made her pause until the flicker of flames showed through the windows.

With her mobile in her hand, she kept her distance from the spreading pall of smoke until she saw the whole scene. A long trailer on blocks, a flight of metal steps leading up to a door, all large and modern, began to give off shimmering waves of heat.

Alex slammed the phone to her ear.

'Which service?' a male voice asked.

She opened her mouth to yell, 'Fire,' but suddenly a man staggered into the open, slapping at his smoking trouser legs. 'Ambulance,' she cried. 'At the Hill construction site near Winchcombe. Fire in a trailer. It's going up . . . it's happening quickly. Send help now.'

While she watched, and listened to the dispatcher give instructions, she tried to get closer. The man with smoking clothes fell to the ground and rolled, shouting, but not screaming. She couldn't hear what he was yelling.

Alex struggled out of her coat and kept going until she felt heat closing around her. She dashed at the man and threw her anorak over him, started beating him with her hands and arms, following him as he rolled.

She heard a loud crack and saw flames shooting into the air at the front of the vehicle. The top of the trailer bubbled and swelled. The skin rolling away from the metal bones of the thing, left it standing in outline, black and insubstantial. Everything appeared to melt in the intense heat.

'Ambulance on the way, madam,' the disembodied voice said from her mobile. 'Don't hang up.'

'We need fire trucks, too.' Alex's voice sounded like a series of loud croaks now, but the dispatcher said he understood and repeated his order that she stay on the line. 'Fire on their way already, madam.'

Throwing aside the phone, Alex beat at the man on the ground with everything she had, smacked at his legs, worked to roll him in her coat.

The smell of burning, the sooty smoke, brought tears, but the urgency subsided a little. He lay, heaped, partially wound in her blackened coat, while diminishing smoke wafted away from him.

Another explosion sounded, louder than the first. The burning structure sent a spray of ragged pieces jetting from the back.

She knelt beside the man. 'The medics are coming,' she told him, trying for a calming voice. 'I expect it's painful but you'll be OK. Hold on, they're coming. Thank God you got out of there.'

He let out a sound that was more a muffled moan than a shout, and grabbed for her hands. 'Did they?'

He squeezed his eyes shut and arched his back.

Alex shook him, wincing at the thought of causing him pain. 'What do you mean? Speak to me.' She jumped up, turned this way and that, hoping to see someone, anyone, coming in their direction. 'Who are you?' She knelt beside the man who looked to be in his mid-fifties at most. But who could be sure when he was covered with soot?

'They're in there.' He gasped the words out, coughing every few seconds. 'Couldn't get to them. It was so bloody hot. Oh, my God, what am I going to do?'

Sirens sounded, shrieked, growing closer. The volume suggested every fire station and constabulary for miles around had emptied out.

A voice came distantly from her mobile and Alex picked it up. 'I'm still here,' she said. 'We may have people inside the fire. I don't know what to do.'

'You do nothing,' the dispatcher said, kindly enough, but all efficiency. 'Who is the victim you have.'

'Just a minute.' She turned to the man on the ground who sat up now, scrubbed at his face, and she realized tears were coursing through the black muck on his cheeks. 'Your name, please? The emergency services want it. The vehicles are getting closer.'

'Thank God,' he said. 'Bob Hill. That's my name, Robert Hill. I have so messed up.'

TWO

Medics had lifted Robert Hill onto a stretcher and moved him rapidly to an emergency vehicle. Although its lights still flashed, the siren was silent, but fire service activity made enough noise to cancel out any lessening of the racket from elsewhere.

Alex shivered, not just from cold but from horror. Alone and beyond the zone where people were intent on saving what they could, she felt useless.

There was a good reason why firemen were called fire fighters. They were fighting now, aiming powerful jets of water toward the all but demolished trailer, running swiftly about their determined struggle to douse the flames. The men worked as a practiced team, totally focused and confident, but forbiddingly intent.

Weren't they worried the water would smash what was left of the trailer, float it away even? What did she know?

A man scuffed toward her in his heavy, rustling gear and boots, his face already blackened beneath his helmet.

'You Alex Duggins?' he shouted. 'You called in the alarm?'

Shifting from foot to foot she told him, 'Yes,' and a familiar prickle of anxiety ran up her spine. 'I just came up here to see the place because I've heard so much about it and I was curious. Everyone's talking about it.'

He bore down on her purposefully. 'The man who's hurt talked to you?'

'Yes.'

'What did he say about the trailer? Dispatch reported he'd said something about others who didn't get out?'

Without her anorak and with the sweat cooling on her skin, even in a thick jumper and wool slacks Alex shivered and wrapped her arms across her body. 'He wasn't very clear but his trousers had started burning. We put that out but he's bound to be hurting.'

'Yes.' The tone suggested he wasn't interested in obvious details. 'But what did he say? The medics won't let us speak to him yet.'

'He said "did they?" after I talked about being grateful he got out. Then he said he couldn't get whoever he was talking about out. He was really . . . he was as upset as anyone would be.'

'Right. Don't leave. The police are on their way and they'll want to talk to you. We'll get your particulars from them in case we need to contact you.'

'Can't you just take my address and I'll get on my way there now? The Black Dog in Folly-on-Weir.' She avoided using her actual home address since she didn't spend a lot of time there.

'I know where it is,' the man said, glancing back at her. 'You'll have to wait here for the police, miss.' He nodded toward the entrance to the development. 'Someone's up there to make sure no one goes in or out without clearance.'

'I can't do anything helpful here,' she protested. 'They'll be worried about me in Folly if I don't show up.' She so wanted to get away from here.

The fireman didn't respond this time.

Alex thought longingly of the blanket she kept in her Range Rover and considered going to get it, but she quickly realized she'd have to say what she needed to before she left and looking at the scene there was no one she could consider distracting for an instant. Trying to talk her way past some guard at the gate was a bad idea.

She paced, sending long glances toward the aid car where she could see movement inside. She didn't believe Robert Hill was severely injured but it would take a while to make him comfortable and calm him down.

Talking to anyone in fire response was out of the question. She could feel the intensity there, both in dealing with the fire and in finding out if there were victims inside the burned shell of the trailer.

Robert Hill would have survived well enough without her intrusion, and she couldn't have changed the outcome of the fire. She should have gone straight home after the book sale, as she had originally planned.

Reluctantly she used her mobile to call the Black Dog.

'Good evening.' Her manager, Hugh Rhys answered. 'Black Dog. How can I help you?'

Alex bowed over and stared toward her feet in the darkness. 'It's Alex. I'm held up for a bit. If anyone asks, I hope to be back before too long.'

A short silence, then: 'And that's it? You'd rather not tell me what you're held up with, or if you're all right, or ask me to give a message to Tony – or Lily?'

Hugh was an enigma, a man of means who chose to manage a country pub and who kept his private life, private. For him to ask her questions meant that someone was agitated about her being so late back and had said as much. That would either be Tony Harrison, who was her lover and her best friend, or, just as likely, Lily Duggins – Alex's mother.

'Is my mother fussing?' Alex asked, deliberately avoiding the other possibility since Tony hated any discussion of their combined lives with others. 'Go ahead and tell her I got tied up but I'm fine and having a good time. I hope not to be too long.'

'If you're having such a good time, why are you hoping it ends quickly?' Typical Hugh verbal callisthenics. 'Sounds noisy where you are.'

'Another point to you, m'dear. Hold down the fort, please.' She hung up and considered calling Tony, but another siren made her pause.

The headlights of a vehicle bounced over the higher points in the track to enter the construction compound. A marked police car followed. On the unmarked car a bubble on the roof near the passenger door rotated light.

The sedan paused, its siren whining to a stop and the flashing light disappearing, then the driver cut the engine and both front doors opened.

Two men strode downhill toward the fire trucks and aid car. Alex stared hard but didn't think there was anyone she recognized. That, at least, was something. She wasn't in the mood for any falsely cheerful reunions – not that she could even be certain of any cheer, false or otherwise. Her too frequent encounters with the Gloucestershire Police had set up an 'interesting' dynamic between her and several detectives.

'Sir!'

A fireman's shout captured her entire attention. One of the men who had been using a hatchet on the smoldering trailer framework jogged back toward one of the trucks. They'd found something. Alex scrunched the neck of her jumper between her fingers. Someone? Or what was left of them? You didn't need a working knowledge of what happened to a human inside a conflagration like she'd just seen to know what it would do to a body – or bodies.

Intent on the dark and moving silhouettes in the huddle of police and firemen, Alex didn't notice one figure separated from the rest until a torch beam landed at her feet and flashed away. The man with the light jogged toward her, coat flapping, his hat tipped forward over his forehead.

When he drew near he looked up and called, 'Alex? For God's sake, you do get around. What are you doing here?'

She groaned and took a step backward.

Detective Sergeant Bill Lamb in the flesh. It never took him long to make her feel superfluous, a nuisance and a few rocks short of an otherwise fine dry-stone wall.

'Hello, detective sergeant,' she said formally but in what she hoped was a cheerily impersonal tone. 'You're all over the place yourself. Welcome.' Now she sounded as if he was visiting her patch, darn it.

'Where's your coat?' he asked, coming even closer.

This was not a good moment. 'It got ruined because of the fire.'

Even in the darkness she could read the disbelieving expression on his face. 'In the fire? This fire?' He hooked a thumb over his shoulder.

'Not exactly.' At least he couldn't see her red face. 'Or, well anyway, I suppose . . . I was wearing my anorak when there . . . a man ran from that trailer and his trousers were singed and smoking so I threw the coat over his legs and helped roll out any fire. He was on the ground then, of course.'

The detective's notebook appeared from an inside pocket and he started scribbling with the aid of his torch. 'So, he's a friend of yours?'

'No!' Alex sucked cold air in between her teeth. 'That's not what I said and it's not the case. I just happened to be here looking at the development. Everyone in the area is talking about it, so I wanted to take a look for myself.'

'"Just . . . happened",' he muttered as he wrote. He looked up sharply with bright eyes she knew too well were disturbingly light blue and unblinking when you got a good look at him. 'You drove all the way over from Folly just to "take a look" at this – in the dark on a Sunday evening?'

He was so good at ruffling her. Why could she never control her reactions to him? One of her trusted friends thought he was a wonderful man so it had to be something to do with her own muddled impression.

'Bill,' she began firmly. They were on first name terms and any formality was pointless. 'I was on my way back from Stanton late in the afternoon. I saw the sign for the development and drove here. It was later than I thought and getting darker than I expected, but here I am. And it was probably a good thing because that man needed help.'

More writing in silence but for the sound of Alex's own breathing.

'Bill! Over here!'

That was one more voice that was well known to her, Detective Chief Inspector Dan O'Reilly. And now another awkward encounter was in the works.

'Come with me, please,' Bill said and called, 'coming, guv.' He shrugged out of his raincoat and settled it over Alex's shoulders, already moving back toward his boss.

Alex said, 'Thank you,' and shuffled along beside him, hitching the coat above her boots.

'Can we speed this up, Alex?'

Darn it! You couldn't snap at a man who just lent you his coat on a cold night. You probably shouldn't think nasty things about him, either. All this was going to take some explaining when she got back to Folly – especially to Tony. Tony took her tendency toward what he called, 'impulse excess' with indulgent, even fond acceptance – most of the time. This one would be convoluted to explain.

'Toward the back of the trailer, sir,' the fireman was saying. 'I'd say there was one of those separate compartments with a couch you can make into a bed across there. That's about gone.'

'No sign of another body?' Dan asked, glancing at Alex and nodding. She raised the fingers of one hand and stayed back while Bill joined his boss.

'Just the one so far, sir,' the fireman responded to Dan's question. 'The fire was pretty intense.'

Alex didn't want to look at the burned-out trailer but couldn't help it. The fire smoldered in places, and hissed, but appeared mostly under control. Several firemen stood to one side at the back of the crumbling wreckage, all staring at what looked like the same area. She was too far away to make out details but she couldn't miss a twisted thing among the debris. That didn't have to be a body but it could be.

'The cavalry is on its way,' Dan told Bill. He said, 'Hello, Alex,' over his shoulder.

'Hi, Dan.' If there was anything else to say, she couldn't think of it.

Bareheaded as he usually was, Dan stood in signature pose: coat pushed back and hands sunk in his trouser pockets. 'Let's do it,' he said. 'Not you, Alex. Stay where you are, please.'

Stomping her feet to try kick-starting her frozen circulation, she did as she was told but wished she could transport herself far away.

The back doors of the emergency vehicle were still open. The darkness was complete now and light shone from inside. How was Bob Hill, she wondered and walked to stand at a respectful distance, but close enough to call out, 'Excuse me. I was with Mr Hill. How is he, please?'

A medic poked her head out, but pulled it back again, talking to someone. 'Come over if you like,' the woman said, looking outside again. 'Mr Hill's doing well. We're making sure he's comfortable.' She jumped down and met Alex. In a low tone she said, 'He's trying to talk himself out of going to the hospital but that's not going to happen. He thinks he can just drive himself home.'

Alex walked beside her. 'Typical male reaction, I should think,' she said, grinning sideways at the medic.

The woman made an athletic upward leap into the vehicle. 'Your friend who was with you is here, Mr Hill.'

Already clambering in, Alex started to say she didn't know the man but had to concentrate on getting herself and Bill's raincoat up slippery metal steps.

Bob Hill was laughing.

'He's had something to settle him,' the second medic said with a meaningful look at the patient, 'but he's a feisty one.'

'I didn't know him before this evening,' Alex said, grinning at Hill who didn't seem to be feeling any pain at all. 'We met out there after the fire had broken out. How are you, er, Mr Hill?'

'Call me Bob and tell these nice people I'm perfectly capable of driving myself home now. Thanks, by the way. You saved the day for me. Don't even know if I've got a mobile. If I do, I don't know where it is.'

'Glad I was here,' Alex said. Hill had a slender good-looking face and straight dark hair, well-cut and flecked with grey. 'They're going to get you checked out at the hospital. That's the best way.'

'I've got my own car,' he said, grinning broadly. They had cleaned his face – a vast improvement. He tried to sit up but was promptly eased back onto pillows.

'Someone else will drive it home for you,' Alex said. 'Where do you live?'

'Temple Guiting. Knighton House.'

'What's the number there, sir?' the male medic asked. His nametag showed he was Pain, which Alex thought an unfortunate name.

'No point calling?' the patient said, less jolly now. 'No one there. All away.'

Pain looked at Alex. 'Not far, anyway,' he said. 'You can drive his car, can't you? Follow us to the hospital. I don't think they'll keep him in. The police will want to speak to him before we leave if he's up to it. How are you doing, Bob?'

'Tickety-boo,' Hill said. 'Absolutely, bloody marvelous.'

'That's good to hear.' Bill Lamb had arrived quietly and leaned in to see Bob Hill. 'Are your wheels in a safe place, sir?'

'Safe as houses,' Bob said with what sounded like a giggle. He sobered again. 'I'll get it later. Or my new friend will drive it to the hospital for me. Good girl, she is. Couldn't have managed without her.' His eyelids drooped.

Bill didn't look at her but said, 'The DCI told you to stay where you were,' very quietly. 'Questioning witnesses isn't your job, remember?'

She ignored him. 'Could I write something for him?' she asked Murdock, the female medic, who gave Alex a notebook and pen.

'This is my name, address and phone number,' she said, writing. 'For you, and for Mr Hill if he needs them.' She tore out the sheet and handed it over before jumping out onto the crackling, frozen ground.

'And I wasn't questioning him,' she said. 'Just asking how he was.'

'That was nice of you,' Bill said. 'You obviously saw a good deal – if not everything.'

'Well—'

Bill cut Alex off. 'I'll put you in a car to wait for DCI O'Reilly. He'll deal with you now.'

THREE

Tony Harrison scarcely made it into the saloon bar at the Black Dog Pub and Inn, when his dog Katie shot away from him and zipped between tables like a sandy-haired, slightly well-padded slalom racer. Tony watched her make straight for the Burke sisters' table in front of the fire where flames bent and sparked over the blackened breast of the wide chimney, and reflected on polished horse brasses hanging from the thick, age-darkened mantel. Joining Bogie, Alex's terrier mix (otherwise known as Standard British

Breed), on the blue tartan blanket kept there for them, she looked around as if waiting to receive welcomes from many friends.

Harriet and Mary Burke, well wrapped up in winter woolies with wide scarves around their necks, gave both dogs attention and suffered serious dog-lick attacks in return.

Hugh Rhys stood behind the bar looking directly at Tony with an expression that suggested he'd not only expected him, but needed some sort of help – immediately.

Making his way to the counter, Tony greeted the regulars that called out to him. But it was Hugh who held his attention.

'Ambler?' Hugh said, picking up a pint glass.

'Make it Macallan,' Tony said. 'Double. What's up?'

'I think you already know.'

Tony gave a brief nod. 'Alex said she called you. Did you make more sense out of what she said than I did?'

'I got the feeling she didn't want to make sense,' Hugh said. He gripped the edge of the counter, locked his arms and straightened his spine. 'Said she was tied up and going to be late. And, no, she couldn't give more details. Since Lily got in she's been up to her eyes checking late arrivals to the inn – for which I'm grateful. They've got a pretty good crowd over there in the restaurant, too. Busy.' He indicated the passageway from the bar to the restaurant on the ground floor beneath the seven guest rooms. 'She's not a happy woman and giving her Alex's message didn't improve a thing. Those two are having a silent battle – or is that just my imagination?'

'No. And I'm not being told what's going on either. I did think Alex would be back by now though. How long ago did she phone you?'

Hugh frowned and put the whiskey in front of Tony. 'Hours,' he said. 'Two, no, three.'

'She called me an hour and a half ago. Are you OK, Hugh? You don't look it.'

'Damned if I know. Intuition isn't high on my list of reliable instincts, but this bar has been giving off waves of negative vibes tonight and I can't call what I've been feeling anything but intuition.'

Nothing helpful occurred to Tony.

'Can you feel anything?' Hugh asked. 'Or do you think I'm a mad man?'

Hunching his shoulders, Tony slowly shook his head, no. 'Pretty grim in here.'

'Lily's not helping,' Hugh said. 'She's been in such a prickly mood recently and that's being kind, but she can't be more than just a part of the reason it feels like doom approaches. She couldn't pull this all on her own.'

Turning his back to the counter, Tony studied the room. The place was full, as it usually was on a Sunday evening, but there was something different. 'There isn't enough noise,' he announced abruptly, looking over his shoulder at the manager. 'Most of them have their eyes downcast. And all the mouths are moving but it's muted in here.'

'Exactly,' Hugh said through his teeth. 'And this isn't a bloody funeral home, dammit. Some would blast out music and try a joke on every customer, but it's not my style. I'm managing the Dog to get away from pretending to be what keeps other people happy. I'm easy-going enough but I'm not responsible for this lot's moods.'

Tony thought about the other man's comments and faced him as nonchalantly as he could manage. He had never heard him make any comments about why a man of means like him was here in Folly-on-Weir, doing what he was doing. He owned just about the largest house in the village proper, Green Friday, but chose to live in a couple of upstairs rooms here at the pub. Sometimes his house was rented, but only if someone interested got a tip about it and tracked Hugh down.

Hugh looked uncomfortable and Tony decided to shelve any notion of practicing his non-existent psychiatric skills. There were reasons he specialized in veterinary rather than human medicine. Discomfort with poking into patients' minds as well as their bodily ills was only one of them. Animals had personalities, too, strong ones in many cases, but he could trust his rapport with them to be his guide. He didn't have to wait and hope they would talk – or not talk too much.

He picked up the brass bell on the counter and rang it energetically. 'Everyone bought their raffle tickets for the church hamper, have they?' he cried. 'I know there's going to be a whopper of a turkey with vegetables and pies from the Derwinters, beer and wine from the Dog, afternoon tea at Leaves of Comfort, served by our very own Harriet and Mary Burke, *and* a free exam and teeth cleaning from the great local vet. Dogs, cats, guinea pigs, gerbils, hamsters and other animals only – prior evaluation of any specimen bigger than me, or that I can't identify. No pets with opposing thumbs. Got your chances?'

A 'yes' chorus went up amid laughter. Some gave a negative answer and raised a hand to show they wanted to buy. Liz Hadley who was working tonight as she did most nights, took a roll of tickets from under the counter. She grinned and chatted while she made the rounds.

The noise level rose.

'Good going,' Hugh said. 'You've got hidden talents, man. Next time it turns chilly in here I'll know who to call.'

'Yes.' Tony got more edgy as time passed. 'Have you tried to call Alex back?'

'Twice. How about you?'

'Twice for me, too. It goes straight to messages. She only went over to Stanton – supposedly.'

Hugh tapped the back of Tony's hand. 'We'd be better off not to speculate, you know. She'll be back safe soon enough.'

'It's already long past soon enough.'

'And here comes Lily again.' Hugh sighed. 'I knew the peace couldn't last much longer.'

'Peace?' Tony gave a short laugh and took a swig of his Macallan. 'Everything in here is strung tight enough to snap. I'm expecting the windows to blow out. Alex going missing is the last straw.'

'She's uptight, too,' Hugh said, keeping his voice down. He spoke up as Lily approached. 'Everyone checked in, Lily? Anyone else still expected?'

Tall, much taller than her daughter, Lily arrived at the counter with pinched lips and her almond-shaped green eyes wiped of all expression. She didn't answer Hugh's question.

'Hello, Lily,' Tony said.

'Have you heard from Alex? What did she tell you?'

'Yes, and not much,' Tony replied. 'She got delayed on her way back from the book sale in Stanton.'

Lily wore her dark hair longer than Alex. Strands of gray streaked the older woman's curls. Height and hairstyle aside, that they were uncannily alike wasn't a stretch.

'Will you let me buy you a drink?' Tony moved closer to her. 'You're upset about something. Is it just Alex?'

'I'm not upset.' Lily lowered her lashes. She didn't convince him.

'How about that drink?'

'No, thanks. Why isn't she answering her phone? Can you even guess at that?' She put her elbows on the counter. 'I can, but what I'm thinking isn't good. Yes, you're right, I'm upset. How can you stand here while Alex is out there on a night like this and we don't know if something horrible has happened? She's not cruel, never cruel. This is so damned cruel.' Lily put her hands over her face.

Tony and Hugh looked at each other. Carefully, trying not to draw attention, Tony put an arm around Lily's shoulders and leaned closer. 'Let's get into the kitchen and decide what we should do. You're right, we can't just keep on waiting.'

Things got quieter in the bar, swelled briefly, and fell silent.

Tony glanced behind him and straight into Detective Chief Inspector Dan O'Reilly's serious face.

FOUR

Brilliant entrance, O'Reilly, the perfect example of the calming arm of the law. 'Evening, all,' he said, stuffing gloves into his raincoat pockets. 'We ran into Alex and she said it was time we stopped in.' *F for improvisation, O'Reilly.*

'Where is she?' Tony and Lily asked in unison. Lily's rigid face was colorless. Tony's forward-leaning stance suggested he wanted to hit someone. From what he could see, Dan was the only target in range.

'She's parking,' he said. 'I'll take a black coffee, please. One for Detective Sergeant Lamb, too. He'll be right in with Alex.'

Tony straightened away from the counter and moved in close. 'O'Reilly, I'm not in the mood for games,' he said very quietly. 'What are you playing at this time?'

'I don't seek you people out,' Dan said, equally quiet. 'You just turn up at my crime scenes. Or, to be accurate, Alex has a way of turning up at my crime scenes. And I suggest we take this conversation somewhere private. Where can we go?'

'I'm coming with you,' Lily said. 'There's nowhere in here. It's too busy everywhere. It'll have to be outside. But if you look around you'll see it's too late to hope we won't have a lot of questions from customers later. You could have used the back door and avoided this.'

He wasn't a family liaisons officer, or a shrink. 'If you had held down your reactions, both of you, we would have been fine. What is it with all of you anyway? I'm here on police business. Now, back through the bar, or through the kitchens?'

Lily said, 'Forgive me,' and seeing her flush he felt callous.

Touching her arm briefly, following her behind the bar, he said, 'It's been a bad night but I should be better at holding my temper.'

As they passed, Hugh said, 'There's fresh coffee back there.'

Scoot Gammage was in the kitchen cleaning off trays of glasses and loading them into one of the dishwashers. When he saw Dan he gave a little nod and hurried to finish what he was doing.

Scoot smiled. His face was thin, his hair blond, thick and straight, and his body kept on getting taller and rangier.

'Time to go home?' Dan said. He liked the boy, admired his courage in working to help take care of his younger brother, Kyle. The two of them had been through difficult family times. Tony's father, Doc James, and Lily, had taken them under their wings and stepped in when their aunt wasn't around. That meant they spent a lot of time between Lily's Corner Cottage and Doc's house in Bishop's Way.

'Doc should be here to pick him up shortly,' Tony said,

joining the kitchen gathering. 'How are you coming with the driving lessons?'

'Great.' This time the boy's grin was wide. 'Doc says I'm a natural. I never thought I'd get to drive anything like that new Lexus. I'm taking my test soon.'

'Good for you,' Tony told him. 'I bet my dad's a lot more patient with you than he was with me. But you probably got a bit of practice out at the cottage, right?'

Scoot nodded and showed no unhappiness at the mention of the cottage that was their home when their aunt showed up to be with them for a day or two. 'Kyle did, too.' He glanced at Dan. 'Only on the farm, of course, not on the roads.'

Perhaps there would be a chance to get his own boy, Calum, together with these two when he finally came from Ireland to visit – supposedly for longer next time, Dan thought to himself. He stared into space. After spending Christmas in Spain with his mother, Calum was to have come to England for a school term and to stay with Dan. They had so many plans, but in the end, Corinne had backed out. She couldn't face letting Calum go for more than the periods the court had granted Dan during the divorce. He still cared about that woman, blamed himself for what had happened to his family, but surely she sometimes regretted how Dan felt living without his boy?

The door from the parking lot out back opened with the force of the wind behind it. Alex came in along with Bill Lamb. Flurries of snow made their way inside before they could shut the door.

'Doc's out front waiting for you,' Alex told Scoot. She didn't make much eye contact with anyone. 'Go quickly through the bar. I think Kyle's in the car, too.'

The boy hung up his heavy apron and waved before pulling on an anorak. 'I'll be here the same time as usual tomorrow. It's just as quick to go out here and cut around to the front.' He slipped through the door and yet again snow blew in.

'Nice boy,' Dan said, well aware of the strained atmosphere all around him. He met Bill's eyes and they both raised eyebrows a fraction.

'The gang's all here,' Bill said, droll as usual and no hint of a smile. He took off his hat to reveal his thick, crew cut, sandy hair. 'Just like old times.'

'Right.' Only Tony looked remotely amused. 'I suggest we talk here rather than outside in the snow. Is this going to take long, gentlemen? I should be getting Alex home. She looks worn out.' He frowned at the blanket she wore draped around her shoulders and her disheveled appearance. She looked very tired.

'We'll keep it short,' Dan said. 'There's nothing sweet about it. We were called out to a suspicious fire with possible deaths. Near Winchcombe. The new development being built by Hill Development and Construction. Alex happened to have chosen today to go up and take a look at the place. She tells me there's a lot of talk about it. I've seen the articles in the papers.'

'It's going to be lovely,' Alex said, surprising Dan by sounding defensive.

'Well, that's as may be,' Dan told her. 'Not my concern. But Alex was there for the whole event. She helped Robert Hill – the owner – when he got his legs burned and ended up observing and being part of enough that we needed to ask her questions. There will be more but not tonight.'

'Why?' Lily's voice rose. 'She doesn't know anything about all that. You shouldn't have gone up there, Alex. That kind of poking around never ends well. You know what I think about opportunists and that's what the Hill man is.'

Alex didn't respond. She went to stand with Tony who gave her a hug.

'Now, how do you know that about Mr Hill?' Bill said and Dan was glad to be saved from asking the question.

'I don't,' Lily snapped back. 'But I've been told about it by people who know that he's not really a dedicated local. They say other people have tried to buy pieces of that land to build on and they couldn't get anywhere. He wouldn't sell and they were warned they probably wouldn't have got building permission if he had. And now, when it suits him, he's back and he can do what he likes, when he likes. So much for protecting the land from overbuilding.'

'We'll soon know all about that,' Dan said. 'We followed Alex here because she had to stay later than she would have if nothing had happened up there, and the weather really turned. I'll request that you don't share anything you know with your patrons, Alex. They'll learn what everyone else learns soon enough but we'd appreciate it if they didn't get any extra details to spread around. That goes for all of you. I had to assume you would share what Alex knows among you or I wouldn't be talking to all of you like this. Gossip can do harm and you've got some champion gossipers in Folly.'

Not well-put, he supposed. And from Lily's narrowed eyes he'd say she didn't think so either.

'Do you know much about Hill, Lily? You seem to dislike the man. Have you had dealings with him in the past?'

'Me? Why would I? I doubt I've ever laid eyes on him.' She grabbed mugs and poured coffee from an urn. 'Warm yourselves up before you go back out there.' She put the filled mugs down on a counter.

'Thank you,' Bill said, taking one for himself and another for Dan.

Alex put cream in three more mugs of coffee, for Tony, Lily and herself.

'If you hear or see anything you think we might want to know, please get in touch.' Fidgeting in a breast pocket of his jacket, he pulled out several cards and set them on the side. 'You already know where to find us but it might help to keep one of these handy.'

'Is there any reason why I shouldn't check up on Mr Hill tomorrow?' Alex said. 'He's had a horrible shock and the burns will be so painful. Perhaps I can do something for him. I felt awful.'

'Possibly,' Dan said. 'Check with us in the morning. We've got a lot of work ahead of us on this one. Burning—' He stopped himself from saying 'deaths'. 'Burning adds a lot of complication to an investigation.'

'Why would it?' Lily turned on Dan, her tone cutting. 'This Mr Hill's got burns on his legs. Surely you know how that happened by now. *You* do, don't you, Alex? Dan says you were there.'

'I don't think that's the point, Mum,' Alex said. She drew the blanket more tightly around her. 'It was a big trailer that burned. One person didn't get out in time. They've got his body. And they don't think his death was an accident, isn't that right, Dan?'

He barely controlled the urge to roll his eyes. 'I really couldn't tell you that, Alex. We won't know until later.'

'After the post-mortem?' Alex said, turning gray. 'How can they do that on a burned body?'

'Leave that to the experts.' He looked from face to face. 'And this is exactly what I don't want you talking about out there.' He hiked his thumb over his shoulder. 'We need a few hours – at least that much to try to get ahead of the press and the ghouls. We're aware of all the talk surrounding this building project – a lot of it negative. There are people just looking for ways to stir the pot and if we don't get a lid on it, this will be whipped up more than it may need to be.'

'Wasn't it an accident?' Tony asked quietly.

'An arson team's on it,' Dan said, cursing his ill luck that he might not be able to control the narrative on this case. 'They'll be the ones to decide that.'

Alex blew into her hands, fixing Dan with a hostile gaze. 'There's nothing the police like better than an easy solve. Mr Hill was there and you think Mr Hill had something to do with it, don't you? That's ridiculous. You might as well call me a suspect, too.'

FIVE

'It's weird,' Alex murmured to Tony and Hugh at the bar. 'There's no point pretending my mother isn't behaving like someone I don't know. Look at her.'

'I know,' Hugh said, sliding wine glasses into overhead racks. 'I'll finish these and go upstairs. She's working something out and I think the fewer people around to watch her, the better.'

Alex put a hand into Tony's on the bar to make sure he didn't think he ought to leave, too.

He gave her a quick smile. 'Lily's a very even-tempered person, very reserved, but she's got a right to get upset sometimes. Something is really hurting her.'

Hugh dimmed the lights behind the bar and went around the room turning down wall sconces before locking doors on his way to the inn and his rooms. He wished goodnight to Lily and the Burke sisters when he passed. The three of them leaned their heads together over the circular oak table. Mary's one-eyed ginger tabby, Max – curled up on the table as he was most of the time – having arrived in the covered shopping cart the sisters used for his transport. Katie lay on her side before the fire with Bogie resting his head on her back.

'Look at them,' Tony said. 'Someone ought to paint them. Maybe you. I haven't noticed you talking about painting in that studio of yours lately.'

'I couldn't do them justice. Not my style but they do make a lovely group.' She looked across at them. 'That's the oddest part. Harriet and Mary wouldn't have stayed tonight if Mum hadn't asked them to. They're never here at closing, let alone after closing. It's as if they're her most trusted friends in the world.' She took a deep breath and let it out slowly.

'You're hurt,' Tony said. He ducked his head to look into her face. 'Aren't you? Please don't be. Lily knew the sisters when you were very young, she's said as much. And I've always had the feeling there was a special relationship between them – an understanding, if you like. If they can help her deal with whatever's bugging her, let's celebrate.'

'Wise as usual.' She touched his jaw. 'And right. I wouldn't say I can celebrate, but I can try to be a grown-up.'

'Why didn't you take a coat today?'

She took an instant to change focus. 'Oh, I did. I threw it over Mr Hill's legs to help put out the sparks. It's in the back of my Range Rover but I'll have to bin it.' Her mother caught her eye. 'I think my mum wants us to join them.'

They took their beers and went to pull extra chairs up to the table. Lily shifted closer to Harriet to make room for them – just.

'I was still a teenager, wasn't I?' she said to the sisters. 'When Alex and I came to live here.'

Alex glanced at Tony. This wasn't a subject she would ever expect her mother to raise.

'Just a girl,' Mary said. 'Not quite twenty. Hard times, I'm sure, aren't you, Harriet?' Both ladies were overly pink-cheeked.

All three women held the stems of sherry glasses. A bottle of Harvey's Bristol Cream Sherry stood on the table, another first-time event in Alex's memory.

'Yes,' Harriet said. 'But I think parts of it were happy, too.'

'A lot of it was.' Lily kept her eyes downcast. 'I knew what I had to do by then. You were good to me. Not everyone was, but they didn't bother me as much as they wanted to.'

Alex's mother never ever mentioned the history of how she came to live here. Growing up, Alex asked about and got the barest details of her early life. It had been obvious Lily didn't intend to reveal more and eventually Alex had stopped asking.

'We lived in Underhill,' she said tentatively. 'But you worked here at the Black Dog. I remember coming here after school from when I was little and playing in the garden in the summer. When it got colder I went in the snug if it was empty, or one of the rooms upstairs. I went to pre-school at the rectory. I remember bits about that.'

'There's nothing interesting about all that,' Lily said. She flapped a hand. 'All in the past.'

'What's the matter, Mum?' Alex said. 'Can you tell us? Do you want me to come to the cottage with you tonight?'

'Anything I can tell you, I can tell Tony. That's how it should be when two people are as close as you are. And he's like his father – he keeps his own counsel.'

Lily and Doc James enjoyed each other's company when they had time free from their busy lives and the mutual affection they held for each other was well known.

She stroked Max, who was supposed to be invisible when he was on the table, and gave a small, bitter laugh. 'Harriet and Mary are my oldest friends.'

'We'll take that as a compliment,' Mary said, her eyes huge behind very thick glasses.

'We've been talking about old times,' Lily said. 'But I need to share this with Alex, too.' From a pocket in her dress, Lily removed a legal-sized envelope. She put it on the table in front of her and smoothed her fingertips along the ragged opening.

The revolution in Alex's stomach wasn't a new experience but she hated the feeling. 'What is that? Mum?' She leaned forward and shook Lily's wrist. 'Mum?'

Lily's skin was clammy, her face ashen.

'Would you like to lie down?' Tony asked. 'You're not feeling well, are you?'

She shook her head, no. 'But I don't want to lie down. I want to know why this makes me feel anything at all.' She lifted the envelope and stared at the typed address. 'I've had it for weeks.'

'Lily—'

'It's just that I thought . . . I more or less thought she might have died years ago.' She stared into Alex's face. 'She promised she'd come back. That was when I was ten but it was in the back of my mind all these years and I couldn't help hoping she'd come through the door. Sometimes I still look for her among faces in the street, or in shops.'

Alex didn't dare speak. They sat listening to silence but for the spitting fire.

'My mother died in July last year,' Lily said. She raised her chin. 'It's all right. I should have expected it, but I didn't, not really. I suppose it's normal to take a while to accept these things. There, out of my system. And you belong with Tony tonight, my girl.'

SIX

A police constable at the door to Bob Hill's hospital room surprised Alex. Winchcombe seemed a laid-back little town – but there must have been more than the obvious attached to last night's fire to justify extra precautions surrounding Robert Hill.

Alex drew back and slipped into a small, empty waiting

room. And she immediately pulled back her shoulders, left again and walked up to the policeman.

'Good afternoon.' She smiled at him and his countenance softened. 'I was the one who helped Mr Hill last night after his legs were burned. I'm just dropping by to find out how he is.'

'Are you family?'

Here we go. 'No. But I'm a friend of Detective Chief Inspector O'Reilly and Detective Sergeant Lamb.' Some slight exaggerations were forgivable. 'If you give them a call I'm sure they'll tell you I told them I planned to come. How is Mr Hill? Do you know, Constable . . .?'

'Finney, miss. Michael Finney. I know Mr Hill had himself a good breakfast. I'd just come on duty. Did you ask at the desk if you could visit, miss?'

With the smallest twinge of guilt, Alex said, 'The desk was right on my way in.' It had been unstaffed and she'd peeked at the list of patients to find the right room.

'Good enough then.' Constable Finney had a lovely smile. 'In you go for a while.'

Irish accents had a pleasing effect on Alex and she was more relaxed as she tapped on the door to Hill's room and stepped cautiously inside.

It was a single room but the curtain was drawn halfway around the bed. 'Mr Hill?' Alex said quietly, ready to flee if necessary. 'It's Alex Duggins from last night.'

'Come in.' He sounded good, or perhaps normal was a better word. 'Come in, come in. Ah, there you are. I thought I might have to grill the police for your details to get in touch.'

She automatically rose to tiptoes and advanced to the bottom of the bed. 'How are you feeling?' The sheets were tented on some sort of cage over his legs. 'I hope it's not too painful.'

'Not at all.' His voice was deep and cultured. She hadn't noticed it the previous evening. 'This thing is probably not such a poor idea to keep any weight off, but I'll be out of here very soon. I hate lying about, especially when there's work to be done. Sit here.' He indicated a chair beside him.

'Are you sure? I don't want to tire you—'

'I'm not an invalid, Alex. It is Alex, isn't it. I heard you called that. And you just said you were . . . perhaps I'm not entirely myself yet.'

She sat on the metal chair. 'Yes. Alex Duggins. I live in Folly-on-Weir – or near enough. Up on the hill there. The Black Dog is my pub.'

'You own a pub?' He studied her closely but seriously. 'Unusual for a woman.'

'Doesn't seem unusual to me.' Giving him more details about her life didn't seem necessary. 'Folly's a lovely place. It's home to me.'

'And is there a Mr Duggins? Forgive the curiosity but I'm enough older than you to get away with it. Perhaps there are young Dugginses?'

'No, and no. Not yet anyway.'

'Well, at least you don't sound like one of those young people who want nothing to do with marriage or having children. It doesn't have to mean you'll do either, but being open to trying things that come your way and may turn out to be good is important. Could I ask you a couple of things, Alex? About last night?'

'I thought you might want to although I'm not sure I know as much as you do.'

Hill glanced toward the door which he must know was open. 'Why were you at the site?'

The flush she so hated began to rise. 'I was curious,' she said honestly. 'There's been so much chatter about the development. People have a way of forming opinions without much information to go on. I probably shouldn't have gone there so late but afterwards I was glad I did.'

He reached a large, long-fingered hand toward her, palm up, and she automatically set her own on top. He held her lightly and shook his head a little. 'You don't expect to meet a lot of principled people, which is a good thing, because you don't.' Then he laughed and it made him look younger. He was handsome, she realized.

'What's so funny?' Alex leaned toward him.

'I'm running on, which is not my way. You were inconvenienced last night and it probably royally messed up your evening, but you're glad you were there to help out. I like that, Alex Duggins of the Black Dog. What on earth made you buy a pub, or did you inherit it?'

'No. My mother worked there from when I was little. Later . . . well, much later, I married but was divorced a few years afterward. I went home and it looked like the Black Dog would be sold, probably to strangers, so I stepped in and kept it in the village, so to speak.'

'I see. Good for you.' He looked serious again and frown lines dug in between his definite brows. 'Have you ever thought of opening another place? In a neighboring village or town?'

Alex puffed up her cheeks. 'Mmm, no. I haven't. It's taken a while to get the Dog running well again. We have an inn as well, and a small but successful restaurant. I sound as if I'm bragging, but it's been hard work and I am proud – or perhaps I should say thrilled about it.'

'So you should be. Do you—'

'Alex, what did I say about this?' Dan O'Reilly, signs of little sleep weighting his eyes, pushed the bed curtain aside. 'I told you we'd have to see how Mr Hill was before you were cleared to visit.'

'Hello Dan,' she said, and her smile cost her considerable effort. 'We've got a busy day ahead and I wanted to have time to make sure Mr Hill was all right.'

'Call me, Bob. OK, Alex?'

'OK.' She widened her eyes at him, knowing Dan couldn't see.

Dan cleared his throat. 'Isn't that nice, now? If you've had your visit, I'd like to speak to Mr Hill myself – on our own.'

Alex got up hurriedly.

Bob Hill tightened his hold on her hand and urged her to sit again, which she more or less had to.

'I'd like Alex to stay, please, chief inspector . . . have I got the title right?'

'Yes, sir,' Dan said. He didn't as much as glance at Alex. 'Some of what I may say could be very private. Are you sure you want an audience?'

'Is there some procedural reason why my friend shouldn't stay?'

Alex almost heard Dan grind his teeth. 'No, sir. That's up to you. I didn't realize you were such old friends.'

Nodding, giving a tight little smile, Bob Hill held her hand firmly. 'Go ahead, chief inspector. And thank you for all you did last night. I'm sorry to have added to your workload.'

'It's my job,' Dan said. Still he didn't look at Alex. 'A man died in the trailer fire last night.'

That wiped any vestige of a smile from Bob's face. 'I was afraid you'd tell me that. I've been asking for more details but nobody had any, or they said they didn't.'

'We know he was Lance Pullinger, the architect working for you on the Winchcombe site.'

'Lance.' Bob bowed his head and was silent after that.

'Were you inside the trailer last evening, Mr Hill?'

Alex heard the man sigh. 'No. I tried to get in but the door was jammed or something. Stuck. I went there to see Lance. He's been a close friend for years. And he's a brilliant architect. Do you know how it happened?' He raised his face.

'We have a number of facts and some deductions.'

'How did the fire start?' Bob looked stricken. 'It's always a fear with trailers but we take every precaution.'

'I'm sure you do,' Dan said with no expression in his voice. 'When the post-mortem is done we'll know more.'

'Do you get much from a post-mortem on a badly burned body?' Asking the question made Alex feel sick. 'The fireman said they found the body on a couch in the back and that it was a bad fire.'

'In the sleeping compartment?' Bob asked. 'Do you think he was asleep when it happened?'

'Possibly. I'll see all the evidence later today.'

'Was there another body?' Bob asked and Alex almost missed what he said, he spoke so softly.

'Who would that be?' Dan asked. He had his notebook and pen in hand and asked his question casually.

Bob didn't answer.

'Mr Hill. Who do you think might have died with Mr Pullinger?'

'I don't know. Sometimes he has an assistant with him or someone just watching him with his drawings. He's so good, chief inspector.'

Dan took off his hat and tossed it on the bottom of the bed while he wrote rapidly. 'We'll find out all about Mr Pullinger. Can you give me his address, please?'

'Well . . . he moved again recently. He's, er, he's had some personal problems. I don't know the details. I learned a long time ago not to hem Lance in. He told me what he wanted me to know.'

'Sounds unusual,' Dan said, still writing. 'As if he had something to hide. Any idea what that would be?'

'Not really. He had some issues, that's all. I try to accept the people I care about without abusing friendships.'

Dan clicked the point of his pen in and out. 'Does that include people who do things outside the law?'

'If you think you've got some bombshell to drop, drop it, chief inspector. I don't know anything else that might help you. I was on the site yesterday to look at progress – particularly on a couple of houses people are interested in buying. I went to the trailer expecting to find Lance there. He works all hours. There was a fire. The rest you know.'

'Thank you,' Dan said. 'If I find a bombshell, I'll drop it for you, Mr Hill. Until then I'd like you to be available at your home. Knighton House in Temple Guiting, is that it?'

'That's the place,' Bob said.

'Good. I know it. Forgive me for interrupting your visit, Alex, but I'd like you to come with me.'

The door to a family waiting room stood open across the corridor. With a look at Constable Finney to let him know his poor decision to allow Alex into Hill's room hadn't gone unnoticed, Dan waved her to the room and shut them in.

She stood in the middle of shiny beige linoleum with her hands in the pockets of a red body-warmer. He could almost hear her trying to anticipate what was on his mind. This was a good time to unsettle her a bit to see if his hunches were right and she was hiding information.

'Why was Lily so skittish last night?' He could tell that wasn't a question Alex expected. 'Sit down. We'll be a little while.'

She sat on a chair with a yellow padded seat and rested an elbow on the table beside her.

He remained standing. 'Your mother was either looking for trouble with us, or very upset about something. You'll admit she was in a nasty mood.'

'No,' Alex said, narrowing her eyes at him. 'No, I won't admit that. You don't know anything about my mother. Why should you? She'd been worried about me being gone for so long when she expected me back hours earlier.'

'You still have to do what your mother wants?'

She put a fingertip between her teeth and he wouldn't be surprised if she wished it were his and she could give it a painful bite.

'Mum and I keep each other aware if we're going somewhere. That's normal in some families. It's kind. Perhaps you have different expectations in yours.'

What family? He couldn't afford to be diverted by snipes she knew might bother him. Alex was aware that he was alone, divorced, and looking forward with near desperation to a visit from Calum. His son was the only bright spot in his personal life.

'You could have phoned, Alex.'

'I did, but I couldn't keep on calling and I was later than I expected. The weather was bad, remember. Slippery.'

'And you've been driving on ice or snow or whatever for years. But I don't think that was all of it. Why would she be angry about a building development? What's really made her so unhappy?'

Alex pulled at the knees of her jeans and bent forward. What was different here? He had an inkling but needed her to open up.

She folded her arms and looked at the floor beside her.

'Alex?'

Straightening in the chair, she looked directly at him. Her eyes were brimming with tears. 'Yes. Leave that, Dan. It's nothing of interest to you. My mum's having a difficult time with something very personal, that's all I will tell you.'

'Understood.' He had to turn away or he wouldn't deal with this as he should. A box of tissues on the table caught his attention and he moved to slide them toward Alex. Then he waited a few moments, registering great flakes of snow driven to the window by the wind that had come up that morning.

'Seeing you at that site yesterday was a shock,' he said, moving closer to the glass and touching a cold pane. 'You know Robert Hill, don't you?'

'What? Oh, I do now but I didn't before the fire.'

'I'd like to believe you. Lying has never been your style.' Talking to her like this didn't sit well with him. 'But there's a reason you don't want to tell the truth. You wouldn't stay away from him last night and here you are this morning – after I asked you to wait for word from us before coming.'

'He's a nice man and he had a horrible shock. Showing kindness comes naturally to me. I didn't realize how unpleasant you can be.'

'Dammit.' Swinging to face her he spread his hands. 'You've been a difficult read ever since we met. One minute I think I almost know you, the next you're a stranger and a mystery.'

He dropped his arms to his sides.

'You held hands,' he said. He hadn't intended to go there but it niggled at him. 'People who just met don't usually do that. He called you his friend and when he looks at you he likes what he sees.'

Alex shot to her feet. 'That's horrible of you, Dan. Bob is still shocked. You can tell that. And he's upset about Lance's death – very upset. They've been friends a long time.'

This wasn't the time to make an enemy of her. 'I may have come to the wrong conclusion. We'll be checking out Mr Hill's movements, and yours. You'll understand that's routine. This is one of those situations when I can't ignore what I've seen – and heard. He's a lot older than you, but that doesn't have to rule anything out. Or you could have some other ties you're not talking about. There's nothing personal.' And he wished he believed that completely.

'May I go now, please?'

Before Dan could respond there was a knock on the door and LeJuan Harding put his legendary woman-killer face around the door. 'There you are, guv.'

'In the flesh, Sergeant Harding.'

LeJuan's smile became blinding. 'Thanks, guv. You heard.'

'I usually do when one of my constables passes his sergeant's exam. Congratulations. What have you got for me?'

'Your hat.' LeJuan stepped all the way into the room, all well over six feet of lean and muscular black confidence. 'Hello, Alex. It's always a pleasure to see you.' He bowed and Dan narrowed his eyes.

'Congratulations on your promotion,' Alex said quietly.

A sensitive man who read atmosphere well, LeJuan raised his brows. He gave Dan the hat. 'You left it on Hill's bed,' he said. 'I really need a word with you, guv. I'll wait outside.'

'Alex is going. We can talk here.' He held the door open for Alex to leave and closed it again behind her. 'Fire away,' he said, with a falling sensation in the pit of his stomach.

'Our lovely police surgeon is on a tear again. Dr Lewis wants to know why the hell you aren't dancing attendance on her right now.'

Dan frowned. 'Because I'm here. If she'd wanted me at the post-mortem, she should have said so. Her office told me she'd rather not put up with my "inane" questions when she needed to concentrate on a complicated case.'

Sucking in the corners of his mouth, LeJuan didn't do a perfect job of disguising a smile. He cleared his throat. 'That's not where she wants you. She says it's a dereliction of duty for you not to be at the second site by now.'

'Bloody hell. What's she talking about? What second site?'

'Christ!' LeJuan rubbed a large hand over his face. 'They didn't reach you, did they? Another victim—'

'From the fire?'

'Nothing to do with the fire – or not the way you mean. This one's in Winchcombe itself. Female. Cause of death not yet determined. Bill Lamb is on his way there and he said to tell you to get your skates on. He said this one could be connected to the one yesterday.'

SEVEN

Why hadn't she known she ought to speak to Harriet and Mary Burke? Why hadn't that been the first thought into her mind after seeing them with Lily last night. She should have done it first thing that morning – or before that while her mother had been quietly angry for weeks. No matter how much she tried to tell herself that she had never noticed a particular closeness, a familiarity between Lily and the two older women, she was not being honest. How could she miss it? But perhaps that was forgivable because when something had always been there and never changed, you might not think too hard about the reason or the meaning.

Alex's mother and the Burke sisters treated one another like . . . like members of a reserved family who got along well, trusted, and probably took their relationship for granted.

The morning had been in the realm of a very puzzling and uncomfortable experience that she would mostly rather forget. Dan O'Reilly's behavior had floored her, embarrassed her, made her feel guilty when there was nothing to feel guilty about. He'd acted like an all around jerk.

None of those things would she have expected of Dan. Too much emotion had rushed in since yesterday and it muddied her thoughts. This pile up of personality clashes made a hard time harder.

The walk from the Black Dog to Pound Street and Leaves of Comfort was short and she was glad the snow had stopped, at least for a while. In addition to the tea rooms, the Burke sisters incorporated the sale of new and used books and sold myriad locally made handcrafts.

What was left of the beautiful garden that bloomed for so many months sported a fresh blanket of snow. Alex went up the garden path past dormant beds where crocuses and snow-drops would be among the first flowers to appear, to a pair of deep blue doors. Side-by-side terraced cottages had been combined into one and both front doors remained – the left for customers and the right for the sisters, although they both opened into the tea rooms. Harriet and Mary must have chosen the right-hand door for themselves because it was directly in front of stairs rising to their flat. The second set of stairs had been blocked off and turned into storage.

Snow mounded on the gabled porch and traced leafless wisteria vines that climbed the wall. Although she could see customers at tables inside, there was little to hear but birds on the forage and the snapping of sticks under the snow's weight.

Considering for only an instant, Alex chose the bell for the flat and gave it a push. The tea rooms were open for afternoon tea so the ladies might not be upstairs, but this was a personal, very personal visit.

She stood back to look at a window upstairs which usually opened to allow Harriet or Mary to call down and ask her up. Instead, the door on the right opened and one of the women who worked at Leaves of Comfort smiled out. 'Hello, Alex. They just went up for a bite of late lunch. Said to send you after them.' So, she'd been seen from the windows as usual.

Winifred Sibley, who comfortably filled out a floral, wrap-around pinafore, waved Alex inside. 'Get in quick. It's cold enough to freeze the bottom off a brass monkey.' She winked and went back to serving customers.

Among the items displayed for sale around the rooms on high, antimacassar-draped shelves, were small china dolls dressed entirely in handmade lace and fine lawn. These were Winifred's work and Alex owned one which she kept in the library at Lime Tree Lodge in company with her extensive collection of children's books.

'What's taking you so long?' Harriet Burke called from the top of the stairs to the flat. 'The kettle's on.'

Banging snow from her boots onto the doormat, Alex waved at Harriet and spread greetings to those she knew – which was most present – having tea at mismatched wooden tables, any of which was for sale together with their handmade cloths.

Taking the stairs two at a time she paused to scratch Oliver the sinewy gray tabby between the ears. Oliver was the stay-at-home member of the family. No carousing in pubs for him.

'We thought we might see you,' Mary Burke said from her spindle rocker. Today's Spanish comb – she always wore one in her white chignon, minus the mantilla – looked to be made of pink coral and was quite beautiful.

At the sound of a kettle's whistle from the kitchen Harriet stood up from her overstuffed chintz chair. 'I'll make that tea. We've the best custard tarts from George's. One of the good things about growing old is that one can eat tarts for lunch, or pudding first at dinner. What would we do without George's? That bakery may not know they are our partner, but we could never manage without them.' She went into the kitchen but popped out again and said, 'I mustn't forget about Gladys. Did Gladys Lymer come to see you about a job?'

Alex shrugged. 'No.'

'She's a bit shy about it,' Mary said. 'Life at Major and Mrs Stroud's isn't working out very well anymore. Not enough hours and, well, you know only too well how the Strouds are.'

'Gladys is a housekeeper.' She wasn't prepared to talk about this now.

'She's also a fine cook and we did sort of drop the idea that you're busy these days and might be able to use capable extra hands in the restaurant kitchen.'

'Gladys?' Puzzled, Alex paused in the middle of taking off her coat. 'I always thought she was settled with the Strouds.'

Neither sister responded.

'Yes, well . . .' Alex didn't want to be distracted.

Harriet said, 'Her husband is Frank. I don't think he's kept much work for some time. Gladys is looking for another job. She's such a good cook and we were thinking you might be able to use her.'

The timing was bad for this discussion. 'I . . . I might be able to. She should come and talk to me. Good cooks aren't so easy to find out here – not reliable ones. My chef is Phil Jenkins. I'll talk to him, but have Gladys come to me. I've known her forever.'

'That's wonderful,' Harriet said, beaming. 'And I think Mary should have said, we *hoped* you'd come today. You must be on edge, Alex dear. I know we are. And we're worried about our Lily. But let me get that tea.'

'I want you to sit down and relax,' Mary said to Alex, indicating the rather lumpy rose velvet sofa reserved for guests. 'And I don't want you to worry about your mother. I'm certainly not concerned. It's Harriet who always overreacts in these situations.' Mary wound a cutwork linen handkerchief tightly back and forth through her fingers. 'I've given up trying to be a voice of reason. My sister must just work these things through on her own.'

Rather than sit immediately, Alex finished taking off her long, green, down-filled coat and went to the window that overlooked the pretty churchyard abutting the Burke's back garden. St. Aldwyn's plain little Victorian church was made beautiful by grand deciduous and coniferous trees. 'The snow makes things so pretty,' she said, not ready to start what might feel like an inquisition. 'But I like to think of all the climbing roses in the churchyard when spring and summer come.' What she would really like was to get rid of the dread closing in around her.

'Here we are.' On a trolley, Harriet brought in small sandwiches, tea and cakes, and the custard tarts on their own pretty china plate. She caught Alex's eye with sharp intensity. 'This is going to be a conversation we should have had years ago, but Lily wasn't ready. I had begun to believe she never would be.'

Alex served Mary and took tea for herself. She didn't feel like eating.

'So,' Harriet said, resuming her seat, 'what don't you know?'

'Everything,' Alex replied. 'I don't know a thing.' She stood near an electric fire in the grate, presently flanked by Oliver and Max.

'That's what I was afraid of,' Mary said. 'What we can't decide is how much of a problem that presents.'

'What does that mean?' Alex made herself go to the sofa and sit down. Being with Tony had helped but still she hadn't slept much last night and there had been too much to take in for the past twenty-four hours.

Since silence had met her question she decided to wait them out rather than push for answers.

Mary's cup clattered into its saucer, rattling the teaspoon. 'Please ask questions, Alex. We'll answer what we can, what seems appropriate – or perhaps I should say the questions we know answers for. It's not my place to have opinions on other people's lives but, of course, I do. I hope Lily will want to talk to you herself soon. She's amazing – very brave – but she's paid a price for sharing so little with you. She thinks she's been shielding you.'

'I'm sure she does,' Alex said. 'And she has a right to guard her own feelings but don't you think it could do harm not to let me know more about myself? At least now?'

'Yes,' Harriet said simply and clearly. 'That's why I said we hoped you would come to us.'

'What would my mum say about us talking?'

'We haven't discussed it with her. Last night we talked about her mother and let her get some of the sadness out. It was beyond painful to be abandoned, as any abandoned child would tell you. I was surprised – and pleased – when she went so far as to admit she never stopped hoping her mother would come back. I think the fear of totally losing a parent is enormous to a child. When you're young, the only constant you have in your life is the person, or people, you're supposed to look to for protection. She lost that.' She paused a moment. 'There are far too many children who never feel safe because even if they have parents, they're not there for them.'

Alex leaned forward, listening intently, feeling the sting of tears in her eyes. 'I was never afraid my mother wouldn't be there for me. Yes, I had the childhood fears that something could happen to her because my world revolved around hers, but I didn't think she could stop loving me, or walk away and leave me.' She set her cup and saucer aside and dug in her pocket for a tissue. 'She talked to you about her mother?'

Harriet leaned back in her chair. 'When we first met Lily she was almost twenty. You were about two. She'd spent a good deal of her childhood in foster care and she only has good things to say about the family she was with.

'She had been here to the Cotswolds from London on some sort of outing – from a summer school camp for young people who hoped to go to a university. That was when she was about seventeen. I should say an outing with the camp which was also in the Cotswolds. As far as we can remember she's never said where the camp was, but this was the area where she felt she wanted to make a life. Then when she got back to London she found out you were coming along and the foster family couldn't manage everything, although they tried. She had to go to a place where she could stay until you were born. Lily never doubted she wanted you. What she did fight against was having to give you up for adoption after you were born. She was told she would have to give you up, you see.'

Harriet looked down into her cup and Alex saw her throat jerk.

'This is awful,' Alex said, gulping breaths. 'I mean awful to think of Mum going through it all. How frightened she must have been. But she would never tell me anything about it.'

'Her mother . . .' Harriet looked to Mary, a plea in her eyes.

'Her mother had no childhood to speak of.' Mary carried on for her sister. 'Angela, her name was. We don't know the last name because when we met Lily she was already using Duggins and she avoided her real name. Later on she changed it legally – said she found the name in a children's story about a poor family that never thought they were poor because they were never afraid and they got by.'

Alex rubbed her eyes and covered her face. Was this harder because it was all coming now, when she had accepted there was nothing she would know about the past?

'Lily's early years were spent in some sort of commune. She was brought up by a group of young people her mother had gravitated to. Lily said they all treated her like their child, more or less, until there were other elements that turned your grandmother's life . . . it got bad.'

'Just tell me about it,' Alex said. She had imagined so many scenarios about Lily's life and about her own early life, but not this.

'Lily talked in a kind of code but we understood there were drugs and alcohol and Angela got drawn into a bad place. Lily with her. Eventually Child Protection Services were alerted and intervened. Lily was taken away from Angela then.

'As she more or less admitted in front of you last night,

Lily had hoped she and her mother would be back together one day. When she was ten, she saw Angela for the last time. We'll probably never know what life was like for her after that. Lily doesn't even know for sure how she was tracked down with the letter from Angela she showed us last night. She has to go to an office somewhere – in London, I think – and sign for some final effects. We doubt there's much, but Angela expressed wishes that after she died – and I gather she was ill for a long time – her letter was to be sent to Lily who would decide if she wanted to collect the things her mother left behind. Obviously, she hasn't decided yet but we think she will go.'

Alex didn't bother to wipe away the tears. She cried silently while her throat burned and ached. 'What about . . . do you know anything else about my mother – and her mother?'

This time the silence went on and on and when she looked from one sister to the other, each of them kept their hands in their laps and their eyes downcast.

'Perhaps that's for another time?' Alex said when she couldn't stand the heaviness a moment longer.

'Yes,' Harriet said. 'Forgive us.'

'Forgive Lily,' Mary added.

'There's nothing to forgive.' Alex got up. 'I'd better get back. I've already been gone too long.'

'Of course.'

She'd never seen Harriet cry but tears were close now. 'We'll make sure the three of us talk soon, Alex. Allow us to think about this.'

'Yes.' Alex started for the door. She wanted to escape, to get into the clean cold fresh air and empty her mind.

Heavy footsteps hurrying up the stairs startled all of them. 'Let's not talk about any of this now,' Alex said. 'You've done the right thing.'

A sharp rap on the door surprised them all into silence.

The knock came again and Harriet cleared her throat to call out, 'Come in.' She stood up and so did Alex. Mary made a move toward her cane then changed her mind.

Tony.

Lowering his head beneath the lintel, Tony stepped into the

room. He wore blue scrubs and had forgotten to take off his soaked shoe covers. His hair was wet. When he saw Alex, he shook his head. 'I've looked all over for you. And according to Bill Lamb, so have the police. Be grateful they didn't alert your mother.'

'I didn't know you needed to keep tabs on me,' she said, but didn't have the heart or the energy to sound cross.

'Give me a moment to calm down. Bill Lamb called me and actually said they thought they should try not to worry Lily. Amazing. He's the last touchy-feely candidate I'd think of.'

Harriet poured a cup of tea and went to press it into his hands. 'Sit. Now. And tell us what all the fuss is about.'

He sat on the couch and took a long swallow of tea. 'I don't even know if I'm supposed to repeat anything. And I don't know what it means anyway.'

Harriet gave him a narrowed-eye look.

'Tell us,' Alex said. 'You can't rush in like this and not tell us what you know.'

'I don't know anything – not a thing. Bill Lamb asked us to wait for him at the Black Dog. That could take a long time. His words, not mine, but I think they may be onto something important. When he's ready, he expects to find you there.'

EIGHT

Wood, which was dusty and gray with age, covered the hall floor inside the Winchcombe cottage door on the High Street, and continued up the stairs. Threadbare and haphazardly rolled pieces of carpet all but blocked a passage to the rest of the downstairs which must formerly have been a shop.

'How much did you say they paid for this?' Dan asked, pulling on the blue disposable jumpsuit one of the SOCOs had given him.

Slightly hunched to avoid tearing the suit that was too short for him, Detective Sergeant LeJuan Harding – Dan was still getting used to the newly minted sergeant bit – said, 'Don't know the actual figure but the uniforms outside reckoned they heard you could buy several spanking new houses with all the fancy trimmings for less and the negotiations for the bottom floor where there must have been a shop aren't even finished yet.'

'It's probably a listed building,' Dan said, climbing over a pile of grungy carpet scraps. 'For all we know, King Charles II and Nell Gwynn slept here.'

LeJuan chuckled behind him and they climbed the hollow-sounding stairs. 'From the stories, they slept just about everywhere else. But this might be a bit downmarket for him, I'd say.'

At the top of the flight, a uniformed constable stood outside an open door and a shaft of glaring white light shone out and across the landing. Voices inside the room were muted. SOCO went about their tasks with quiet efficiency. Apart from the occasional spot of black humor, the task consumed them.

Not so much silence for police surgeons. Dr Molly Lewis's sharp voice rose above the rest, incisive and often cutting.

Dan heard his name but shut out what was said. Instead he asked the copper at the door, 'What room is this?'

'One of those all-in-one things, sir. All new – or all new old, if you know what I mean. Sitting room, dining room and kitchen. I reckon they were working down from the top of the house, redoing as they went. Won't make any matter now. Not to her anyway.'

'Thanks,' Dan said. He didn't need to ask what he'd find on the other side of the doorway.

LeJuan preceded him and made an immediate overall canvass of a room which, despite being the result of several spaces combined into one, was still a compact area. Cozy, or it would be without the surprisingly small corpse of a long-haired brunette lying partly face-down with her head on the hearth in front of a long-cold fireplace. From the waist down, her body rotated to face upward, legs clad in blue workout tights and bare feet splayed.

'No smoking,' Dr Lewis barked.

Dan had a violent urge to bum a fag and light up, which was odd since he rarely, if ever, smoked. 'What have we got, Molly?' It was always best to attempt jollying her along.

'What do you smell?' she shot back.

He didn't have to sniff. 'Petrol.' And given the putrid stench in the room that meant more than a few drops of fuel.

A petite blond woman, Molly Lewis pushed her hood away from her forehead and wiped at some sweat. 'Glad you could join us.'

He let it go. Molly had troubles she had never shared with anyone, even though it was widely known that she drank too much whenever she wasn't working.

Dark hollows underscored her eyes. 'I just want you to take a good look at this in case there's something being missed.' She indicated a winged armchair upholstered in green tartan tapestry, blotched tapestry now, with a garment, probably a coat, crushed in a sodden heap at the back of the seat. 'It's been photographed from every angle. Once you're satisfied I want it taken to the lab. I think almost all the petrol dumped out is on the coat, not that I'm an expert on things like that.'

She was an expert on most things. 'Right.' He looked at it from all sides and checked photos a technician showed him. 'How about under the cushion? And the coat? Anything identifying on that?'

'Could we get it out of here first, Dan?' His old friend Molly showed through for an instant. 'That's a smell that gets to me. If it all goes up in here . . .' She was afraid of fire, he realized, more than afraid.

'There isn't all that much petrol here but you're right. Preserve the integrity and get it to the lab, boys and girls. They'll know how to deal with it. Any idea how long—'

'Don't even go there,' Molly said. 'You know I don't guess at these things.'

'I wasn't asking about the time of death, Molly,' Dan said calmly. 'I was thinking about how long the petrol or whatever has been here. Probably makes a difference to how flammable it is after a while. Better get the carpet from underneath, too.' To his untrained eyes the rug looked valuable, old maybe, possibly Chinese. But what did he know?

Technicians lifted the chair, revealing a mostly empty whisky bottle underneath. This was rapidly put into an evidence bag and logged.

'Any sign of whatever the petrol was in? To bring it in here?' Looking around, Dan was met by blank faces.

'Could have been carried out and dumped,' LeJuan said.

Dan knelt beside the body with Molly while LeJuan stood behind them. 'Do we know who she is?' Dan asked. Shiny congealed blood spread under her head and streaked the hearth. More blood had settled beneath the right shoulder where it was twisted forward, partly on the hearth, partly on the highly polished oak floor. Hair, some thick with blood, obscured the face. He looked up at Molly who beckoned an assistant over.

'Her name?' Molly said.

The man consulted notes. 'Driving license in the name of Darla Crowley. Ah—32. Brunette. Blue eyes. 5ft 3ins. This is the address listed. Plenty of mail addressed to her, too, sometimes using the last name, Pullinger.'

'Say that again.' Dan eased back to sit on his heels. 'Crowley was also known as Pullinger, is that what you said?'

'Yes, sir.'

That was the last name he'd expected to hear. 'Other personal effects?' Dan asked. Very carefully, he moved enough hair aside to get a look at her. 'Poor woman,' he muttered.

'When this officer told me about the names, that's when I wondered . . . well, we'll see,' Bill Lamb said, coming through the door from the landing. 'They're taking it slowly. Being very careful. There's an office of sorts one floor up. Looks like a tip. Someone's been at it, unless the deceased decided to have a turn out. I'd put my money on whoever did that—' he inclined his head to the body – 'having a sort through upstairs.'

'You saw the name?' Dan asked.

Bill nodded. He glanced around at the others in the room. 'I thought we'd get to that later. It's on some of her mail and on the bills. But not on the driving license. I'll call in to have someone dig deeper.'

'I saw the name, too,' Molly said. 'Bit of a coincidence – or not a coincidence at all.' She carried on working.

'Pretty woman,' Dan said. 'Nasty blow to the temple but it didn't bleed enough to do all this.' Dan indicated the blood beneath her shoulder. He bent closer. 'Whisky.' He searched around. 'We've got the bottle. Lagavulin. Find any used glasses? There's several on the tray by the sofa.'

'Scalp wounds are bloody,' Molly commented. 'And these are extensive.'

'Unused,' a technician announced. 'No prints. We haven't seen any other glasses like this, including in the kitchen. Looks like it was drunk from the bottle so we may get saliva at least.'

'The sooner I get her on the table, the sooner we'll have some answers for you,' Molly said.

'Small woman,' LeJuan said, almost to himself. 'Must have been easy to knock her around.'

Dan glanced at him. LeJuan had a short fuse when it came to men rough-handling women. Dan liked him for it but hoped it wouldn't put his career on the line one day.

'So, tell me it's more than the petrol, kerosene, or whatever, that makes you think this is connected with the death at the building development yesterday.'

'Much more,' Bill said. 'That's a sideshow. There's much more. I know we need to keep this out of the press for as long as possible if we want an advantage, so I thought it best not to be too specific. I was surprised no one leaked anything to the media last night.' He met Dan's eyes and they both raised brows. 'Someone's got connections.'

Dan grunted. 'Anything strike you, Molly?'

'You first,' she said.

He sighed. 'Why did I expect you to say that? Caution could be your middle name. Does the victim have more than one injury to the skull?'

'Yes,' she answered simply. 'As soon as you're done here, we'll both have a clearer idea what happened.'

'She could have fallen and hit her head, then tried to get up and fallen again,' LeJuan said. 'That could account for two blows.'

'Bit convoluted, maybe?' Dan said. 'But don't stop thinking.'

Molly was making comments for the recording. She finished and turned back to Dan. 'I think we can bag this one?'

He nodded and stood back while SOCO snapped out a plastic body bag and unzipped it. With their usual efficient economy, they transferred the remains of Darla Crowley, or Pullinger, inside, closed the bag and lifted it onto a gurney.

Dan looked, not at the departing body, but the floor where it had lain.

'Remember I told you the scalp bleeds profusely,' Molly said, patting his shoulder on her way out. 'Check in with the morgue later and we'll tell you when we'll be ready. Not that you aren't welcome at the party anytime, of course. We'll save you some cake.'

Shaking his head, he watched her go before studying the angles and blood spatters again, more drips than spatters. 'Get this, will you,' he said to the photographer – superfluously since the clicking was already underway.

'Upstairs, then,' he said to Bill. 'You, too, LeJuan.'

'Boss,' Bill said, stopping on the landing. 'I didn't reach Alex but Tony's on it and he didn't seem worried about her.'

For all that he tried not to be with her too much, he couldn't pretend – not to himself – that Alex Duggins wasn't important to him. Just because she'd made it clear in the past that there couldn't be anything between them didn't mean he'd managed to turn off every vestige of what he felt for her. 'Did you explain to Tony that there have been new developments in the case and we want to impress on Alex that this is potentially very serious?'

'Yeah. If she doesn't show up, he'll call me. I arranged to meet them later.' Bill grimaced. 'I told Tony we could be late but one or both of us would catch up with them. I didn't mention tracking down the rest of Bob Hill's family.'

'Why would you?'

'Only that it could put it even later before we get to Tony and Alex again,' Bill said.

Dan nodded. 'We need Alex to stay away from Hill. Even when she's trying to mind her own business she mixes things up.'

'She means well,' Bill said, surprising Dan.

The flight to the next floor was even narrower than the last one. They went, single file, to a small office where, as Bill had warned, there was chaos.

'What do you think on the two Pullingers?' Bill asked. 'Married? Brother and sister?'

'Cousins?' Dan added. 'Major coincidence? I didn't see that coming. How come Hill didn't mention it, I wonder.'

'He must have known we'd find out,' Bill said.

'Yeah,' Dan said. 'If *he* knew, and he's innocent. But if he's our killer who knows what stories he's whisked up?'

'Bloody mess here,' Bill said.

There were heaps of scattered papers, books pulled from a wall of shelves and tossed wherever they fell, a filing cabinet spilling contents from sagging open drawers and desk drawer contents visible where drawers had been yanked out and dropped; beneath all this they could see an expensive antique desk and leather swivel chair. A small floral armchair faced the desk and between the detritus a silk Asian rug showed.

'So, someone mislaid their bus pass,' LeJuan said, deadpan.

With effort, Bill scraped the door shut over fallen papers. 'How long do you think we can keep the truth about last night from the public, boss? You can only plead accident for just so long, especially with this second body in the picture.'

Dan had known this was coming. If Bill hadn't asked, he'd have introduced the topic himself. 'I didn't think we'd make it this far without the media overrunning us. But since we have, I hope we can put them off until we talk to Molly later.'

'As soon as it gets out, we'll lose our advantage,' Bill said.

LeJuan shifted restlessly. Waiting to be put in the picture. He knew enough not to ask what he didn't know about the previous night.

'True, but only part of it. The trick then will be vigilance. We'll expect movement from somewhere and we'd better be watching to see where that is. But I don't see the connection between last night's and today's victims.'

'You will.' Bill pulled an evidence bag from an inside pocket and held it up. 'Whoever did this search was sloppy. Otherwise they would have found this.'

Dan frowned. 'Is that logged in?'

'No,' Bill said. 'But it will be when it's eventually found.'

'Christ,' Dan said. 'Just don't tell me, or anyone, how you intend to reintroduce it.' He moved closer and peered through the plastic bag at a passport opened to the bearer photograph. 'Where was this?'

'Passport dropped down behind the bottom desk drawer, probably when the top drawer was manhandled out.'

'I don't know this man,' Dan said and LeJuan shook his head, no.

'Just read the name. You know that.'

Dan fished out glasses and peered closer through the distorting bag. 'Holy hell,' he said in a harsh whisper. 'Lance Pullinger. Now we need to find Darla's passport.'

Getting Molly Lewis out of the morgue to talk about a case wasn't easy. When she finally came toward Bill and Dan in the deserted Remembrance Garden provided for grieving families, she moved at a trot, her blue puffer coat turning her into a small blimp on tiny ankles and feet. A black wool cap covered her short blond hair.

Bill and Dan stood up. 'Thanks for coming, Doc,' Dan said. 'Take a pew.'

She planted her feet apart. 'I'll stand. Why the cover-up?'

An expert at innocent expressions, Bill's pale blue eyes popped wide.

'That's why we wanted a word now,' Dan said. 'This is the first opportunity we've had to get you on your own. We don't know how long we can let the press run with their assumptions but we're making the best of it while we can. We couldn't tell you in there, but Lance Pullinger's passport was found in Darla's house – not her house. We now know it belonged to Pullinger. He bought it eight or nine months ago. But her name was on monthly bills, credit card bills and everything else left there. Sometimes she's Darla Crowley and sometimes Darla Pullinger. If the men's clothing in a closet and men's toiletries aren't Pullingers we've got another puzzle but we're pretty sure they are. We think Lance and Darla were in a close relationship.'

'And I couldn't have been told as soon as you knew?'

'When would we have done that, Molly? We didn't know till after you left the Winchcombe cottage.'

She skewered him with her eyes and raised a single fine

brow. 'Let me guess, you both lost your mobiles. You'll have to do better than that. The more details I have, the better job I can do. It might not make any difference but it could.'

Dan dug in his raincoat pocket for a bag of sherbet lemons – his drug of choice – pried one of the sticky sweets free and put it inside his cheek. He sucked fiercely for a few seconds.

'OK,' he said finally. 'Sometimes it's kinder not to be blunt but here it is, bluntly. A lot gets said during a post-mortem and it isn't all strictly professional. Doesn't matter a damn to me except we're scrambling to keep what we now know quiet, and hoping someone will say what they shouldn't know. There, that's it. The whole story.'

Molly sat and he dropped down beside her. 'You don't want anyone to know the truth about—'

'That's right,' he said quickly. 'And if I'd had a chance to explain in person I'd have asked you to keep schtum until it was common knowledge anyway. A word in the wrong place and we'll have a different ball game. We'll deal with that when it comes. When the first body was found, it was dark and the firemen who dealt with it had the sense to ask us what we wanted said. Were your people surprised by the condition of the body? Did they say anything?'

'No. They don't tend to get surprised – at anything. Apart from generalities there was no discussion ahead of time.'

'So, what do you feel like sharing with us?' Dan asked.

'Nothing.' She smiled and her face became the impish one Dan liked so much. 'But, since it's you two. Darla was body number one, not body number two.'

Dan and Bill stared at one another. 'And neither of them was a suicide?' Dan asked.

'Absolutely not. A lot of rage went into both killings. I avoid saying this, but I've never seen anything quite like it before. Similarities in both cases, but if Lance Pullinger hadn't been drunk out of his mind – which he was, soused to the gills – he might have fought it off.'

'Appropriate description,' Bill said mildly.

Another smile pulled at Molly's mouth. 'Very funny. Didn't I hear you were fond of a nice mackerel?'

Bill grimaced and shrugged inside his trench coat. 'I may never touch another one.'

'As I was saying,' Molly continued. 'Pullinger was fit, a strong, muscular man. If he had been in possession of his faculties, the outcome might have been different. I think he was incapable of doing more than thrashing around. Now, are you going to tell me the reason why he's not burned to a cinder and why there are multiple bone fractures and he's got cuts all over his face – and inside his mouth? And throat?'

That bought her blank stares. Frowning, Bill said, 'We don't have the complete report from Arson, but they think a petrol bomb exploded and he was blown through the back window – that big, wide affair – with minimum fire contact.'

'Fits,' Molly said.

'Makes sense the blast and subsequent impact could cause the broken bones. Glass from the window is the obvious reason for the cuts.'

'More or less,' Molly agreed. 'But we've got work to do on the oropharynx. The base of the tongue and the vallecula – that's the space between the base of the tongue and the epiglottis. About at the level of the hyoid bone. Lacerations are random and . . . why don't I show you what I mean? I left them working on the areas in question and it'll take some time. You can get an up-close look.'

'I think we've got the general picture,' Dan said. 'You'll spell it all out in your report. If and when we need more detailed explanation – probably in court – I'm sure you'll be there to make everything crystal clear.'

This time she didn't smile. 'I don't think Darla's death was planned. It has all the marks – and again, we're not finished with the finer points – of looking like another wild reaction to the unexpected. The only thing that didn't fit that scenario was the petrol. You'd expect that to have been planned and brought in. But you'll want to see if that was already easily at hand and an afterthought. Could be the perpetrator had a fleeting thought to burn the place down with the body in it, then changed his mind. The second time around, he went prepared.'

Dan would kill for a pint and a pork pie. There hadn't been

time for lunch and from the way things looked, they wouldn't get dinner either. He squeezed his features together and rubbed his face. 'How long between the two deaths?'

Molly pulled off her wool hat, scraped her fingers through her blond hair, and jammed the hat on again – all the way down to her eyebrows. 'I don't have a bloody crystal ball. How many times have you asked me questions like that and how many times have I said I need more time?'

'Just a guess please, Molly?' Dan wheedled.

She thought about it, propped her chin on a fist and thought some more. 'Not really so long, I'd say. But don't quote me,' she added rapidly. 'I think he didn't intend to kill her, went mad about something and did it, then didn't know the hell what to do. But Lance knew something that could be a threat to giving everything away so within hours the killer found and killed him, too. The killer isn't professional, or practiced even. All just a theory, of course. And the question would remain, will he run? Has he already run?'

Dan avoided acknowledging Bill's knowing little grin. But he knew his partner was thinking how much people like Molly liked to lay out their interpretation of a crime pattern, then step back to admire it and wait to be proved right.

Sometimes they were.

He didn't think Molly was this time and dread turned him cold. He wished whoever did these things would make a run for it – fast – and that they'd catch him before he fixated on the next victim, the next one he feared could give him away.

NINE

This was usually Alex's favorite time of the business day; after the early evening rush but while the Black Dog was still busy, filled with happy customers and decidedly mellow. The prospect of Bill Lamb arriving with questions designed to unnerve her spoiled the mood. The detective inevitably made her edgy and awkward.

Things at the Dog were good. She no longer worried whether the business was making enough money and she'd come to feel warm about the regulars, the folks who came in most nights to relax and share their good and bad times.

This evening, each time someone came in, she checked to see if it was Tony. He'd had to deal with an emergency at the clinic but she hoped he'd get back before Lamb arrived.

'Thoughtful, hmm?' Juste Vidal said in her ear. She stood behind the counter, watching the activity and Juste, her frequent help over several years, stood beside her, tray in hand. 'A good night, I think.'

'Good, yes. I have nothing to complain about.' Other than the heap of unpleasant questions that had piled in during the past couple of days.

Juste was French, from a town on the Loire, just hours south of Paris. He was in his final year as a divinity student in Chichester. He'd become a fixture at the Dog and much loved by many.

Alex had started to feel grim about the day when they'd have to do without him.

'I read the papers,' he said, and pushed his round, wire-framed glasses up his nose. 'It is too bad you happened upon one of these horrible deaths again. I believe it must happen because you have something to offer – for the good, Alex. You'll argue with me, but I see you are troubled.'

'No, I won't argue,' she told him. 'I'm very troubled. I can't believe I decided to go to that development on a whim and . . . well, look at all that's happened.'

'We don't control much that happens to us.'

She looked sideways at his serious, slender face. Often Alex had felt sympathetic toward the young women who had watched him with moonstruck eyes and almost swooned over his irresistible accent, not that she expected him to remain unattached. But for now, he seemed to care only for his calling, although he took time to know the people of Folly-on-Weir and Alex harbored hopes that he might eventually find his way to St. Alwyn's here in the village. An unlikely dream, but why not dream?

'Juste, do you think our fervent hopes can have any effect on what happens to us?' She wondered that on many levels.

He turned his honest, green eyes on her. 'I think they may. I believe in prayer, so how can I not believe in hope?' He smiled and the simple charm was melting. 'I shall clear some tables and glasses and hope all will be well, for all of us.'

Alex inclined her head to see the Burke sisters. Max curled up on their table – they no longer attempted to hide him – and they each had a half pint of shandy. She smiled, thinking of how much they meant to her. Earlier, she had visited with them by the fire and given reassurances that nothing would change the closeness they shared. Still she had felt their anxiety.

A tap on the shoulder brought her attention back to the present. 'Gladys Lymer's in the kitchen,' Hugh said. 'She says you're expecting her.'

'Oh, good,' she said. 'Where's Mum? I want her with me for this, too. Gladys has asked if we have a job for her. She's been recommended as a good simple cook. Could be really useful. You have the final say on hiring, of course.'

'I thought she was with the Strouds,' Hugh said, frowning.

'She has been, but apparently it may be time for her to make a change. What do you think? I should have asked you before I agreed to see her.'

He put an arm around her shoulders. 'I don't think we have to worry about ceremony,' he said. 'Phil gets overwhelmed, particularly when we do Sunday brunch. And we could use a cook on hand at breakfast time in here. I think there's a possibility for working up a good group of morning regulars if we have the labor.'

'I didn't think of that.' She smiled up at him. 'I knew you were a winner the moment I saw you, although I still don't know why you stay . . .' Her voice faltered and she felt hot.

Hugh gave her a serious look. 'I've never been happier than I am here. Sometimes we make really good decisions. I did when I came to you and I hope you keep on thinking you did, too.'

Before she could come up with an appropriate answer, he said, 'Here're Lily and Doc.'

Doc, tall, broad shouldered, unaffectedly good-looking and with an almost uncanny resemblance to Tony, entered into the pub and was immediately pulled to a halt by Major Stroud who threaded an arm through his and spoke meaningfully into his ear. If Tony's hair eventually became silver, like his father's, they would be doubles separated by a generation.

Lily wore a black jacket and red scarf, casually knotted, with a long black pleated skirt and slim heeled pumps. Looking at her gave Alex a lot of pleasure. Tonight Lily seemed her old, even-tempered self.

She beckoned her mum behind the counter and told her about Gladys. 'I meant to explain to you earlier but it's been crazy today. Anyway, I didn't think Gladys would come so soon.'

'I know she's a good cook,' Lily said. 'The idea of cooked breakfasts is good as long as we have enough help for the clean-up, too.' They went together to meet Gladys who shifted awkwardly, rubbing her hands together and looking overheated. Lily immediately reached to hug her and Alex could see how good her mother was at these things.

'I really like the idea of doing breakfasts,' Gladys said, smiling widely. 'I'm comfortable with anything you have in mind.' Her bleached hair was freshly permed and she wore the fake fur coat they usually saw when she came out for an evening with her husband, Frank.

'I have to ask,' Alex said. 'Do the Strouds know you're leaving?' Knowing the major was in the bar, she kept her voice down.

'Oh, yes.' Gladys struggled out of her coat. Her cheeks glowed now. 'I gave notice but the major said I could leave right away. You know how he is. He was very shirty with me.'

'I can imagine.' Lily grimaced. 'How will it be when you see him here?'

'He'll have to put up with it. He wouldn't want me telling anyone how difficult . . . well, he won't like it but that doesn't worry me.'

'Alex.' Hugh stepped past the wall of bottles that stood between the saloon bar and one of the kitchens. 'Lady here to see you. Esme Hill? She seems excited or nervous. Not sure which. Do you know her?' He gave Gladys a friendly smile.

Alex shook her head, no. She held up a hand and turned to her mother. 'Perhaps I do know her, in a way. May I leave Gladys with you for a while, Mum?'

Lily and Gladys both looked curious, as if they would like to check out Alex's visitor.

'How soon could you start?' Lily asked Gladys.

'Whenever you like.' Gladys's relief was in her voice and her eager face.

Alex turned back to Hugh and lowered her voice. 'Any idea who this woman is? What do you think?'

'I don't know her but she looks nice to me,' he said. He laughed. 'Actually, she's a knockout. There's a man with her. A lot younger but that's not so surprising anymore.'

Alex ran her fingers through her hair and followed Hugh into the bar. The name, Hill, hadn't escaped her.

'Hello.'

Before she could take stock of who had arrived, this dramatically-featured red-head with large blue eyes pressed against the counter, a huge bouquet of tropical flowers clutched in both hands.

'Hello,' Alex said, taking a quick look behind her to be sure this woman was talking to her. 'May I help you?'

'I'm Esme Hill,' the woman said. 'This is my son, Grant.' She waved vaguely at a confident-looking young man whose brown hair waved over the collar of a grey duffel coat. 'You're Alex Duggins, aren't you? My husband described you.'

Alex nodded. 'Yes.' Now she was sure who the woman must be.

'Bob's at home now but he told me all about how you helped him after the horrible fire.' Her face paled and her mouth became a tight line. 'Bob wanted to come himself but he's not quite ready to get out yet. Horrible thing that's happened. I can't believe it. I've got to thank you for being with Bob when that terrible thing happened. If it wasn't for you the burns would have been much worse. That's what they told me at the hospital. I was in London for a couple of days. Awful timing on my part. These are for you.' She thrust the brilliant flowers into Alex's hands.

'Thank you. But I didn't do anything anyone else wouldn't

have done.' Alex grasped the bouquet, feeling horribly uncomfortable. 'I just called the emergency services, that's all.'

'Thank *you*,' Esme Hill said earnestly. She reached out a hand and Alex automatically let the woman take hers in a firm grasp. 'I don't think you understand what could have happened if you weren't there. Bob's impetuous. He could even have tried to go back into the fire.'

Alex didn't mention that Bob Hill hadn't managed to get into the fiery interior of the trailer a first time. 'I'm glad it's working out as well as it is.'

Esme Hill stood straighter and flexed her shoulders. Her eyes became moist. 'We can't believe Lance Pullinger is gone. Poor man. Things so often didn't go his way but he will be terribly missed. Who would have done that to him?'

'Aren't the police still thinking it could have been an accident?'

Esme puffed out hard. 'Lance was a careful man.' Tears stood in her eyes. 'I suppose he could have been drunk too . . . that's not the point now. He didn't smoke, you know.'

At a loss for the right thing to say, Alex smiled and shook her head.

Esme leaned close to Alex. 'Would you help me with something? Would you not tell Bob I came to see you? He hates feeling what he calls "looked after". But he doesn't look after himself. If I can tell him you got in touch and said everything was fine from your end and he didn't need to worry about you, it would help him find some peace. He takes on everyone's problems and tries to solve them.'

Alex almost said she didn't have any problems, but she held back and studied the woman for an instant. 'Of course. Whatever will help.' But she wondered if Esme Hill wasn't too overprotective of her husband. Or even too controlling. It didn't matter to Alex.

'Bless you,' Esme Hill said. She looked at her son. 'Isn't this a lovely pub, Grant?'

Grant's dark eyes were cool. 'I like it,' he said. 'I'll have to get everyone to come here.'

Alex smiled but the outward warmth didn't come close to what she really felt. She didn't think she would like Grant Hill even if she ever came to know him.

'Almost forgot,' he said. 'Dad was going to get these to you since you run a pub. We're planning a pub and restaurant in the new development by Winchcombe. We're tossing names around. He thought of holding a contest. To be honest I don't think he thought of it until he was trying to come up with ideas of ways to thank you. He's having a "name the pub" contest and he wants you to have the entry forms for your customers.' He pulled a sheaf of papers from his pocket and set them on the counter in front of Alex. 'A thousand to the winner. Should interest one or two.'

She was rarely at a loss for words, but these two had arrived like steamrollers.

'Will you hand them out and make an announcement?' Esme asked. She lowered her voice. 'I think it's possible that a Black Dog entrant is slated to win the prize.' She smiled conspiratorially.

Alex collected herself. 'Surely your husband will wonder how the entry forms found their way to me if you were never here.' She let the idea hang there.

'Shows you how much experience I have with working these things out,' Esme said. She pulled her lovely red hair away from her neck while she thought about what Alex had said. 'Grant, could you have taken it into your head to run them by? To do something nice for your dear old dad?'

Grant rolled his eyes. 'Go ahead and tell him that. I'll back you up.'

This wasn't behavior that made Alex comfortable but there seemed no way out. 'Well, good,' she said. 'I hope your husband recovers quickly, Mrs Hill.'

'Esme, please. And I already think of you as Alex. Grant's younger sister – she's nineteen now – was almost Alexandra but Carmen won out. Bob thought it was more sophisticated. I still think he was wrong.' She smiled again. When she stepped back from the bar Alex saw a stunning figure in black and gray workout tights and a torso-hugging top that matched. Over one arm she carried a long alpaca cardigan which she now slipped on.

'I should have offered you a drink,' Alex said. 'The gorgeous flowers distracted me. Thank you so much for them.'

Esme waved a dismissive hand. 'They're nothing but I'm glad you like them. We'll say goodnight, then.'

'Good night,' Alex echoed, watching them leave.

Before she could return to the kitchen, Grant Hill came back. He pulled a glove from his pocket, put it on the bar and immediately picked it up again. 'Thank goodness,' he said, grinning. 'I thought I might have lost this altogether.'

Alex only stared at him until he leaned closer across the counter and said quietly in her ear, 'Just a friendly suggestion. Best you stay away from anything to do with my father. I'm telling you this out of kindness because you helped him.'

TEN

'No good deed goes unpunished.' That was one of Oscar Wilde's, but so was, 'A good friend will always stab you in the front.' I wonder what he said about someone you aren't sure is a friend anymore.

There's only one way to be safe: don't trust anyone and never let yourself feel safe.

I shall never again feel safe.

I hate driving at night and I hate this bloody sleet. I hate snow more.

And another load of that will be next. Look at this, the way the wind hurtles sleet at the headlights. It fills the beams and turns them into mirrors to make sure you see only what stops you from seeing what matters. Some good that is.

And the wipers are useless. I'm not supposed to have any nerves. I'm in control, always have been, and that's what I am now and I'll keep telling myself so. But there is a cost and I shall pass it on.

If something crosses in front of me, it's dead. I couldn't stop in time if I wanted to. I wouldn't try.

No one ever thought I'd make any waves. I'm the calm, trustworthy one. That will be my advantage because I've only just begun to make waves but they will turn into a man-killer of a tsunami. Man, and woman-killer if necessary.

Why did this have to happen? I was so careful. Paths have crossed that should forever have stayed separate. Everything is twisting. If people did exactly what you told them to do, and if no one unexpected chose to wander into the picture, it would all be easy and right now I'd be on my way to fixing the mess other fools have made. I've worked too long and too hard to watch it all destroyed now.

Black and white.

The world is black and white out there with no room for nuance – and it wants to take away everything that is rightfully mine. I've got it made, right? Wrong, or it will be wrong if I don't stop them from opening doors I locked a long time ago. I locked them and I didn't just throw away the keys, I melted them down. I covered my tracks, but not without considering what was best for everyone concerned.

I've done a lot of good. People are better off because of me. They may not think they are, but they don't know how I straightened things out for them and ensured they didn't make bad decisions. They may be about to find out the truth, then we'll see what must be done about them. What they do afterwards will make up my mind for me. I deserve to win.

One thing I am sure of; ingrates are no friends of mine. I'll stab them wherever is most convenient to me.

ELEVEN

'It's damned cold out there,' Tony said, walking into the snug at the Black Dog. 'It's snowing again now. Seriously snowing. This is turning into one hell of a winter.' He had kept on his heavy Barbour coat, zipped and snapped, and he tucked his jaw into the rolled neck of a heavy jumper. But still he couldn't control the shivers.

With a dog flanking either side of her on an upholstered banquette, Alex eyed him somberly. 'At least you're dressed for the weather now. In those cotton scrubs you had on this afternoon, you could have got frostbite.'

He knew when argument was pointless. 'Yeah. Perhaps I was too worried to think straight.'

'And I'm supposed to feel guilty? OK, I feel guilty. How much longer are we expected to wait here? Bill Lamb told you he'd be here hours ago. It's after midnight.'

Tony rubbed chilled hands together and stamped his feet. He didn't know the answer to the question and she wouldn't like the only thing he might tell her.

'Tony?'

He sat on a chair facing her and tried a smile. 'It's always nice in here. How about an Irish coffee?'

It amused him when she smiled but was trying not to. 'We closed some time ago, sir. Hugh's still back there but he shouldn't be.'

'I make a very good Irish coffee myself.'

'But you're not so good at avoiding topics you don't like.' She got up from the worn tapestry seat, went to the hatch into the bar and leaned through. 'Hugh, are you in a generous mood?'

A minute or so passed before Tony heard Hugh speaking from behind the bar. 'I'm in a lousy mood but for you, dear lady, anything. What is your pleasure?' Given his Welsh name, his Scottish accent might surprise a lot of people.

'Two Irish coffees,' she said although she didn't sound enthusiastic. 'Tony's freezing and I'm in a nasty mood. The coffee might help.'

'Put like that, how can I refuse?'

Alex returned wearing a slight smile. 'See. My smooth talk does it every time. Poor Hugh. He's getting it from all sides.'

'From customers pushing questions and demanding answers, from you and from Lily, do you mean? The police are behaving as if everyone's satisfied with their story of an accidental fire. They don't know the sharp minds of our people here. No wonder there are questions.'

'Nothing's getting any better between my mother and me, either,' she said, sliding back into her seat and readjusting the dogs with their heads on her legs. 'Mum's started putting on a much better front for other people, but she won't talk about anything personal at all now. You heard what went on last night – or the night before last by now. She let just so much out the way she did, then clammed up. I thought she was ready to be open with me. But I tried talking to her one time and didn't even get a full sentence out of my mouth.'

He met her almond-shaped, green eyes and didn't want to look away. 'Concentrate on me, Alex. On what I'm trying to get through to you. Perhaps it would be a good thing to leave Lily to come to her own decisions. I think she'll talk to you when she's ready.'

'And when is that likely to be? I've waited long enough and just when she finally starts . . .' She raised both palms.

Hugh ducked to look through the window into the snug. 'Two Irish coffees. My patented formula and guaranteed to cure whatever ails ye.'

'Thanks.' Tony hopped up to get the coffees. He dropped his voice. 'Bear with us if you can, Hugh. But if you know anything that could help with whatever's going on, call me. Anytime night or day.'

'Gotcha.' Unlike usual, Hugh's dark eyes weren't smiling. 'I wish I didn't feel there was something really big and nasty creeping up on us. I've never seen Lily the way she is.'

'No,' Tony said. 'My dad said the same thing.'

He returned to his seat. 'Did you know that?' he asked when he'd set the glass Irish coffee mugs on the table. 'Even Dad has backed off from asking Lily much and you know those two share things they wouldn't tell us.'

Alex cocked her head. She looked into the distance as if following a new train of thought.

'What is it?' Tony asked. He hadn't passed on Bill Lamb's warning to stay away from Bob Hill, and anyone or anything else to do with the case. It needed to be done.

'Nothing.'

'Freakin' rubbish, Ms Duggins. That busy brain of yours just jaunted off somewhere new, didn't it?'

She colored and stirred her coffee furiously with its cinnamon stick. 'Bonkers,' she muttered. 'It's all completely bonkers. I don't know what I should think about first, or if I should think about any of it at all.'

'I'll let you decide on that.' Not that he could decide anything for her. He did know that suggesting Bob Hill could represent danger wouldn't ease her mind.

'The coffee's good. Thanks for the idea. I'm sorry, Tony – for being irritable. This thing I'm dealing with shouldn't be your problem.'

'Really? I thought we shared our issues, not just the good times.'

Propping an elbow on the table, Alex held her mug in mid-air. 'Of course, but that doesn't stop me from feeling guilty when I'm a drag. I've got to step back and let it go – for your sake and for mine.'

He grinned, couldn't help it. 'I love it when you grovel.'

Alex laughed aloud. She tapped the back of his hand. 'I might as well confess that I tried to call Bill. Couldn't reach him. Same thing with Dan. Finish up your coffee. We're leaving and going back to your place – enough is enough.'

How good that sounded. 'Promise you'll still say that when I tell you the truth, the whole—'

'Tony! About what? What haven't you done?'

'When I spoke to Bill after I found you, he asked me to bring you back here and . . . he said he needed to know where you were for when he could get back to see you.'

She shook her head slowly. 'You didn't say that before. When did you talk to him?'

He said, 'When I got back to the clinic.' And added quickly, 'He called me.'

'That was hours ago.'

'He said it could take hours.' Tony dropped his voice but it didn't sound any better. 'He wasn't sure when he could get away but they want to be sure you don't leave.'

'I haven't. No, I'm not having that. Lamb doesn't leave secondhand messages for me and expect me to follow instructions. I'm out of here. Come with me, or stay and apologize to Bill for letting me get away. He's probably forgotten all about us and gone home by now.'

Easing the dogs to the floor, she got up to leave.

'All right. I didn't want to say this, but Bill Lamb said that if you aren't here when he arrives, a warrant will be put out for your arrest.' Darn, why did he avoid what he found difficult by making jokes?

She laughed at that. 'I'm scared to death. Come on, you fibber.' Without warning, she sat again – thudded down and scrubbed at her face.

'Alex?' He moved beside her. 'Are you ill?'

'No. Not the way you mean. Weirded out and confused, but not ill. I wasn't going to say anything about it but there's stuff we probably ought to know and I don't see how we can.'

'Come on, sweetheart. Don't keep me in suspense.'

'Is it definite that the architect – Lance Pullinger – didn't die because of an accident? It could have been, couldn't it?'

'It could.' He gripped her shoulder and shook gently. 'But they know those things pretty quickly. The police wouldn't be involved the way they are with an accident – not once they ruled out foul play.'

'That's what I think. I told you about Esme Hill coming here. That was strange, Tony. She made a good show of charming me, but I didn't like any of it. She was telling me to stay away from her husband, I think, in a way. And Grant, her son, actually made an excuse to talk to me on our own and came right out with a warning. He flat out told me not to go near his father. What can that mean? I've thought about telling Dan and Bill but I've got to think about it.'

'They said these things to you here.'

'Right at the bar. With smiles on their faces like they were discussing the weather.'

At the sound of the door to the inn and restaurant slamming, Alex squeezed her eyes shut. 'Say that isn't Bill Lamb. We were almost out of here.'

Tony said, 'We haven't finished our coffees.' But he didn't feel either flippant or remotely comfortable.

Footsteps and a shadow passed the glass door to the snug. Tony and Alex looked questioningly at each other.

They didn't even have to strain to hear Bill Lamb say, 'Hugh. Good to see you. Alex didn't leave, did she?'

'Cheeky bastard,' she mouthed and Tony had to smile.

'I don't know,' Hugh responded in a slightly raised voice. 'Let me check out back.'

'Put Hugh out of his misery,' Tony murmured and opened the snug door. He went into the saloon bar where Bill Lamb waited, a knowing smile on his lips.

'Be grateful I don't have a short temper,' the detective said. 'You people do stick together, don't you? I suppose Hugh was giving you a chance to decide if you'd talk to me. Not a good idea if you want things on an even footing.'

'Alex and I are in the snug,' Tony said, ignoring Bill's comments. 'We're both pretty much all in but we knew you had a couple of questions for us.'

'For Alex,' Bill said, his face expressionless as usual.

'Is this an official interview?' Tony asked, standing his ground.

'Not at this point. Just a friendly exchange.'

'Good.' Tony went ahead of him into the snug and slid into the banquette beside Alex who had already resettled herself between the two dogs who now sat at alert, ears perked.

Bill threw off his trench coat, tossed his hat on the next table and settled in the barrel chair opposite. He took a notebook from his inside jacket pocket. He sat back and closed his eyes for an instant, ran a hand through his sandy crew cut.

'How about a beer?' Tony said. The man was tired and it showed. 'Or coffee?'

'Are you hungry?' Alex added.

When Tony looked at her he saw concern and a little pity. 'Yes, Lily leaves sandwiches in the kitchens.'

Bill looked from one of them to the other. He gave a short laugh and Tony wondered what it meant.

'What the hell. Half a pint of Doom Bar – I like to stick with a favorite. And if there's a sandwich going spare, I'll take it. Thanks.'

It was Alex who hopped up, taking Bogie in her arms, and left the snug.

Tony was certain Bill would have preferred to be left alone with Alex. 'Long day?' he said, and draped an arm around Katie, whose body shivered with tension just under the skin.

'They all are,' Bill said. 'But this is the job I chose. I must like it.' His smile didn't reach his eyes.

'I didn't quite get to warning Alex about Bob Hill,' Tony said. 'Is there something else I could help with while she's busy?'

Bill rubbed at his brow. 'Let's wait for her. If you need to leave, I'll make sure she gets home safely.'

'Thanks,' Tony said, but he wouldn't be leaving Alex alone. 'I'll stay as long as Alex wants me.' He'd seen nothing to suggest Bill had any hold over Alex's actions.

'Radhika likes working at your clinic,' Bill said, surprising Tony. 'I'm glad she feels safe and settled here.'

His own smile was automatic and genuine. 'She's loved around here, Bill. Who wouldn't be glad she's part of the community?'

That got him a speculative stare. 'Doesn't always follow that nice people are accepted, not if . . .' He looked at his hands.

Tony considered but only for an instant. 'Not if they're of a different race? I suppose that's true, but not of the people who matter. She's one of us now. She's a lovely, caring woman. We're lucky to have her here. I'm certainly lucky to have her.'

Bill raised his eyes slowly. 'You won't get any arguments from me.'

Why not take the plunge? 'You're fond of each other, aren't you?'

Crossing his arms, Bill nodded. 'Yes. Very. I've never met anyone like her but I don't fool myself there aren't cultural hurdles. Not between us so much, but . . . well . . . no, there aren't any between us but she's gentle, fragile. In the past she's been hurt, but you know that. Anyway, that's my problem.'

'And something tells me you're happy to take on the problem. Am I right.'

'Yes, you are. I hope I can find a way to work things out for us.'

Tony took a swallow of his cold Irish coffee and decided it tasted just as good cold or hot. 'You've got our support,' he said.

Alex walked backward through the door, a tray in her hands,

and Tony was grateful to see her. 'I thought we might all like something to eat,' she said, sliding the tray on the table.

Bill took his Doom Bar while Alex passed out plates and put a heaping platter of sandwiches on the table. She placed a brandy snifter in front of Tony and another on her own side of the table. 'If you want brandy, Bill, just speak up.'

'This is just the thing,' he said, downing half of his beer. 'Tell me what you know about Darla Crowley who also used the name Pullinger sometimes.'

Alex had picked up a cheese and pickle sandwich. She set it on her plate. 'Who is that?'

'You don't know?' Bill gave her his pale blue unblinking stare. 'Are you absolutely sure?'

She looked blank. 'I've never heard the name. Who is she?'

'What about Lance Pullinger?'

Alex shook her head, no. 'Yes, yes. Forgive me. Bob Hill talked about him being the man who died in the fire. So did Esme—' She clamped her lips together and picked up her snifter to swirl the brandy inside.

'Yes. Lance Pullinger. Did you ever meet him?'

She was pale and growing paler. 'No.' It was barely more than a whisper. 'This is horrible even to think about.'

'Who is this Darla?' Tony asked, unable to help himself.

'You'll find out in good time. We rather thought Alex already knew. Being so close to Bob Hill.'

'I'm not close,' she said quickly. 'I met him because of the fire at the construction site. That's it. I never saw him before in my life.'

Bill opened his notebook and scribbled a few lines. He took another swallow of beer and picked up the first sandwich he came to. 'Why was Mrs Esme Hill here earlier this evening?'

Tony saw Alex start. She leaned forward, her nostrils flared. 'Perhaps I should just tell you she wasn't here and I don't know who she is. Then you'd have to explain yourself.'

'I'll do that anyway. But you can't go back and I did hear you mention Esme just now. Mrs Esme Hill – and I think you'll agree she'd be hard to miss – was seen coming into the Black Dog.' He flipped back a couple of pages in the notebook. 'With a young man. Who was he, do you know?'

The mutinous set of Alex's features didn't bode well.

'Mrs Hill came to thank me for helping her husband on the night of the trailer fire. The man is Grant Hill, Mr and Mrs Hill's son.'

Bill made a few more marks in the notebook. 'What did you talk about?'

'Very little.'

'Right.' Bill's tone suggested the answer was what he'd expected. 'Alex, you're going to have to drop the act eventually. The sooner you do, the easier it'll be all around.'

'What act?'

'Have it your way.'

Tony's muscles tightened. He didn't like the direction this conversation was taking but knew he'd best keep his mouth shut for now.

'How do you know Mrs Hill was here?' Alex asked. 'Do you already have someone watching me.'

'We do.' Bill ate another sandwich in three bites.

'Why?' Alex's voice rose. 'I've done absolutely nothing to deserve that.'

Bill took a long swallow of his beer, looking at her across the rim of the glass, and set it down. 'Perhaps we're watching you because we think you could be in danger. Have you thought of that? Do you think we do whatever we do to be annoying, and because the force has such huge extra funds it can afford to play silly buggers?'

He got up and Tony glanced at Alex who tipped up her face to watch the detective. Her eyes had widened and her lips parted.

'The answer to that is, no. I'll leave you with one thought: if there's anything you're holding back please come to us immediately and if you know who Lily Mary Edwina is – or was – and I think you do, will you tell me why someone would want to remove a plaque with that name on it from a bench in the graveyard?'

TWELVE

Smoke from cottage chimneys rose straight into the still, pink-tinged, early-morning sky. Snow sliding from the bare branches of an oak tree swished to softly pepper the drifts below.

The *tic-tic-tic* of a robin drew Alex's eyes to a little bird, perched alone on a rickety bird-feeder hanging from a low branch.

'Wait,' she said quietly, closing the lychgate into St. Aldwyn's graveyard. She pulled on Tony's hand and he stopped at once, looked down into her face with the questioning, worried expression he wore too often lately. 'I'm OK. Honestly. I want to think a while before I charge into this – not that I think it means much. Bored kids getting into mischief, that's all it is. I'll replace the plaque and forget all about it. And I'll make sure this one is sturdier.'

'I didn't know you'd had a bench put by the church. It was a nice idea.'

'It's been there for months.' For once she wished Tony hadn't been there the night before when Bill made his announcement. He didn't need to be constantly reminded of her lost baby. 'I thought I did mention the bench last year. That was last year when I was thinking about putting it here but we don't need to look at it now. We've both got busy days ahead, and—'

'And it's going to make you sad to be reminded about your baby?'

Cold struck through her feet. Her hands tingled as if they had been flash frozen and just begun to thaw. She stood very still, even when she felt Tony's hands close firmly on her upper arms.

'Alex?'

'You're probably right,' she told him, keeping her gaze on the front of his coat. 'It's past time I was over it, anyway. See, those books you've been reading on cognitive behavior are paying off.'

'Hey, lady, what's going on with you? I haven't read . . . I didn't mean to upset you.'

'I'm only joking.' She glanced at his face. 'I was going to say something about making me face fears head-on but it's not funny. Anyway, it's time to stop pretending. I'm not in such great shape. I wish we could have stayed at your place all day. In bed.' The look she gave him was supposed to be defiant, teasing as well.

Tony didn't laugh. 'I'm not joking,' he said. 'I would like us to be together and away from whatever is going on here now. You're frantic about your mum. Having the police breathing down our necks again is twice as confusing as it is scary, although the deaths are tragic – and on top of that someone chooses now to pinch the plaque from your little one's bench. Not funny – any of it.'

Her smile came easily now. 'Thanks for that. What I need is a plan. What's the order of these things? Which should I try to deal with first?'

'Sounds logical. And I've got another question – is there something that ties all of these things together? Sounds bizarre, but they do all seem to be coming at once.'

'The deaths can't fit with my family issues, Tony.'

He shook his head, no. 'You're right. But darn it, why does everything have to hit at the same time.'

A clear tenor came from the path beside the church, or Alex thought that was the location. Singing confidently, it got closer and Tony made owl eyes at Alex.

'So pretty,' she whispered. 'What's he singing?'

Tony shrugged and they both listened. '"Morning has Broken",' they whispered in unison. 'There's a Cat Stevens version,' Tony added. 'Or is it Aaron Neville?'

> Mine is the sunlight, mine is the morning
> Born of the one light, Eden saw play
> Praise with elation, praise every morning . . .

When Juste Vidal caught sight of Tony and Alex, his warm voice trailed away. He waved, his reddish hair bright against the snow, and he waited for them to join him.

'Is he working at the Dog this morning?' Tony asked.

'Not as far as I know.'

She had no choice but to advance to the bench where Juste, in a thick black windcheater, black roll-neck jumper and black cords, stood smiling a welcome.

'Morning to you,' he said, inclining his head. 'How beautiful it is like this. Made clean with the snow.'

'Do you walk here a lot?' Alex asked.

'Quite a lot,' Juste said. 'Sometimes I help Reverend Ivor early in the morning – if I have a later class. Then I catch a bus.'

'You have a good voice,' Tony said.

'No,' the man said promptly, 'but I love to sing. I must be honest. I came this way today because I know Detective Sergeant Lamb was going to tell you about the missing plaque for little Lily Mary Edwina and you might come to look at the first opportunity. I hoped I could offer to deal with it so you need not be distressed.'

'You're kind,' Alex told him. 'I wonder how long it's been gone. Just a day or so, I expect.'

'Two weeks,' Juste said promptly. 'Or I found it was missing two weeks ago. Sometimes I sit here to think, although I confess this is the first time I've returned since that morning.' He sat at one end of the pretty cedar bench with its fan of curved spokes along the back. Where the plaque had been, there was evidence of a tool having been used to pry it loose.

'Come on.' Tony led Alex to sit between them.

'It was the reverend and his wife who told me you put this here.' Juste smoothed the arm beside him. 'Sibyl, Mrs Davis was distraught and Reverend Ivor wanted to get another to replace it at once, but I'm afraid I thought you should both know and make your own decision. You are not people who hide from the truth.'

Clearing her throat, Alex glanced at Tony to see if he might think, as she did, that Juste assumed her baby was his.

Tony smiled. 'Little Lily was the baby Alex lost during her first marriage. I wish she had been mine.' Color spread across his cheekbones and his very blue eyes deepened to almost navy.

The silence that followed wasn't long, but it was uncomfortable, although Alex very much wanted to kiss Tony.

Juste patted Alex's hand. 'Children are a blessing – not that they aren't also a pain in the neck sometimes, as you British say. I should like to have my own one day, just as I will pray that you have yours – both of you,' he said with an impish smile.

The sound of a car engine spoiled the moment. Tony leaned to see past the lychgate to a tiny overflow car park beside the row of cottages on Pond Street, two of which comprised Leaves of Comfort, Harriet and Mary Burke's tea rooms. A dark car, very new looking, pulled in but the engine remained running.

Alex glanced up at the back windows of the sisters' flat but was relieved to see the curtains were still closed.

'Who is it?' Juste asked. 'You know the car?'

'I think they're lost,' Tony said, and promptly the engine was cut and the driver and front passenger doors opened. Bill Lamb got out of the driver's side and Dan O'Reilly stood up beside the car with a mobile to his ear.

'When did the police start driving Jags?' Tony said. 'Nice car. I've always liked dark gray – especially when it's clean.'

Lamb walked through the lychgate first and O'Reilly followed at a more leisurely pace. When Bill got close he grinned at Alex and Tony. 'I'm not surprised to find you here. But I didn't expect you to interfere, Juste.'

'That was not my intention,' Juste said. He moved away a little and stood quiet and unmoving.

'He's not interfering,' Alex protested. 'Don't forget he's the one who found the plaque had been taken, not that I think it's important other than as an example of how unruly the kids are getting around here.'

'Whatever you say.' Bill waited for Dan to catch up. 'Surely you know we aren't the ones who usually bother with petty vandalism?'

Just what she'd been thinking. She didn't answer.

'Who else knew about the bench?' Dan asked, although he smiled, softening the atmosphere. 'I agree we've got an upsurge in unruly youngsters but that's the story all over.'

'I don't know who knew,' Alex said. 'Probably . . . well, no, I don't know because I didn't talk about it. Why would I?'

'You never saw anyone else visiting here?'

'No – apart from a few close friends. We planted annuals and the roses will be back in bloom soon enough. We'll start lavender this year.'

'Very nice,' Dan said with no suggestion of ridicule. 'I like this little church, and the grounds.'

That surprised Alex. Dan didn't usually go in for platitudes.

'Well,' he said, 'I'm sure the uniforms are on the mystery of the missing plaque. That's not why we're here. We were told you and Tony might be here, Alex.'

Tony frowned at her. 'Nobody knows where we are.'

She was being watched, Alex thought. Apparently every move she made which was a disturbing thought.

'It was a guess and it was right,' Bill said. 'But that's not important. We went to Corner Cottage to speak to Lily. She's not there and she isn't at the Black Dog yet.'

'I should hope not,' Alex responded quickly while she digested the idea that her mother might not be at her cottage. 'How can you be sure she's not at home?'

'She didn't answer her phone or the door, and her car's gone from the back of the Black Dog,' Bill said. 'We know that's where she keeps it. We went to ask Doc Harrison what he knows and he said he couldn't tell us anything. That might have meant, he wouldn't tell us anything, but we didn't push him. He was dealing with the Gammage boys. Good man, your dad, Tony. Boys and their sports, their homework and a new cat and being the local GP, he's something else.'

'Yes, he is,' Tony said.

Alex hardly dared to look at him. 'My mother helps a lot with the boys and their activities and Naruto is a darling – the cat, I mean. We all help out and both Scoot and Kyle are capable, aren't they, Tony?'

She heard Tony's long, indrawn breath. 'If every pair of teenage brothers were as reliable, it would be an easy world to live in. Kyle puts in some hours helping at my small animal clinic, which Bill probably knows from Radhika. She is very attached to the boy. Scoot works at the Black Dog. Terrific boys.'

'Did we say they weren't?' Bill asked.

'Back to Lily,' Dan said. 'We'd like to question her – informally, if possible. We'd appreciate it if you helped us find her.'

Alex looked straight ahead and pushed a hand under Tony's arm. They looked toward the lychgate, watching Dan and Bill get into their car and reverse to a wide spot where they could turn around and drive away.

When they were out of sight, Alex let out a long breath and said, 'Why would they be so interested in speaking to Lily?'

'We should have asked them that,' Tony said. 'My mind was going in several directions. But I probably shouldn't call and ask now.'

'No, please don't,' Alex said. The less they gave the impression that they were concerned about Lily's movements, the better.

Juste cleared his throat. They had forgotten he was there. 'Perhaps I can help.'

He joined them and they stood in a huddle on the cold morning of a day that didn't seem destined to warm up.

'We'll take any hints,' Tony said. He folded a hand over Alex's on his arm and smiled at her. 'We aren't making out too well in the investigating department. Some silly young churchyard kleptomaniacs can't have anything to do with . . . anything, I suppose, but why would the police want to see Lily.'

'If she was here, where she's supposed to be, it would be easier to believe they don't have a reason at all.'

She leaned on Tony and looked up at Juste, who was silent, but frowning in a way that didn't help her relax. 'What is it?' she asked him.

Juste studied his feet – for a long time.

'Juste!' Alex said urgently. 'What is it? You're frightening me more than I was already frightened.'

'OK. I didn't understand when it happened and I still don't

understand. You must ask Lily why she did it, but I told her I would try not to put myself in the middle of it. This is between all of you. I am merely a bystander who wants the people I care about to be happy. And I will do anything to help with that.'

Alex reached for Juste's hand and he took it firmly.

'Will you listen to me when I tell you this small thing, and may I rely on you to do nothing about it until you have thought it through?'

'What would we do?' Tony sounded bemused.

'Nothing, of course. I had the terrible little thought that you might tell the detectives if you knew, but that is foolish of me. If it is important, Lily will explain herself. When the detectives came just now I was afraid they already knew, but now I'm sure they don't. They were here for a reason we don't know.'

Alex's legs felt weak. 'I would never tell the police anything about my mother.'

He inclined his head. '*C'est ça*. Of course that's the way it would be. And I'm certain this was unimportant. It was Lily who took the plaque from the bench.'

'That doesn't make any sense,' Alex said. 'How do you know?'

'I saw her with it. She must have hidden it in the church and she was putting it in her bag. She doesn't know I observed her. No one does but you two.'

THIRTEEN

Lily tromped through clumpy, wet grass to an overgrown path close to the Thames. From there Windsor Castle was massive atop it's chalky bluff and she could make out the Union Jack snapping above the royal residence. No monarch in residence today, if she remembered the rule properly.

A mossy bench beneath the leafless branches of a weeping willow glistened with moisture. She took a croissant and bottle of Starbucks Frappuccino from a plastic bag and used the latter to keep her coat from getting too wet on the seat. The canvas tote she carried was heavy enough to make red marks on her wrist and she balanced it on her lap, keeping her elbows propped where they guarded the bag against her.

Her car was parked on the other side of the river, the Eton side. Only foot traffic was allowed on the Windsor Bridge and although she barely remembered much about it, this, or somewhere around here, must have been where her mother brought her on one of the rare times she'd taken Lily out from her foster home for a day.

They would be serving the lunch crowd at the Black Dog. Lily's hands were cold. She blew on first one, then the other. The mountain of overwhelming guilt at having run out on the people who relied on her had become a numb place in her mind. James knew where she had gone, as closely as she could explain, and he would manage to cover for her – or at least stop Alex from panicking too badly.

Angela had brought her seven- or eight-year-old daughter Lily here. They had looked up at the castle and gone by bus to Runnymede where Angela had read aloud a memorial commemorating the signing of the Magna Carta, although it had meant nothing to Lily who couldn't really concentrate on anything anyway. Being with her mother was all that mattered to a little girl who spent so much time waiting for such a day.

There was a house, a big house with tall trees and lawns, flowers, and water fountains spraying into pools. Lily remembered people riding by on horseback, laughing and talking. They took no notice of Lily or Angela. Immediately after that Angela had held her hand while they ran through trees again to a big gate.

Where had that house been? Quite close to Eton and Windsor, Lily thought. And it had a name but she didn't remember that, either.

She must eat. The croissant was still faintly warm – probably from clutching it too tightly. When she unwrapped the flaking pastry it was squashed and pieces sprayed her coat but she started eating and found she was ravenous. The creamy coffee tasted good cold. Lily drank it down quickly and put the empty bottle on the bench.

Ducks swam closer, light catching emerald green feathers on their heads. They nattered and fussed and Lily broke off bits of the croissant to toss among the birds. The flapping and bustling brought her an instant's smile before she looked down at the tan bag she held tightly on her lap.

Angela had come to see her once more, when Lily was ten. They went only as far as the playground beside the tall block of flats where Lily lived with foster parents and four bigger children who weren't interested in her. They did leave her alone when they were at home and they weren't mean.

It rained that afternoon but Lily didn't care. She and Angela sat side-by-side on swings that creaked and screamed with every small move.

'Do you remember when I took you to look at Windsor Castle?' Angela asked. 'You were really little then so you've probably forgotten.'

Lily looked at it again now. *'Of course, I haven't,' she'd told her mum. 'I never will. Cross my heart.' Grown-ups didn't seem to understand how little kids had good memories for happy stuff.*

'Would you like to go there again—?'

'Yes, yes!' Lily jumped off her swing. 'Can we go now? I can go and get my mac.'

'No, Lilababe, not now.' Mum hadn't called her that for ever so long. Lily liked hearing it again. 'I was thinking that it would be a lovely place to go back to one day. For something special.'

Lily kept her head up and smiled. She wouldn't look disappointed, or cry like a little kid might. 'I'd like that,' she said, climbing back on the swing.

'We need to go in,' Mum said. 'My friends are waiting for me.'

With hurt in her throat, Lily nodded and frowned as if she was thinking hard about something serious. 'Do I know your friends? Are they some of the ones we lived with sometimes?' She must not let her voice wobble or her mum wouldn't come back ever.

'I don't think you met these friends,' Mum said. 'Come on.' She got up and reached out a hand.

Lily held on tight and smiled her very best smile. She had all her teeth again now and sometimes she was told they were nice.

All the way back to the block of flats where her foster family lived Lily skipped. Was she too old to skip now? She wasn't sure but she stopped and lifted her mum's hand to kiss it. Mum stood still and gave her a hug, rested her face on top of Lily's curly hair.

They took the smelly lift to the right floor and walked to the black front door with all the kick marks.

'Remember,' Mum said, 'for something really special I'll take you to see Windsor Castle again – and sit by the river. We'll take a picnic.'

'Oh, yes,' Lily had said.

Her mum went away quickly and didn't look back to wave once. Lily couldn't swallow at all. Tears escaped and ran down her cheeks. They tasted salty on her lips.

This probably wasn't the actual bench they'd sat on but it was close enough for Lily's memory to make it so.

Angela had not returned, not to the awful flat, or to the two other homes where Lily had been placed before, at fifteen, she was taken by a couple who were so kind she thought she had finally found her forever place.

The bag on her lap wasn't really heavy, just awkward. Her mother had promised her that they would come back to this place for something special and in a way, they had. In the bag were two wooden boxes and several sealed envelopes of various sizes. These things were all she would have of Angela, and a past Lily had never known – her mother's past, or that's what she expected to find. Lily had brought them here because it seemed the right thing to do.

She put a hand into the bag and pulled out a box. Perhaps two inches deep, it had enough weight to make her wonder if it could have only papers inside. The second box, cheap but carved and painted in garish colors, looked as if it was one of many the same, perhaps from a market. Lily had a fleeting memory of Notting Hill. How could she remember when she must have been no more than five? And Portobello Road Market, her hand held tightly. Big girls like her mother in long, colored skirts. They shrieked with laughter and strands of beads clicked from their necks and wrists. Their hair was long and so was the hair of the men with them. They all laughed and they tickled her until she laughed, too. And they bought her ice cream and candy floss, and toffee apples.

The colored boxes, of all different sizes and shapes, were piled on a table covered with a bright yellow cloth that flapped in the wind. One of the big girls took a box and put it in Lily's hands . . .

She looked at the box she held now. Had this been the one she was given? Lily didn't remember. She put both boxes on the bench beside her.

The envelopes did contain papers. One held a child's crayon drawings and she knew they were hers, that Angela had kept them. Childish notes in big, rounded letters: 'I'm being good, Mummy?'

The second envelope bulged with photographs, a lot in black and white, a scrap of faded lace, a small envelope of fragile pressed flowers. Inside pieces of creased tissue paper lay a tarnished silver frame containing the black and white photograph of a young couple smiling at the camera. The man had a rose in his buttonhole and the girl held a bunch of flowers.

Inside the final envelope were several sheets of paper folded together with a notecard paperclipped to them. Lily eased the card free and read:

> *I understood that you should know these things, but not when would be the right time to give them to you. When you get this, the decision will have been made for me. I can't tell you what to think or feel, but I can ask you to understand that we are all no more than human and we are weak sometimes. I love you. I always have and I wish I could have been better at finding a good path for both of us.*
> *With love,*
> *Mummy (Angela Picket Devoss)*

Devoss?

There was folded paper, lined, torn from a notebook. Lily's hands trembled as she pulled off the paperclip and opened the sheets out flat.

I am Angela Picket Devoss. My parents worked for the Devoss family on their estate in Windsor. That's where I was born and grew up.

Simon Devoss was the youngest of three sons and my friend for all of my childhood. We played together as children, but as we became teenagers Simon was told he must not be around me. He was not someone who did as he was told unless he thought it was the right thing. Simon thought, as I did, that friends as close as we were should be together.

I was eighteen, Simon was twenty – we knew we would always be in love. We ran away and married in a registry office. Two of Simon's friends were our witnesses. Afterwards we tried to tell our families. Simon's parents wanted to take him home and send him back to university, but said I would never be welcomed by them. They wanted our marriage annulled. My parents wouldn't see me.

We lived in a little flat in Slough and Simon got a job as an accounting clerk. He intended to be a lawyer but we knew it would be hard to find a way to do that with little money. I worked in a sweet shop.

It wasn't a sad time. It was very happy, the most happy in my life.

Four months after we married, Simon was killed by a car that overtook a bus when he was crossing the road. His family held his funeral but wouldn't speak to me. I understand they thought it was all my fault. In a way it was. But for me, Simon would never have been near that bus. I couldn't change any of it.

Lily could hardly breathe, or see. She wanted to hold her mother, to comfort her. Too late. Too late so long ago.

I had just found out I was pregnant with you, Lily. My family continued to work for the Devoss household and were so ashamed and angry they said awful things to me and said I should do what was kindest for them after I caused so much trouble. They would send me to Ireland, to relatives, they said.

The only relative there was an aunt who put me into a convent where they took in what they called fallen women, including those who were pregnant and not married. I was not supposed to leave at all and my baby would be taken away and given to a family in America. The sisters made money by selling the babies but they pretended it was best for everyone. I was told, over and over, that I wasn't married because there was no church wedding.

A young nun, Sister Mary Edwin, helped me to run away. I wish I knew what happened to her but there was no way to stay in touch. I put her name on the back of your pendant, Lily – that was the prettiest gift I gave to you, my child. I came back to England and never contacted my family again.

I was so lucky but so young. I was too immature and frightened to look for help in the right places. A group of young people, about my age, had the top floor of the house where I rented a room. I was upset all the time and very pregnant. I couldn't hide it anymore. What little money I had was running out and the group upstairs took me in. They loved that I was having a baby and when you were born, they loved you, Lily. Without them I don't know how we would have survived. I couldn't stop thinking about Simon – your father – and all we had lost.

That's almost all of the story. Lily, you were our child, all of us. We all looked after you but not well enough. We did a lot of things we shouldn't have done and got into trouble. We got into trouble many times and eventually it all fell apart for us. Stupid people, we were. But I don't want anyone to think my friends weren't special. They were. Silly, but kind. I have never forgotten how good they were to you and me, Lily.

You were taken away from me and put into foster care. I wanted to get you back and I tried for a long time, but then I stopped trying.

The best thing I ever did for you was stay out of your life, I got out of your life before I damaged you forever.

Forgive me.

Lily pulled the child-sized medallion from beneath the neck of her sweater. She had long ago had to put it on a much longer silver chain than the one Angela had given her as a very small girl. At last she knew the reason for using the names, Mary Edwina.

How long had she sat there, watching the ducks, watching a lone oarsman propel his scull past with the smooth rhythm of an expert?

Too long but Lily couldn't seem to make herself move. The day had grown darker, the sky hanging heavy with snow.

She must call Alex and she must go home.

Her mobile was in the tote. She fished it out and turned it on, tried not to look at all the calls she had deliberately missed. It would be easier not to talk to Alex yet – cowardly, but easier, and she needed to gather her strength and her wits.

Lily dialed the pub number. If Alex answered, so be it.

The phone rang a number of times before it was picked up and a breathless voice said, 'This is the kitchen – I mean this is the Black Dog. Hang on and I'll get someone.'

'No,' Lily said quickly. 'I'll talk to you. Who is this?'

Before the woman could answer, Lily remembered that Gladys had started work today.

'Hello, Gladys. This is Lily. How did breakfast go? I was sorry I had to be gone on your first day.' Her heart beat hard. If she stretched this out too long, Hugh or Alex would come on the line.

'It went really well,' Gladys said, still breathless but sounding pleased. 'We had a lot of customers.'

'That's really good. Listen. I've got to get on the road. Please let Alex know I won't be too late.'

She thanked Gladys and before the woman could get another word in, hung up. Gladys always left Lily with a warm feeling.

She wasn't demonstrative, but had been there when Lily first went to Underhill and was so kind to her and little Alex.

The Ford was in a car park on the Eton side of the Windsor Bridge. Lily gathered her things back into the tote and set off at a brisk walk. The sooner she was on her way, the better, even though she wasn't sure how she would explain her absence. Perhaps with the truth. Like Lily, Alex had a right to know these things. It could be that if she had discussed her own history much earlier, she would have had the courage to tell Alex hers.

By the time she reached her car, snow began to fall lightly. Her hands were cold and she rubbed them together, smiling as a gaggle of kids rushed by screaming with laughter. They attempted to scrape enough snow for snowballs but the results fell apart in the air.

The mobile rang as Lily opened her car door.

Her first thought was that Gladys had already told Alex about the call, but when she checked, she saw 'unknown caller'.

In the front seat, she continued to look at the phone and eventually sighed, relieved when the ringing finally stopped. She closed and locked the doors, started the car and turned on the wonky heating system. It would take a while to warm up and clear the inside of the windows.

The mobile rang again.

The readout was the same.

A lot of people preferred not to broadcast their numbers. She took a breath and answered. 'Yes. Who is this please?'

'Where are you?' It must be Alex and she sounded muffled, as if she was crying.

'I just had to get away for a bit. Too much seems to be happening so I wanted to have a chance to clear my head. I came to a place I knew when I was a kid. This is . . . I've never been back before. I'll be on my way home again soon. Don't worry.'

'Are you in London?'

'No. I was, but I love it here by the river. I'll tell you all about it later. All of it, this time.'

Alex didn't answer but Lily could tell she was still on the

phone. 'I came here with my mother, Alex. It's difficult to talk about on the phone. Let me come home first.'

Nothing. Lily held back tears. 'Say something, please.'

'I'm a friend. An old friend, Lily. Don't you recognize my voice? You'll hurt my feelings if you don't. But I recognize yours so please just listen to what I want to tell you. We have some catching up to do. It's for your own good so listen carefully.'

Shocked, Lily hung up. Her hands might be cold on the inside but on the outside, they were sweating. She rested her forehead on the wheel. Who was it? What did they want? A woman's voice but husky the way people who smoked a lot had husky voices sometimes. She must have got the wrong number. But she knew Lily's name!

Once more the phone rang and she pressed the talk button, took the instrument to her ear.

'Don't do that again. It's not wise. Just listen. This is Beverly Irving. Your dearest friend, remember? I'm the one who rescued you when you had nowhere to turn.'

Lily breathed through her mouth, gulped air through her mouth. It couldn't be. The memories flooded back and mingled with thoughts of Angela, and her own childhood. Some might look at Lily's life, at Alex's beginnings, and say, 'like mother like daughter', but it wasn't the same. Angela's story had been different.

But Beverly Irving wasn't supposed to find them again. Lily had changed their last name – even though Beverly had eventually promised not to come near them again. Lily had worked hard to find a new life for Alex and herself, away from Beverly Irving, social worker, with designs on Alex.

Beverly started laughing and Lily clutched the phone tightly.

'Take a proper breath, Lily. You always were an anxious little thing and I can't have you dying on me now. You might draw attention we don't want. I know you've been to pick up the things your dreadful mother left for you.'

Lily slapped a hand over her mouth to keep the exclamation in.

'Unfortunately, I wasn't able to get to them first, but we all trust the wrong people from time to time. Another lesson learned for me. Now. I can imagine some of what has been passed on to you. Take it with a pinch of salt, my dear. Forget it. More important, you are not to drag up anything that happened while we were together. I have worked too long and too hard to build my own life and I like it. I cannot have you or your daughter spreading lies that could upset my family. You don't know my family and never will – that's as it should be. So, forget any ideas you may have of digging up the past. You were well paid to forget but I have reason to doubt that you have kept your end of our bargain. Regardless, you will get nothing further from me.

'If you ignore what I'm saying and go to the police, I'm afraid someone you care for will suffer. Goodbye.'

FOURTEEN

'That Hill woman's here again,' Hugh said, sitting beside Alex at a table in the restaurant.

She was going over room bookings, trying to bury her anxiety about Lily, who hadn't shown up or checked in all morning, or even by the middle of the afternoon. Doc and Tony had devised a plan they didn't share with Alex although they assured her they would have good news the next time they spoke.

How could they know?

'Alex?' Hugh smiled when he had her attention. 'Our visitor?'

'Can you get rid of her?' she asked. 'Why would she be back again, particularly so soon?'

'I don't know the answer, luv. She's got another woman with her – very upper crust. Silver bob and velvet hairband – probably expensive surgery. That type. Major money, if I had to guess. Quiet but watchful – or what I can make out behind her dark glasses looks as if she is.'

'You make her sound appealing,' Alex said, keeping her voice down. Not that she would be heard from the saloon bar if she shouted. 'Thank goodness we didn't have many for lunch today. The weather's keeping people away. Gladys Lymer fitting in OK, is she?'

'You bet. Even starchy Phil is singing her praises and he's never been one to like new people in his kitchen.'

'Good. Any breakfasts ordered this morning?'

Hugh's expressive brown eyes sparkled. 'Word got out. We served thirty. I didn't expect that. We got people using the snow as an excuse to be late to work, I think. And some of the regulars showed up as well – probably to support Gladys.'

Alex remembered to close her mouth. 'Wow. That's stupendous. And she can do that almost on her own, right?'

'You've got it. Liz Hadley came in to give a hand and it ran like silk. If word gets around we could have standing room only on our hands. I think we wore Gladys out on her first day. I've packed her off home. Er, Alex, what about—'

'OK, OK. I'll go and talk to Esme Hill but I can't think why she's here again. I'd rather forget about that horrible fire.'

'Did you see the articles in the papers today?' Hugh made a face. 'Nasty stuff.'

'I expected to see something a couple of days ago. I think O'Reilly must have some sort of magic inside help with keeping the lid on things.'

Hugh crossed his arms. 'Or someone with influence does. But even a magician can't keep that up for long. It all sounds complicated to me – the case, I mean. Lance Pullinger doesn't come off as a nice type. But there's always speculation mixed in with fact. There're copies of the papers in the kitchen if you want to see them.'

Alex took the route from the dining room, through the short passage past the snug into the mostly empty main bar. The two women she sought sat at a table near one of the front windows and she had a chance to observe them briefly.

Esme wore another set of workout clothes, these turquoise and black, but the body warmer zipped on top was of glistening black fur, sable perhaps, and a wonderful foil for her red hair. Her long legs, elegantly sloped to one side and crossed at the ankles, ended in boots coated with dark fur from knee to ankle.

The same alpaca cardigan she'd worn before was tossed over the back of her chair.

The silver-bobbed companion of the major dark glasses was porcelain-faced with pouting, earth-pink lips which parted to reveal perfect and very white teeth when she spoke. Her body was also encased in spandex, this outfit in grey and black pinstripes with deep pink gussets. These were two majorly fit and eye-worthy figures.

The pair looked as if they'd accidentally wandered into Marks & Spencer on their way to Brown's.

Liz Hadley, tall and elegant herself and still struggling to keep a ladies' dress shop afloat in Broadway, appeared and set down two drinks Alex couldn't identify from her vantage point. As soon as Liz left, Alex stood as tall as 5'3' could manage and went to the table.

'Hello, ladies,' she said, with her best welcoming smile. 'Esme, I didn't expect to see you again.'

Esme Hill looked up at her. 'You should have. Places like this are gems, my dear. I believe in encouraging people who try so hard.'

Alex's smile felt fixed. 'Thank you.'

'Join us,' Esme said. She stirred her drink with a plastic stick and took a sip, followed by a long swallow. 'Lovely,' she said. 'I adore a good mojito. Your man knows how to muddle his mint.'

'Welcome back,' Alex said. 'I'm pleased we made such a good first impression on you. I really shouldn't stop now. We're short staffed, so—'

'Oh, come on, darling. Being the boss has its bennies.' Esme pulled a chair closer to her and patted the seat. 'Sit by me. I insist. Meet my good friend Audra, Lady Mekins. Audra's husband is Sir Hillary, the surgeon. Audra, meet Alex Duggins, landlady and owner of the Black Dog.'

The woman extended a well-manicured but capable-looking hand and gave Alex's a surprisingly firm shake. 'Nice to meet you, Alex. Please call me Audra. What's your poison?' A pleasant, husky but rather quiet voice.

'Thank you.' Alex sat and caught Hugh's eye. 'I think I'll have coffee. I've still got a long day ahead.'

Hugh sauntered over beneath the approving gaze of the two women.

'Is there coffee?' Alex asked in a raised voice and, as she'd intended, with a wave, he turned back. 'How far did you have to drive? It's treacherous today.'

'Audra and I take yoga. That's where we met *ages* ago. We also do high impact aerobics and pilates, just not all on the same day.' She chuckled at her little joke. 'I doubt any weather would keep us from our appointed classes. We came from Temple Guiting, where I live. Dear Audra comes down from London to stay with me regularly and keeps us both on our toes.'

'Good for you.' Alex smiled. 'I have to make do with running around here and exercising my dog. But I promise myself that when I'm older and have more time . . .' *Speaking of little jokes.*

Audra tipped back her head and laughed. She wiped at tearing eyes beneath her glasses and sniffed. 'Indeed. When my son was younger I didn't seem to have much time for myself. Of course, I had a nanny but I was one of those mothers who had to see every little thing he did for the first time – or the tenth time. Winston was a wonderful child. He's still wonderful. Do you have children?'

'Afraid not but I still live in hope.'

Liz brought coffee and cream with a plate of Bourbon biscuits and Alex thanked her. 'I expect Hugh told you how well breakfast went this morning,' Liz said. 'Gladys left you a little note on the cork board. She was bubbling about the good turnout.' She went away before Alex could say anything.

'That's Liz Hadley,' Alex said. 'She has that lovely dress shop in the arcade – in Broadway. All Shades, it's called. Take a look if you go that way – or make it a destination.' These were the type of clients Liz catered to.

'We might just do that,' Audra said. She hadn't taken her veiled eyes off Alex since she arrived at the table. Not a comfortable feeling.

'Your people like you, don't they,' Esme said. 'They seem happy. That's rather sweet. Did you read the articles that came out in the papers today about the suspicious deaths? I must say I thought they were a bit lurid. Lance was a good man and he certainly didn't deserve to die like that. Not that I'm any the wiser about exactly how he did die. But they paint him as a sneaky lothario of some sort. Completely unnecessary. My husband doesn't show much emotion but he's very upset. Lance was his dear friend.'

'I'll read them,' Alex said, wishing she could get away and start now. 'Was there something you wanted to talk to me about, or is this just a lovely uncomplicated pleasure stop?'

Lady Mekins reached across the table to press one of Esme's hands. 'Have some of your mojito darling. I just know everything's going to be all right.'

'Of course it is.' Esme sounded snappish. 'Forgive me, Audra. I know you want to help and I'm grateful. This is just so unexpected. And it doesn't help that Bob is a basket case and Carmen's sloping around like a lovesick calf while she supposedly sympathizes with him.'

'Bob's got a lot on his mind,' Lady Mekins said. 'And Carmen adores her daddy. She's probably worried to death about him. Alex, I've heard how you walked into the whole thing with that nasty fire. Did you see all of it?'

'Not all, but enough,' Alex said. She looked at her watch. As soon as she could get away she would try to call Tony. Radhika at the clinic might have heard something.

'So you were there when the fire people arrived. How long did it take to put out the fire?'

Alex gave the woman a speculative look. This started to sound like an interrogation. 'They were very efficient. I don't know how long it took. I was a bit disoriented by everything.'

'Lance's body. You saw it?' Audra Mekins had the grace to blush. 'Forgive me for being curious but one can't help trying to work out how everything happened and how the two deaths were tied together. I expect the police told you something about that.'

'No, they didn't. And I didn't see the body, thank goodness. I was too far away. It's not the police's way to talk about cases to civilians.'

Audra leaned back in her chair, a downward jerk at the

corners of her mouth. 'You're being coy. We know all about the wonderful help you've been to the authorities on more than a couple of occasions. You must have some ideas about all this. What do you really think?'

Showing offence, or worse yet, annoyance, would only make this woman more certain she was right – which she was – at least about past cases in the area.

Alex frowned thoughtfully. 'You know, I think it's all very puzzling. And the police may be puzzled, too. I don't have the faintest idea what happened.' Soon she might be able to give lessons in how to pontificate and say absolutely nothing.

'Bob's so upset. Beside himself, really. He seems to think he should have been able to get Lance out but some suggest it would have been too late regardless.'

Alex inclined her head at Esme. 'What does that mean?'

The woman shrugged eloquently. 'I'm not sure, but what do you think? Could they be suggesting Lance was dead before the fire, so getting to him wouldn't have made any difference?'

Alex wanted desperately to ask who the 'some' were but decided that was a question she'd share with Tony. Then they'd decide if O'Reilly and Lamb might be interested in the comment.

'I have no way of even guessing what that suggestion might mean,' Alex said. A cold frisson climbed her spine and she looked around. For an instant she'd thought there was someone watching her but the three of them were the only people in the bar now.

Esme cleared her throat. 'I think . . . oh, I mustn't speculate.' She stopped, waiting, probably hoping Alex would jump in, which she didn't. 'Well, the fire could have been set to destroy evidence – to make it so they couldn't be sure how Lance died. The body must have been just about incinerated. Those trailer fires are infernos I've heard.'

'It did go up pretty fast,' Alex said. 'But the fire department got there quickly and they did a wonderful job. They saved more than I would have expected.' She recalled the way a group of firemen gathered in a circle around something on the ground a little distance from the trailer. It could have been a body. Or they could simply have been having a discussion.

'Oh, dear.' Esme swallowed more of her drink. 'They'll have to look for signs of arson. Oh, damn, I'm worried.' She put a hand over her eyes and propped her elbow on the table.

The sensation of contracting skin attacked Alex again, more ferociously. She must be even more upset than she'd thought. Little wonder with Lily having done a runner.

Alex put a hand on Esme's shoulder and rubbed gently. She looked sideways at Audra who had turned her face partly away – although behind the almost opaque shield of the glasses, her eyes, at a strained angle, were trained on Alex. She was being watched again, covertly this time.

'Perhaps I should get you home,' Audra said, looking fully at Esme. 'You're overwrought.'

'I hate that word. So Victorian.' Esme leaned very close to Alex and all but whispered, 'I know I shouldn't say this, but I have to trust the ones who understand. I'm afraid they're going to try pinning this killing on Bob. They could say he was only pretending about trying to get in to rescue Lance. Couldn't they? They could try to prove Bob killed him, then set the fire to cover it up.'

'Rubbish,' Audra said. The woman had good ears, Alex noted. 'And I suppose Bob murdered that Darla person, too, whoever she was.'

Esme made a strangled choking noise.

'Who owns the Bentley Mulsanne?' Hugh called delightedly, coming from the gaming room on the other side of the pub entryway. 'That is one gorgeous piece of car flesh.'

'For my sins, it's mine,' Audra said. 'Which reminds me, we'd better get back, Esme. I'd rather drive while there's still fairly decent light.'

Alex frowned at the white scene outside the nearest window. 'My mother is still out. She's so independent but I don't like her driving around in this.'

Esme chuckled. 'We do all worry about the people we love.'

All three of them rose from their chairs. Esme opened her bag to get her wallet.

'On the house,' Alex said. 'It was lovely to see you again. And to meet you, Audra.' In fact she wasn't sure she liked the woman at all.

'Don't forget the entries for naming our new village pub,' Esme said. 'I'll pick them up in a few days if that's all right. I'll call to remind you.'

With an unpleasant feeling that she'd rather Esme didn't come back, Alex nodded and busied herself replacing chairs. By the time she'd picked up empty glasses and her own mug, she and Hugh were alone.

'So what was that all about?' he said.

'It felt funny to you, too? Well I don't get it at all and I don't think I want to.'

'I heard most of what was said. Could it be that Esme Hill would like to find a sympathetic witness to be on her husband's side?'

Alex thought about it. 'You could have a good point. How horrible if it was Bob Hill who caused the fire . . . but it wasn't. I hardly know him but I don't make such monumental mistakes about people. Not usually.'

She carried the empties into the kitchen and pulled a folded note addressed to her from the cork board.

Gladys had written, 'Your mum called and said she would come home soon. She was sorry to be so late.'

'A message from my mum and I wasn't here. Darn it. How long ago?'

Hugh shook his head. 'Hours, I suppose. Before I sent Gladys home and that was around one this afternoon.'

FIFTEEN

'Good night for housebreaking,' Hugh murmured in Alex's ear.

She gave him a questioning glance. 'Weird thing to say.'

'Think about it. There's nobody home. They're all here.'

Alex smiled. If her mum had shown up or called, she could have coped with anything. Lily still hadn't checked in again. 'Ha, ha.' She hadn't been in the mood to smile for what felt like forever. 'Good night for us if it keeps on as it's started out.' The bar was full and so was the up-room – the overflow area one step up from the main saloon bar where customers often ate at high-backed wooden banquettes around scarred tables. Ceaseless ringing came from the slot machines in another room.

'The roads are too bad to encourage people to go far,' Hugh said. He swiped a cloth along the counter, took an order and started pulling pints.

'What will you have?' Alex asked Kev Winslet, gamekeeper at the Derwinter estate.

'What I always have,' Kev shouted over the din. 'Pint of the best, please. Where's your mum? Not feeling good?'

Her mother rarely ventured far from the pub on nights like this when it was busy. Especially in bad weather. 'She'll be in soon enough,' Alex said, silently praying she was telling the truth. 'There you go.' She slid Kev's beer in front of him.

'We heard there was a swanky Bentley out front earlier. Don't see many of those around here. Tell me it's yours, Alex. I'd love to spread that around. Major Stroud takes whisky, right?' When Alex nodded, Kev said, 'Make it a double. He's an interesting sod and I like having the familiar bunch around me. And a half of black and tan for Frank Lymer – the big drinker. He's waiting for Gladys to show up. All he talks about is what a whizz she is at cooking breakfasts. We'll all have to come and give it a try.'

She pulled fresh glasses from overhead and smiled at him. 'You must be short of gossip, Kev.' Alex grinned up at him. He was florid, big and getting bigger. 'Sorry I can't oblige on the Bentley, although I wish I could,' she said to him.

'A Bentley Mulsanne, was it?' A young man wearing a heavy wool overcoat leaned to put an elbow on the counter beside Kev. 'White?'

Kev looked at him. 'I reckon it was. Don't tell us it's yours.' He guffawed.

'I think it's my mother's friend, Lady Mekins's,' the man said, unruffled. A green paisley silk scarf hung loose around his neck. 'I haven't seen another one like it in the area – or anywhere in the sticks come to that. I'm Grant Hill.'

He stuck out a hand and Kev changed his beer to his left hand to shake.

Of course. Now Alex recognized him and remembered Hugh talking about the Bentley. 'I'm glad you made it back to us,' she said. 'Your mother and her friend were in earlier.'

Grant smiled and she could see strong signs of his mother's good looks. The girl with him didn't look old enough to be in the bar but Alex waited for a less conspicuous moment to check.

'My sister, Carmen,' Grant said. 'And she's nineteen even if she does look about nine.'

His sister punched his arm lightly and slid her driving license out. They had the same chin and mouth but Carmen was fair and very feminine.

Alex glanced at the license and immediately remembered Esme Hill saying her daughter was nineteen.

'We came on a mission,' Grant said. 'We risked life and limb to get here rather than keep on listening to Ma and Pa nag. I'll have half of Guinness – I'm driving – and Carmen likes a Babycham.' He made a face and got a harder punch to the arm for his efforts.

Major Stroud, red faced and doing his customary roll from heels to toes, butted in and took his whisky from Kev. 'Thank you, old man,' he said, slurring a little. 'Awfully good of you, I must say.'

Alex got the Guinness and looked under the counter for a Babycham. It used to be one of the most popular drinks with the ladies, or so they said, and it was coming back, also so they said. She found the green bottle with the blue label and a picture of a stylized golden doe on the front, and poured the popping champagne-style liquid into a matching glass. 'There you go.' She smiled at Carmen. It was rather sweet to see a youngster choose such an innocent drink. Alex still liked it herself.

'So what brings you here on a ghastly night like this?' she said to Grant.

Hugh served steadily but she felt she needed to be hospitable.

'We have to decide on a name for the pub at the new village.

I'm hoping some customers here may have given their ideas. The prize is a good one.'

She smiled at Grant. He remained straight-faced as he looked around the room. Then he caught her eye and grinned.

'Juste Vidal, our helper extraordinaire, did pass out the entries,' Alex said. 'And he left some extras out. Let's see if anyone brought them back.'

A couple came into the bar and she barely remembered not to stare. Bill Lamb ushered Radhika, Tony's Indian assistant, across the room. Alex started coughing and took a drink of water. This was a first.

With his hand at Radhika's back, Bill guided her to the table by the fire where Harriet and Mary Burke sat with their one-eyed cat, Max. She watched the interchange when Radhika got there. Bill bent over the sisters to say something and they smiled as if delighted. He pulled a chair from another table for Radhika to sit with the ladies. Gold threads in her purple sari glinted. When she looked at Bill her lovely eyes shone. The light touch he passed over her hair made Alex's tummy turn. Bill was heartless, right? A mean-mouthed clod who could make anyone feel guilty, even when they'd never done anything wrong.

He came to the bar. 'Could I have two Harvey's Bristol Cream sherries and an orange juice please?'

'Of course,' she said, smiling at him.

'Perhaps I could have a rum and coke for myself. I'll come back for it shortly.'

'Will do, Bill.' She made sure her face showed no particular reaction. 'Busy days for you, I expect.'

'No rest for the wicked. But that's the way I like it.' She had put the juice and sherries on a tray and he carried them away.

Hugh rang the bell on the counter and raised his voice. 'Any entries for naming the pub at the new village near Winchcombe?' Obviously, he had heard what Grant said and wanted to do his share. He knew how much Alex disliked announcing anything.

People started to leave their tables and come forward. Folded entries were placed on the counter. Even Frank Lymer, bundled in a hand-knitted muffler and a tweed cloth cap, surreptitiously approached and added an entry.

'I'm surprised,' Hugh muttered. 'I thought they'd all ignore it.'

'A thousand pounds will buy more than a fish and chip dinner,' Grant said.

Alex stared at him, wondering if he was making a dig at the Black Dog's clientele. 'Not much is better than a good feast of fish and chips,' she said. She didn't look at anyone else when she said it.

At last the entries stopped coming. 'Read some of them,' Grant said. 'Entries don't close for a few days. These will inspire competition.'

'You do it,' she told him. 'It's your contest.'

The way he leveled a stare at her was odd. 'Evening, everyone.' He raised his voice and the din quieted. 'I'm Grant Hill. We're the ones building a pub over at our new village near Winchcombe. This is great. Lots of you have given your ideas. I'll read a few of them and then you'll know what you have to beat by the time the contest closes in a few days.'

The shift in the bar atmosphere didn't feel comfortable.

'This is clever,' Grant said. 'Through a Beer Glass Darkly.'

From the silence, Alex got the impression that the effort fell flat.

'Winchcombe Arms,' Grant read loudly. 'And here's a lovely one. Certainly brings some images to my mind. Horse and Bottoms.' He sniggered and was joined in the laughter. 'Bottoms Up. Now that's good.'

Even Alex thought that wasn't bad.

She suddenly wanted him to wait until the competition closed. This felt painful.

'The Dancing Squire. The Lords' Revenge. Fish and Pickle. Now there's a show stopper.'

Applause followed and cries of, 'That's it.'

'The Cork and Bottle,' Grant continued. 'The Happy Cow. The Badgers' Retreat. The Cats' Meow.'

Immediately Alex looked to the Burke sisters who smiled and averted their eyes. Her traitorous dog had wheedled a place on Bill Lamb's lap. Bogie had a soft spot for policemen.

'For Those Who Serve. Very nice,' Grant said with a sly glance at the major who tried to look detached.

'And Blithely Blunder Inn. Ooh, I like that, don't you?'

The crowd applauded and Alex concentrated on the beer she was pulling.

'You?' Hugh said in her ear.

'Might be,' she said. 'Might not be.'

He started to laugh but stopped abruptly. 'Well, look who's here. Is this what you were hoping to see, or do you wish they had used their heads and avoided coming into the bar like this? Just wait for the gossip now.'

Lily walked from the kitchens with Dan O'Reilly at her shoulder. Tony was only steps behind and Katie almost tripped him up when she made a dash for the bar room, weaving through legs to get to the fireplace and Bogie.

The glass in Alex's hand started to slip and she set it unsteadily on the counter. Grant Hill's was the first face she saw clearly and his half smile could have been knowing – or it could just have been a smile. 'Don't forget your Guinness,' she said in the most level voice she could achieve. He drank, his gaze never leaving hers.

The crowd at the bar pressed in, calling orders. There wasn't time to speculate. Alex worked steadily until she felt Tony beside her. He squeezed the back of her neck gently. 'Take it easy,' he said quietly. 'You look anxious. I drove into the car park behind Lily and Dan. He came in his own vehicle. There was no chance to ask what was going on.'

'Why doesn't my mum come and say something? Why doesn't she help out? She's been gone all day.'

'I know she has but I'm a pretty good pair of extra hands,' he said, leaning toward the next customer who ordered something Alex didn't hear. 'Two gin and orange coming up,' Tony said.

'If Lily's got a lot to tell you, she won't want to make any fuss in front of everyone,' he said, reaching for clean glasses. 'Especially Dan. Give it a chance to calm down a bit and the two of you can talk on your own.'

Alex set out a long breath. 'You're right.'

'Has something happened, Sweetheart? Even Hugh looks wound up.'

She rubbed his arm. 'I'll tell you later. It's been strange although I could be imagining things. I hope I am. Almost forgot, Bill brought Radhika in. They're sitting with the sisters. That's a first.'

'I'm damned.' Tony avoided looking toward the fireplace. 'We both know there's something going on between them, but you don't see them anywhere together. I never expected to see them in here – or should I say, I wouldn't expect Radhika to agree to come with Bill.'

'See all these?' Alex tapped the pile of entries Grant Hill had left on the counter. 'This name contest puzzles me. I'm trying to convince myself the Hills are just trying to be nice because I helped Bob Hill during the fire. I don't know, though, Tony. A thousand pounds prize for coming up with the name of a pub seems a bit much.'

'Yeah. A bit ridiculous, but I think they can afford it.'

She stared up at him and raised her brows.

'OK, they seem keen on being best friends with you. Could be something devious about it – maybe not. I don't know.'

'That's Mr Hill's children, talking to Fay Winslet. Grant and Carmen.'

'I didn't think the Hills lived around here,' Tony said.

'They don't. They're from Temple Guiting, or that's where the family has a home. I doubt they're there all the time. Esme Hill and her friend were in here earlier. Hugh heard them asking me questions. He wondered if Esme was looking for a tame witness to be on her husband's side. Makes me feel strange, but she honestly didn't say anything obvious.'

'That doesn't mean she wasn't fishing,' Tony said. 'Look, I've been wanting to say this so I better spit it out. I wish the Hills would stay away. I wish they would never come near you again.'

She bowed her head. 'Because you think they could spell trouble.'

'I suppose. I can't help wondering what the story is behind the two deaths the police are investigating. And the Hills are connected somehow, even if only because the dead man worked with Robert Hill.'

'I can't argue with a word you say.' Alex looked up in time

to see Dan accompanying her mother toward the snug – or beyond. 'Damn. I want to talk to Mum on my own. It doesn't look like that'll be in the offing too soon. Dan's sticking to her like a limpet.'

Dan paused to speak to Bill who immediately got up with a kiss to Radhika's cheek that brought Alex's eyes and Tony's together.

'Well, well,' Tony said. 'He'd better not be about to pinch the best assistant I ever had.' His smile was decidedly artificial.

Dan, Bill and Lily went through the archway toward the snug and the restaurant.

'I did think my mum would want to tell me what's been happening as soon as she got here.' Alex turned her back on the bar and faced Tony. She blinked back tears. 'This is getting really weird.'

Not more than half an hour passed before the detectives and Lily returned. The men appeared relaxed. Lily smiled, but Tony could feel Alex's tension.

Lily was the only one of the three to join the group at the bar. 'My,' she said lightly, although Tony didn't like the dark patches under her eyes or the drawn lines around her mouth. 'I obviously chose a wild day to go AWOL. Forgive me, Alex. Just needed some hours away and I couldn't know this place would turn into Piccadilly Circus while I was gone.'

'Everything's gone beautifully.' Alex put an arm around her mother's waist. 'Let's hope we get lots more days like it. Preferably without snow storms.'

'Kev Winslet was going on about the contest for a pub name. Apparently, a lot of people are determined to win that thousand.' Lily leaned toward Hugh. 'Don't tell Doc James but I think I'm going to have a Dubonnet. It'll help me sleep.'

'Coming up,' Hugh said and turned away to find the bottle on a high shelf. 'And Doc would approve.' He poured a large glass and gave it to her.

Lily shook her head. 'This should be enough to knock me out. Thanks, Hugh.'

He gave her a broad grin and went into the kitchens.

The Hill brother and sister had left, Tony noted, although he hadn't seen them go. 'The Hills seem like a nice family, Lily. It's too bad they're going through hard times.'

'Yes.' Lily didn't sound interested. 'Gladys gave you my note, Alex?'

'She left it for me. She was bubbling with excitement over the breakfast success. Liz says she'd like to help her out every day. She's got an assistant at the dress shop to open up and I gather the early mornings are very quiet.'

'Is it worth it?' Lily, ever the pragmatist, asked. 'For Liz or for us?'

'I think it might be,' Alex told her. 'Let's give it some time to make up our minds. Is it OK if I ask what Dan and Bill wanted?'

Lily appeared surprised. 'I thought Dan would have mentioned it to you. Seems they are really busy with the case near Winchcombe. Dan said it's proving a lot less localized than they'd thought at first. They haven't had any luck finding accommodations they like elsewhere and they're used to us, so they'd like rooms here. Since we're very quiet at the inn, I agreed.' She gave Alex a worried frown. 'Did I do the wrong thing? I could just say it's not possible.'

'Oh, no,' Alex said with a quick glance at Tony. She knew he didn't like it when Dan stayed at the Black Dog – the man's powerful interest in her was too obvious to Tony. He and Alex had never discussed the subject but they didn't need to.

'Mum, are you all right?' Alex said. She clasped her mother's wrist. 'You seem anxious about something.'

With a somber and direct look at her daughter, Lily said, 'I'm not all right, sweetheart, but I intend to be. You and I have a lot to talk about but first I need to unscramble my brain and decide the best way to approach it all. I wouldn't be honest if I said I hadn't had a shock. But I've learned a lot I didn't know before and it's time I shared it with you. Can you be patient?' Lily caught at Tony's sleeve. 'I can't explain how glad I am for Alex to have you in her life. We both need good people around us.' She sipped at her Dubonnet.

How he'd like to hear Alex say those words to him. He set

his jaw, trying not to wonder how much longer he could just be Mr Wonderful and not need more.

Alex's strained expression said she couldn't be patient, or she didn't want to be. She put her arms around her mother. 'Yes. It won't be easy to wait, but I can. I love you, but you know that.' She pulled away to see Lily's face. 'Is Doc coming for you or are you going home alone? If you're going alone, I'm coming with you.'

'James is coming. The boys' aunt is home for a couple of days so they're at their cottage in Underhill. James and I have Naruto and we'll take good care of that sweet cat. Don't you worry about us.'

Her mobile rang and she answered, smiled and said a few words. 'Off we go,' she told Alex. 'James is out front with Naruto. He won't leave her at home alone – or in the car, of course. Too much responsibility when Kyle's not there. We're going to babysit.' Her smile lighted her eyes and she slipped away to get her coat and leave.

Alex scrubbed at her face and felt Tony pull her into a hug. 'I'd like to invite you on a holiday,' he said. 'Don't you dare say, no, without thinking. We'll wait until things cool off here. Your mum and my dad make a lovely couple, don't they?'

She nodded, yes.

'We do, too,' Tony added. He was too cautious to remind her how much he wanted her, and not just as a best friend and lover. His restraint was getting very thin.

'Yes, we do,' Alex said. 'And we'll make an even lovelier couple if the stinking disasters stop falling on our heads. I'm going to help Hugh close up, then we'll leave.'

The Burke sisters had gone, driven home by Major Stroud in one of his benevolent moods. Radhika was nowhere to be seen although Tony didn't know when she'd decided to leave. Dan was not around and neither was Bill. The bar was empty.

'Best time of the day,' Alex said, raising her face to Tony's who gave her more than a peck of a kiss. She kissed him back fiercely and pushed her hands beneath his sweater.

Hugh cleared his throat.

Tony hugged her closer. 'Ignore him. He's only jealous.'

'You've got that right,' Hugh said seriously. 'Did you know

Radhika's bought a property not far from Green Friday?' he asked.

That got their attention. 'Really?' Alex said. 'That's fabulous. She's stayed in that little cottage too long and I never felt comfortable about it after she was attacked there.'

'Neither did I,' Tony said.

Alex wanted to know everything about this major move for Radhika. 'Seems a long time ago all that happened, but it's not really so very long when you think about it. Is this place somewhere we know?'

'I didn't,' Hugh said. 'And it's practically next door to me. The property is heavily wooded. I looked at it after she told me.'

'She didn't tell me,' Tony said, sounding vaguely put out.

'The sale only just went through so she probably didn't want to let everyone know how much it means to her. But like I said, Green Friday is almost next door so she probably thought I'd see her coming and going and think it was strange if she didn't tell me something.'

Alex raised her shoulders. 'I'm excited. I'm not going to play dumb about it. Tomorrow I'll barge in and ask for an invitation to see the place. Is it big? What's it called?'

'It's not small. It's been empty a long time apparently and she's having it completely redone, including the gardens. She mentioned she may live in a couple of rooms there during renovation. And she mentioned deciding on a name.'

Tony made a face. 'She's not going to want to continue being a vet's assistant, is she?'

'Yes,' Hugh said. 'She is. And if she wasn't, she'd have told you. She's the kind of woman who doesn't fool around – she comes right out with the truth. She told me one of the reasons she fell for the property was because it wasn't too far from the clinic. She's buying a car, too, and learning to drive.'

Alex gave a breathy whistle. 'Oh, dear, I can't imagine that.'

'Well, start imagining it,' Hugh said. He stopped and inclined his head, looking out into the room. 'Excuse me?' he said. 'Um, we're closed, sir. I didn't see you there.'

Alex swung around and saw Frank Lymer emerge virtually from the cover of a long, heavy curtain behind the door.

He stood up and nodded. 'Just me,' he said, sounding awkward. 'I'm waiting for my Gladys. It's too nasty for her to ride home to Underhill on her own. I can put her bike in the back of my pickup.'

Tony clamped a restraining hand on Alex's shoulder but she was rigid. 'She's coming here from somewhere else, is she, Frank?' she asked.

Frank shifted from foot to foot. He took off his cap and his thin hair clung to his head. 'She said things went really well and she thought there would be more work for her to do than you all thought at first. I expect she's still doing dishes in the kitchen.'

Alex looked at Hugh who shook his head slightly.

'Frank,' Tony said. 'Did Gladys know you were coming to pick her up?'

When the man shook his head, no, they all sighed with relief. 'Have you called her?' Hugh said.

'I just thought she must be busy, so I've been waiting in the corner here,' Frank said. His face had grown pale and he wound his cap between his fingers. 'She was coming home this afternoon but when she didn't, I thought I ought to wait for her to let me know when I should come, this being a new job. She shouldn't ride her bicycle home in this weather – not when it's dark.'

'She's not here,' Hugh said.

Frank looked from one of them to the other and rushed from the pub. Alex caught up with him outside and about to get into a small pickup. 'Hold on, Frank. Don't go off like this. She'll be all right.'

'I knew I shouldn't let her come here. There was nothing wrong with her job at the Strouds. She loved it there until you suddenly asked her to work for you. She hasn't been the same since.'

SIXTEEN

What a hellish night it had been.

Twice before leaving the Black Dog Alex had called the Lymer's cottage in Underhill. The first time Frank had told Alex he didn't need her help. In response to the second call he said she should mind her own business because they were private people who took care of their own business. When she asked if Gladys was all right, he suggested she was only pretending to care and hung up.

After that, in the very early-morning hours, she had made a call to the Gloucester Constabulary and tried to explain that she wasn't really putting in a missing person report because she wasn't sure anyone was missing, but she hoped they would keep an eye out for someone looking like Gladys Lymer, just in case. The officer on the booking desk had been polite but Alex could tell he thought she was another whack job. Finally she asked that Dan O'Reilly be informed when he made contact and left it at that. With Tony spreading his fingers over his eyes and shaking his head, she'd been too embarrassed to push further.

Tony persuaded her to go home with him for what was left of the night, not a hard sell when the kindest place she could imagine was in his arms, in his bed.

They both moaned when the alarm and the clamoring dogs woke them in the morning.

It was almost nine in the morning by the time Tony drove them down the ice-slick hill toward Folly with the relaxed confidence of long practice. He held Alex's hand on top of his thigh and the flex of muscle brought her comfort – and a desire to go back up the hill with him. She'd left her anorak in her own vehicle and they had the heat blasting in Tony's, but still his bed appealed more.

'You OK?' he asked.

'OK,' she told him quietly.

As they drove past her mother's cottage, Alex peered at the front windows. All curtains remained closed. 'Mum opens the curtains as soon as she gets up. And takes in the milk.' The milk still sat in its mini metal crate on the front step.

Tony whistled, softly and tunelessly, then said, 'Well, we don't like to think about our parents as sexual beings, but—'

'No, we don't,' Alex said quickly, and felt silly for the reaction at her age. 'But they would have gone to your dad's house anyway. Because of looking after the boys. I expect my mum closed her curtains last night and . . .'

'And?' Tony prodded.

She almost took her hand away but thought better of it. 'The boys aren't at your dad's this weekend. Their aunt's at the cottage and they're with her. Let's forget it. They're grown-ups. Where they sleep is their business.'

He turned in at the Black Dog and gave her a wide smile. Alex pinched his leg.

Tony pressed the brakes. 'What's going on? I just realized how many cars and vans there are here.'

'We don't open for morning coffee for almost an hour,' Alex said. 'Oh, damn, do you think they're gathering here to send out search parties for Gladys?'

'We'll find out soon enough.' Tony backed out onto the road again and parked at the curb a few yards away.

They jumped out of the Range Rover and ran back toward the pub, the dogs in hot pursuit.

'I've got to keep an ear open for my pager,' Tony said, taking Alex by the hand. 'They'll be calling about that mare. If she's not ready soon she'll need some help.'

'Go now.' Alex was panting. 'I'll manage whatever's going on here.'

'I'm not leaving you until I see what's going on.'

The door slapped open and Hugh jogged to meet them. 'I've been watching for you,' he said and grimaced. 'There's nothing bad so don't get exercised. This is really weird but Gladys showed up on time this morning. Frank brought her and came in to make sure one of us was here. That had to be it. He looked around as if a mad axman was likely to jump out from somewhere and attack them. He didn't say two words while

Gladys went back to the kitchen, only put more wood on the fire like he was making sure Gladys would be warm enough in here. Then off he went muttering about how he'd be back to get his wife later.'

Alex and Tony looked at each other. Alex blinked and threw up her hands. 'I didn't remember to put out a sign that there'd be no breakfasts served this morning. What an idiot. I wasn't thinking.'

'I didn't think to do it either,' Hugh said. 'Just as well as it turns out. Come in and have coffee. Have you eaten?'

'No,' Tony said. 'Suddenly I'm starving. If you've got a spare pig you could slap on the spit, go ahead.'

'I might if there was time,' Hugh said, leading the way inside. 'We've been a bit busy. Liz Hadley was able to come in again, thank goodness.' He held the door open for Tony and Alex. Bogie ran between her feet to get into the warmth and she caught herself on the doorjamb. Katie was only slightly slower. 'I think Liz is hoping this turns into a regular thing. She's juggling a lot but seems to manage well enough.'

Alex slammed her boots down on the mat inside the door, knocking off chunks of icy snow. 'We'll have to see if the business stays steady after the thaw sets in.' Once inside the bar she stopped and looked around. 'Amazing. This is more than yesterday, isn't it?' The place was packed, including the up-room, and there were people waiting for tables.

'I wonder how many places serve tea while you're waiting?' Tony said. Those in chairs along one wall and standing in groups, held cups of tea and coffee and looked pleased with the entire situation.

Hugh hadn't put on a coat to greet them and went straight back to work, serving those who liked a little nip – or not so little – with breakfast.

'In the kitchen,' Alex said. 'I need to see if Gladys's attitude gives anything away. I don't care about the excuses – and being private people hardly explains a thing – something happened yesterday and I'm going to find out what it was.'

'Sweetheart,' Tony said, addressing his remarks via an unwavering examination of her mouth, which never failed to reduce her to jelly and with feelings she couldn't explore at this moment. 'If there's anything concerning, it should go to the police. Right away. But what could there be? This is an ordinary couple with an ordinary life. They're happy with it but they could have had a little spat. Happens to the best of us.' He gave her a too-sweet smile.

'I happen to know there are fresh crumpets from George's – gift from the sisters to celebrate the start of a new venture. If you want some – toasted and dripping with fresh butter from Wheedley's Farm and creaking under a mound of home-made raspberry jam – you'd better get into the kitchen now. Or that poor mare will be paging you herself. Just come and give me moral support – not that I'm going to say much. Keep your eyes and ears open. Really listen to what's said.'

Firelight leaped over glittering horse brasses on the fireplace. The room was warm and intimate. Even the garlands of dried hops along blackened beams, showing signs of needing replacement, took on a sunny yellow that was almost Christmassy. Liz smiled brilliantly as she hurried between tables with loaded trays and the customers chattered so loudly the conversations had risen to shouting point.

Tony caught her by the hand and towed her through the room and behind the bar. They passed the two walls of spirits bottles, some exotic ones kept on the highest shelves. These were relics Alex hardly remembered and certainly couldn't be sure what they contained. They would have to be explored one day – when she was older and had much more time.

The heat in the kitchen might have been overpowering if Gladys weren't working with windows thrown wide open. In the absence of wind, at least the still cold of the frozen morning mitigated bone-melting steam from kettles and pans to say nothing of hot and popping fat.

'Good morning, Gladys,' Alex said with enough alacrity to grate on her own nerves. 'My goodness, people love your breakfasts. This is wonderful.'

'Glad you're happy, Alex.' Gladys smiled tightly and worked on without looking up. 'I'd like to add porridge to the menu for tomorrow. If you agree, I'll have sign-ups for it so I can soak enough oats overnight – best that way – and we'll have to make sure Phil won't mind if I store a pot or two in his kitchens.'

Tony stepped in. 'I am a slave to good porridge, Gladys. Let's insist Alex agrees.'

Gladys gave him a shy smile but Alex quickly agreed. 'No problem setting the pots aside. Tell me what you want on the sign-up sheets and I'll put one on each table for you.'

For the first time that morning, Gladys looked genuinely pleased. 'Just have them put their names and a check mark if they want it. Then they can let me know if they like sultanas or currants, or stewed apple. Brown sugar and cream or milk will be automatic. They can suggest variations if they like but I'm not guaranteeing that or they'll want chocolate covered ants or something disgusting.'

Alex laughed. 'Or fried grasshoppers,' she added. Two large boxes from George's stood on the counter nearest the bar. Alex removed three crumpets while trying not to look too hard at all the other goodies lined up there.

'Have you eaten, Gladys,' she said. 'You could manage a crumpet while you're working.'

'I'll have something later.' Gladys said, sliding heaped plates onto the center work island in time for Liz to come and sweep them away.

Drinking coffee, munching on crumpets – with a Bakewell tart apiece mixed in for variety – Tony and Alex stood in a corner of the kitchen, watching and waiting for activity to eventually slow down.

Alex took sign-up sheets around the tables asking for any interest in porridge. The result was overwhelmingly positive and she visualized stock pots lined up in the kitchen come morning. Gladys was quietly thrilled.

Dishes were piled high waiting to be loaded into the dishwashers but Alex knew better than to offend Gladys by starting on that task. Gladys would take the efforts as a suggestion she couldn't manage. But Alex made a note to find someone else to help work the shift by tomorrow and there were plenty of mums in the village looking for a few hours of part-time work.

'Still no sign of Mum,' Alex murmured as the pace relaxed. 'Not that she has to be here until lunch time.'

Tony leaned on the counter, coffee mug in hand, and said, 'But you're about at the end of your rope with wanting to talk to her. I don't blame you. When you can, call her and tell her so.'

She looked at the floor. 'I suppose I'd better.'

The dishwashers hummed. Liz went to take a break and have her own breakfast before going about the final cleanup and Gladys started mopping the kitchen floor.

'Take a cup of coffee and talk to Liz,' Alex said, 'if you've got time. See what ideas she's got. I'll help Gladys.' A meaningful glance passed between the two of them.

When they were alone, Alex poured coffee for Gladys and set it on the island. 'Take a few minutes off,' she said. 'You're working too hard and I don't want you worn out. We could have rioting hoards at the door if you don't show up.' She held her breath for an instant after that unfortunate comment.

Gladys drank the coffee. Her bleached curls looked damp and bedraggled but her satisfaction in the morning's results showed.

Alex took in a deep breath. 'I'm sorry Frank was so worried yesterday. If I'd known he misunderstood what you were doing, I'd have talked to him. He was sitting in the corner of the bar and I didn't really take any notice of him being there.'

'We're pretty easy to miss,' Gladys said. There was no hint of pleasure in her now.

'That's not what I meant.' A fine start, Alex thought. 'The weather was so horrible. If I'd known you intended to go back and forth in that, I'd have made sure we took you both ways.'

Gladys's demeanor had sunk to anxious but glum. 'Not necessary. But thank you. Frank likes to do it.'

That was the first Alex had heard of it. Frank Lymer was famous for his lifelong history of sporadic employment and everyone knew Gladys was the glue that held hearth and home together.

'So you rode your bike home yesterday, then,' Alex said. She didn't feel good about pressing the woman but if there was a problem it needed to be dealt with.

'Yes.'

One of the things Frank had mentioned the previous night was that he hadn't seen the bike. Gladys must have put it in the hut behind their cottage.

'I'd be afraid of sliding,' Alex said. 'But you're more experienced than I am.'

'Some of us learn to make do,' Gladys said.

Alex tamped down irritation at the unnecessary unpleasantness.

'I know all about making do,' she said. 'I lived just about next door to you and Frank when I was growing up, remember. My mother cycled to work over here – at this same pub where you're working now. I understand.'

'Sorry for saying that,' Gladys said. 'You don't deserve it and neither does Lily.'

'Forget it. I thought maybe you got a lift back. It would have been much better.'

'But it's none of your business,' Gladys said sharply. 'I told you I rode my bike.'

Alex tingled with embarrassment. 'Now *I'm* sorry,' she said. 'Frank was so worried about you. He said he'd been at home waiting for you to let him know how you were doing but you didn't call. He didn't want to interrupt you, so he came and waited in the pub. A considerate man you've got there. He must have been waiting for you in the pub when you got home. I expect you had errands to run on your way home.'

Gladys stood up straight, pushed her hair back from her suddenly red face. 'Frank told you we're people who keep to ourselves. It's been just the two of us for a long time. We've no one else to count on. It happens I was tired and went up to rest. He didn't know I'd come in. I fell asleep and he eventually came here because he thought I must still be working. There. Now you know the whole story. Not much to it, is there?'

Alex rubbed a hand over her eyes. In fact she thought there could be a great deal more to this than Gladys was saying, but until and unless some other fact came to light and it had some importance, she had to let it go.

'I'm glad you're safe, Gladys. Please understand how worried and angry Frank was last night. He seemed to blame me. He said I lured you away from the Strouds and we both know that isn't true. So forgive me, OK? I'm so pleased with the breakfast trade and I don't think anyone else could do it nearly as well. Can we be friends again?'

Gladys smiled, back to her shy persona. 'I'd like that. Thank you. I'll call Frank to come and get me unless you still need me.'

'Go home,' Alex said. 'Give my best to Frank.'

Tony's pager had summoned him to a farm in the rolling flat land to the north of Folly and Alex left the Black Dog in Hugh's capable hands. He and Juste Vidal would prepare for the lunch-time influx. Alex had finally found the courage to call Lily and they had agreed to meet at Lily's Corner Cottage in the hour.

Alex made a call to the Gloucester Constabulary to report that her potentially missing person wasn't missing. The disinterested reception dealt with any embarrassment she might have felt.

Leaving the dogs by the fire, she went out of the kitchen door into the parking lot and screwed up her eyes against a new fall of snow, this one soft, the flakes fat and in a hurry to pile up on the crusted remains of the last major snowstorm and the two or three inches added in the night. She trudged over to the Range Rover to get her anorak.

Carefully, grateful for her Hunter wellies, Alex walked around the rear of the vehicle and jutted her face forward to squint at a heap beside one of a row of storage sheds. Her tummy rolled. She'd like to just walk away but she couldn't do that. Best get Hugh.

Grow up, Alex.

She went purposefully to look down on whatever was hidden by at least two layers of snow rapidly being added to by today's plump flakes.

Now was not the time to get sick. This wouldn't be the first time she'd come upon a frozen body. Alex closed her eyes at the memory.

She scraped back some of the soft snow at one end of the pile, then gradually delved deeper, brushing carefully as she grew closer to the shape underneath. Alex pulled on her leather gloves and used the flats of her fingers and palms, moving faster, but cautious in case there was something . . . There was something beneath the snow but it didn't have to be a body.

Abruptly, she stopped. She felt tears on her face. Memories rushed back of the sadness, the futile reality of what people could do to other people. Good people in the wrong place at the wrong time. But here, outside her pub?

She yelled, 'Hugh!' but didn't expect him to hear. Turning back to her task she first revealed rusted black metal, then what was obviously a tire.

'What is it?' Hugh reached her and caught her around the shoulders, almost lifting her away. 'I saw you from upstairs. Alex, what's the matter?' He looked down then.

Together they revealed Gladys Lymer's old bike.

Alex's heart beat so hard it hurt her throat. She crossed her arms over her chest.

The rumble of Hugh's deep laugh confused her. 'It's Gladys Lymer's,' she said.

'Is it? I didn't know. And we thought it was a body. Or I did.'

'So did I. Hugh, please don't tell anyone about it – finding the bike, I mean.'

'OK. But why does it matter? She and Frank must have decided to leave it here until the weather clears up. Shouldn't we stand it up. Here, I'll do that.'

'Please don't. If it becomes an issue, they'll want to know why it was left like this. If Gladys had known it was here, she'd have dealt with it.'

'You haven't said why it's a big deal,' Hugh said, rubbing his hands together against the cold.

'Because Gladys lied to me about it. Obviously, she didn't ride her bike home yesterday. Or if she did, something did happen to her along the way. I think it was bad and it's important. No one else may see this the way I do, but I'm going to find out what it means.'

But first she and her mother were to meet at Corner Cottage for a talk. Alex hoped their discussion could finally be open, but she still had a sick feeling Lily might cut it off at any instant.

SEVENTEEN

Dan paced his office, talking on the phone. Through the window into the squad room he could see team members leaving with equipment. 'Yes,' he said, trying not to sound as unenthusiastic as he felt. He frowned. 'Bourton-on-the-Water? You've got it. See you there.'

He rang off and dropped his mobile into a coat pocket. 'We almost got away clean,' he told Bill who was still pulling files from Dan's cabinets to fill cardboard boxes with case information. 'I thought by coming in early enough we'd avoid diversions.'

'What now?' Bill said. He'd changed personalities since last night when they'd booked to stay at the Black Dog in Folly. 'Why not tell me in the car?'

'Because you don't want to wait another second to hot foot it back to the vicinity of your lady love?'

'Because I want to get on with this stinking case and it's going to be easier from Folly than here in Gloucester. You keep pushing it when it comes to Radhika and me, but it's wearing a bit thin and pretty soon you're going to need a different diversion from reality.

'You saw the papers. We've run out of cover from our very few friends in the press. Maybe we should concentrate on that. Anytime now—probably right now—we are going to be plastered all over every rag. We'll be those amateurs who haven't got a lead to our names. Not that it's true, but since we can't share any leads while we try to break this thing, they'll keep on goading us into giving something away.'

'Which we won't do,' Dan said shortly. 'We'll come up with a couple of leads to feed to the press, and a better one for someone we can trust to use it well. Now, stand where you are and listen.

'Alex Duggins called in with a wishy-washy report. A Mrs Gladys Lymer who works at the Black Dog may have gone missing. She left the pub for home around one in the afternoon yesterday and Alex doesn't know for certain if she's been seen since.'

The box Bill was holding started to tip and he smacked it down on the nearest surface. 'So, what does that mean? Missing person or no missing person?'

'Damned if I know. We'll go after it when we get to Folly. For some reason that eludes me, our friends at the Dog don't seem to know either – and Mrs Lymer's husband isn't talking.

'Let's go. I'll drive. You let the team know we'll be scrambling the minute we hit that sumptuous parish hall in Folly. We can't afford to have a double homicide drag on without any breaks for much longer.'

'Balls Harding has everything set in Folly,' Bill said hefting two boxes into his arms. 'Coffee, tea and snacks arranged from the Black Dog – apparently he thinks his priorities are straight. Spare desks and chairs transported. Computer and communication equipment in place.'

Dan switched over his phone to the front desk. 'I thought that since our resident upstart has made detective sergeant, we'd drop the "Balls" to avoid questions we don't want to answer.'

'Yes, boss, but it slips out. After all, he is about the most ballsy upstart I ever encountered. But I'll try. Detective Sergeant Harding is very efficient, I'll give him that. And I haven't noticed him developing an attitude since he passed his exam.'

'There's something else,' Dan said. 'We've an appointment with Molly Lewis. That was her on the phone. The post-mortems are complete – apart from some long-range lab work that probably won't make a lot of difference either way to us. Not if we get some irrefutable explanations ahead of that. The exotic tests are almost always about stuff that only interests the boffins anyway. We're meeting Molly now.'

'Shit,' Bill said, with feeling.

The Hill's plot, Knighton House on the far side of a wide gentle hill, from Winchcombe, impressed LeJuan Harding – just when he thought he'd become blasé about these excessive country piles.

Knighton was old, very old, just how old LeJuan wasn't sure but he imagined there were more than a couple of hundred years of English privilege cosseted by miles of stone walls backed with yew hedges and dense woods. The house was invisible from any of the surrounding roads, particularly at this time on a snow-cloaked morning. The estate could only be seen from behind and above where the hill rose just enough to give a cloud-darkened view over the trees.

It had been Bill Lamb's idea that LeJuan and Barry set up in Folly before dawn was even breaking and carry on to Knighton before – they hoped – there was enough activity to catch them poking around without an invitation.

Barry Trafford drove the Jeep they'd been fortunate to purloin from the motor pool that morning and from his silence, Barry was enjoying their ride too much to bother himself with minutia.

'What did you think?' LeJuan asked. 'Like it?'

'Wouldn't mind having one of these myself,' Barry said. 'Beats the hell out of my old Nissan.'

'I meant the Hill's place – the estate?' LeJuan smiled to himself. They had dropped down to the level of the estate again and taken what was little more than a track around Knighton. 'Stop here while we figure out how we'll get to the carriage house without being seen. The Hills made it clear we aren't invited to wander around their territory, so asking at the main entrance is out of the question.'

Obediently, Barry pulled the dark blue Jeep onto a verge and up close to the dry-stone wall. 'I know that. Sergeant Lamb looked thrilled to have us leaping from our beds in the middle of the night. But I thought we'd have been told how to approach; instructions about it, I mean,' Barry said. He was not much of a self-starter but he was a sterling bloke and LeJuan liked him. When the chips were down you could trust Barry to be there for you, whereas a lot of more aggressive officers were always looking for a way to get up a ladder – leaving anyone else behind if it suited their purpose.

'We did get this from Lamb.' LeJuan opened a chart across his knees. 'It tells us more than a long-distance view over the chimneys. This is the house,' he said, pointing out a large building shaped like an E without a central stroke. The chart showed that the two end bays no longer existed in their original form. There looked to be a flight of steps running the length of the remaining wing with a front door in the middle and rows of matching windows on either side. A porte-cochère broke up the long expanse and in front of that was a large pool. Vehicles would drive in a circular pattern.

'That was probably where the carriages went in times of yore,' LeJuan said and laughed.

Barry, his blond head bent over the chart, nodded and said, 'I'd have liked to see that.'

LeJuan's black heritage didn't quite stretch his imagination to enjoying the sight of carriages and fine ladies and gentlemen arriving at Knighton, but he appreciated the history.

'Right,' he said. 'You're the whizz at this sort of thing. Where do you think this is? Or should I say, where are we now?' He pointed to squares that depicted small buildings a distance from the back of the house.

Barry looked up. 'That's north. Which means the house faces this way.' He pointed on the chart. 'South. And these buildings are north-east and, if the key is right, about half a mile from the back of the house. These are the kitchens, right? And the kitchen gardens if they still keep them up. There's another wall between the gardens and the out buildings. This says stables. Do you know if they're used?'

'Wouldn't be surprised,' LeJuan said.

'Then we may be lucky.' Barry bent lower over the chart. 'It seems as if they don't overlook the out-buildings. Who would live in those?'

'Wouldn't have thought anyone did now, but this one.' He set a fingernail on one. 'This is the carriage house where our Lance Pullinger had digs when he chose. Apparently, he didn't choose very often but at one point he had it set up so he could go there when he wanted to.'

'So where did he go otherwise?'

'I'm no wiser than you. The house in Winchcombe where the woman was found, I suppose, but if O'Reilly and Lamb know that for sure, they haven't told either of us. The Hills told our boys Pullinger moved out of the carriage house and the place is under renovation now. The boss said Robert Hill was cagey about Pullinger's living arrangements. He answered questions but he didn't volunteer any information. Our job is to get in here—' he tapped his finger on the carriage house again – 'and see what, if anything, we can find to help us with the mystery of Mr Lance Pullinger, architect. Hill sidestepped any suggestion of looking at the place. He said there was nothing to see, just building supplies.'

LeJuan scooted down in his seat and crossed his arms. 'And since we don't have enough of an excuse for a search warrant we'll have to try doing this without being seen. But start thinking up excuses, just in case.'

'I think O'Reilly's hoping there's an easy way around the warrant,' Barry said, frowning and rooting around in his pockets. 'He's always liked the element of surprise. Here. You're better at this than I am.' He gave LeJuan his lock-picking set.

EIGHTEEN

'Hello, me darlin',' Dan sang out, knowing he took his life in his hands if Molly Lewis was in a foul mood, dealing with a hangover, perhaps.

As promised, she waited for them about a half mile from the busy village center of Bourton-on-the-Water.

Seated on a flat rock beside the shallow waters of the River Windrush, she looked toward them. When they got close enough she waved and called out, 'Aha. Good. My entertainment for the morning has arrived. Gird your loins, m'boys. I'm ready to cut you to ribbons and feed you to these fine ducks.'

That, Dan realized, was probably as close as Molly would come to humoring him. She wore a puffy blue coat large enough to exaggerate her small stature, black trousers and boots, and large, dark glasses. Her blond hair was incongruously bouncy and completely at odds with her basic personality.

'Glad you're in such fine fettle,' Dan said. He perched on

the edge of a smaller and very uncomfortable rock while Bill crossed his arms and remained standing. 'I didn't know you were an outdoors woman.'

'This is close to home for me,' Molly said. She turned her face away as if closing the topic.

The yellowing stalks of reeds poked brokenly from the snow-covered muddy riverbank. A sky, so gray and heavy it met the mist-shadowed branches of trees not yet showing as much as a leaf bud, hung like billows of gauze about to burst.

Rivulets of water ran through melting snow between the rocks and the slimy towpath had taken on a gelatinous quality. 'Being outside always cheers me up,' Molly said. 'Mr Pullinger was either dead or close to death when he was blown out of the back of that trailer. I'm prepared to bet on dead.'

Dan looked into the lenses of her dark glasses. Here was a woman momentarily removed from a life dedicated to death. Who, he wondered, was Molly Lewis other than a crack pathologist?

Two small boys squelched purposefully past, each clutching a bag filled with pieces of bread. 'Ducks,' the first, towhead child announced, raising his bag aloft.

Dan said, 'Good for you,' and waited while a woman walked in the boys' wake, casting curious glances at the unlikely trio he, Bill and Molly must make as they hung out beside the river.

'What makes you so sure?' Dan asked when the duck-hunters were well away. 'Or perhaps I should say, why is there a question and why does it matter?'

Molly hiked her feet higher on the rock and fastened her arms around her knees. She chuckled softly. 'Yesterday I might have wondered the same myself but I was missing . . . no, not missing anything, just unaware of all the evidence. By last night it all came together.' She jiggled the toes of her boots and smiled to herself.

Snow, the small sharp flake variety, started to fall and grew denser by the moment.

Seconds ticked by. Bill swiped a hand across his eyes, cleared his throat. 'Are you going to share your great discovery with us?'

'Of course. Why do you think I'm freezing my bum off on

this rock . . . for my health? Lance Pullinger had drunk enough alcohol to put him to sleep for a while. Had he been much smaller, he might have died of alcohol poisoning. But I doubt he was unconscious when the whisky bottle was rammed down his throat to choke him. I think it was held there while he tried to dislodge it and it broke. There are consistent cuts on his fingers and palms, in the mouth, the throat and so on. Unfortunately, the only prints on the bits of bottle they found are his, three of them, and one of those is smeared – probably by someone wearing gloves while they did the deed. I'm piecing this together, of course, but I'm more or less right.'

Relieved to jump up, Dan stood beside Bill. 'Pretty fit fellow, Pullinger, right?' He slapped his arms back and forth across his chest.

'Yes,' Molly said, her face turned up to the weather, a smile showing how much she enjoyed the icy splatter against her skin.

'There must have been one hell of a struggle.'

Molly looked up at them. 'Not necessarily. Anything from Arson?'

'It was arson, all right,' Bill said. 'Petrol start, probably. We don't have anything final.'

'And Darla was what to Lance Pullinger? Wife or lover, which do you think?'

Dan studied the police surgeon. She loved putting as many pieces together as she could manage. He nodded, yes. 'One or the other. That's the way it looks, but we're not sure. She could just have been someone he hooked up with who started using his name. So far we haven't had any luck tracing her before she and Lance Pullinger showed up with what looks like joint lives. She isn't on file as far as we can tell. No prints, nothing. And nothing in HOLMES, but we'll find her.'

'One sharp instrument blow to the back of her cranium,' Molly said. Her eyes were closed as if she had moved into another realm. Her voice had lost both enthusiasm and expression. 'Extensive fracture. Second blow most likely from falling on the hearth. Right temporal bone extending to the parietal. Massive injury. Dead or close to after the first injury, she'd have gone down hard, with her weight behind it.'

'And you're sure she died before Pullinger?'

'No doubt about it. And there was a lot of rage there. Too bad we can't turn it around and magic the two deaths together into a murder then suicide.'

Dan met Bill's eyes briefly. 'Nice of you to want all of our jobs made easier.'

Molly held up a hand and Dan pulled her to her feet. 'Actually, I was thinking of justice,' she said. 'Women like Darla don't get much of that. There are healed and partially healed cigarette burns on the deceased's back, including her buttocks and the backs of her thighs.'

'You didn't say anything about them at the morgue,' Dan said.

'I wasn't finished then and I had to be sure. I wanted a second opinion. Darla had been tortured . . . and I use the word in its real sense. There are more scars from burns where they were unlikely to be found unless she sought help – which evidently she didn't.'

Dan swallowed. 'How do you know she didn't go for help.'

'If she had, it's likely it would have been stopped. Someone would have been in jail, or so I can tell myself. The newest burns were the ones I've already told you about. Most of the older ones, except for the sides of her breasts, were where they were even harder to find and mucous membranes have the capacity to heal very well – and fast. Not so easy to identify. Copies of the reports are on their way to you but I'm sure you can work out what I'm telling you.'

NINETEEN

'I'm here, Mum,' Alex called, closing the front door of Corner Cottage behind her. Her mother had chosen her own home for their meeting. The most comfortable surroundings for her, Alex supposed.

Her mum appeared from the tiny dining room. 'I've got coffee and sandwiches,' she said, with an unconvincing smile.

'I thought I could spread things out on the dining table for us to look at. I don't know what I expected to find when I picked up Angela's things in London but some of it makes me glad I decided to go. All of it does, really, if I'm honest. It isn't a bad thing to shed tears over secrets your mother shares with you.'

Nodding, Alex followed into the room. She couldn't think of anything to say other than how she wished, had wished for a long time, that Lily had shared her secrets with her daughter before. The dining-room table was covered with slim piles of papers and photographs; piles Alex wished were thicker. There were two wooden boxes, one painted with bright colors, faded in places, the other carved but dried out and showing some cracks.

Lily smiled at her. 'Not a lot for a lifetime, is it?'

'We'll make the best of it.' Alex smiled. She couldn't help feeling excited. Apart from what little her mother had shared at the Black Dog with Harriet and Mary at the table, this was the first time she could hope to learn more about who she really was.

Her mum glanced up from studying a photo in a silver frame. 'Are you all right, Alex? You sound really tense. Is it because of all this?' She waved at the things on the table. 'Or has something else happened?'

Alex considered. 'There are some troubling things going on, Mum. Gladys's behavior for one. But really, I only want to think about us – and all this, for now. What's the framed picture?'

Lily picked it up and gave it to Alex. 'You don't have any idea who these people are but they're related to me – and to you. What do you think?'

'I've never seen any relatives before,' Alex said, going to a window to look at a picture of a girl and a young man – scarcely more than a boy either, she supposed. They looked like an incredibly happy pair of teenagers. 'Who are they?'

When Alex looked at her mother she saw she was crying. 'My mother and father,' she said in a choked voice. 'Angela and Simon Devoss.'

Alex stared. 'Devoss? I've never heard that name before.'

'Simon Devoss was my father's name. I didn't know that either, not until I picked up my mother's things.'

Alex looked at the photo again, at the girl's curly hair, her laughing eyes looking up into the man's face – and at him staring back at her, an arm around her back, a big hand possessively clasping a small waist. Angela's dress had a sweetheart neckline and it looked white with small flowers all over the material. Simon wore a dark, flattering suit, white shirt and striped tie. He had a rose in his buttonhole. Angela held several long-stemmed roses of a pale shade.

'This was their wedding photo,' Alex exclaimed. 'Wasn't it?'

Lily made no reply and Alex kept her eyes on the photo.

'I . . .' Lily cleared her throat. She wrapped an arm tightly around her middle and waved the other hand in front of her face as if dismissing both her tears and trembling mouth. 'Don't worry about me. I'm being too sensitive.'

'You are not.' Alex moved closer to her mother and pulled her close. 'You don't have to be stronger than anyone else – and you don't have to be strong for me anymore. You've always been there for me, I never doubted I was safe and loved – and cared for. And you were young when I was born, Mum. Young but grown-up at the same time.'

She fell silent, afraid she would put her mother off from telling all the things Alex wanted so badly to know.

'Read this first,' Lily said, giving Alex some lined paper with a card attached. 'This starts at our beginning really. We don't have anything earlier. Sit down. I'll bring in the coffee and sandwiches.'

Alex pulled a chair up to the table. First she read the card, then started what her grandmother had written on sheets of lined paper that looked as if they'd been torn from a school workbook. When she finished she crossed her arms on the table and rested her face on top.

She closed her eyes and thought about two people with every right to love one another and the cruel fate that had taken that love from them.

'Your mother was punished so many times for what she didn't do,' Alex said when she heard her mother come into the room again. 'She fell in love with someone she'd known all her life and married him. How could her own parents treat her as they did? How could his – especially when she was expecting their dead son's child.' Pausing, Alex thought about what it all meant. 'Mum, you have relatives somewhere. From both of your parents.'

Her mother shook her head. 'No. They could never be anything to me.'

'But I'm related to them, too.'

'Yes, you are.' Lily picked up a pile of papers. 'Would you want to know any of them? These are drawings I did for Angela in the years after I went into foster care.'

Alex looked at one crayon picture after another. They mostly showed a woman and a child and Lily had sorted them to show how they changed as she had grown older. 'I wouldn't want to know those people,' Alex said. Was that true?

Gradually they worked their way through everything on the table. Alex took her time, lingering over photographs of people she didn't know although her mother pointed out herself as a small girl, and some of the people she had lived with when they had taken Angela and Lily under their wings.

'Take it all home,' Lily said, surprising Alex. 'It's as much your history as mine. Take your time. We might want to have the pictures copied properly, make an album for you even.' She started gathering everything up. 'I'd like to hang the little wedding picture in my bedroom.'

Still she showed no sign of talking about the story of Alex. Surely she knew how much her daughter needed to understand her own beginnings.

Reaching back, Lily pulled the long silver chain she'd always worn from around her neck. Alex was so used to it she never gave chain or medallion a thought. Her mother gave it to her.

'My name is on the back,' her mum said. 'And it's got an engraving on the other side.'

'Lily Mary Edwina,' Alex murmured. 'My baby's name, too. I like the cross and the roses on the front.'

'It's yours now. If you want it.'

With a smile, Alex slipped the medallion around her own neck. 'Of course, I want it. Thank you. But won't you miss it?'

'I'll be glad you have it, and so would your grandmother – and grandfather – have been. Let's have this coffee while it's still hot. Then I'll put everything into a bag for you to take home.'

They carried their coffee and the plate of sandwiches into the living room with its small, leaded, bow window and floral damask curtains. A fire in the grate was burning low and Alex put on more wood. Her heart thudded harder and harder. *Please let Mum tell me the rest of the story now. Please don't let her find it too hard to start.*

They sat in soft-seated spindle chairs on either side of the fireplace and Alex's mother pulled a red Chinese trunk she used as a coffee table between them.

'Eat some sandwiches,' she said, setting down the plate. 'You're too thin, Alex. I think you overdo the worrying.'

It was hard not to laugh. 'I'll remember you said that.' And with luck her mum would throw off the unhappy cloak she'd been wearing for weeks and everyone around here would feel better.

'What's bothering you about Gladys?'

Alex felt like standing over her mother and demanding she stop avoiding issues. 'We can talk about it another time. It's probably nothing.'

'I don't believe you. The look on your face says you're worried, or upset.' Lily set down a sandwich without taking as much as a bite. 'Look, Gladys has known us since I first went to Underhill when you were little. She was so good to me – and to you. If I worked in the evening, she babysat for you. Something's happened and you're not telling me.'

Just like part of my entire life happened without me knowing anything about it? 'I think Gladys and Frank had a spat, nothing more.' She didn't think that but it filled a gap for now. 'Mum, why did you decide to live in Underhill?'

Sometimes people turned pale but Lily's face not only became white, it took on a chalky quality. She sniffed and gulped at her coffee, settled her eyes on Alex's. 'I spent a couple of weeks there once and I was very happy. When . . . when I could finally think clearly and realized I had to make a way for the two of us, I went back there and I was lucky. I had enough money to rent that little flat next to the Lymers and I got a job at the Black Dog. I was so young-looking everyone was nice to me, even the younger men who might have been a problem. Yes, I was very lucky to be in the one place where my life had . . . well, I liked it a lot around here. There was this camp they held for young people who intended to go to university.' She turned her face away. 'That wasn't to be but I learned a lot there and I was in the open air for the first time – clean, open air. I'd always lived in London, you see.'

This was it. 'And you had met my father around here, hadn't you?'

Lily looked into the fire and after a while, she nodded, yes.

'Was he as young as you?' If so it would have made it hard to think of taking on a family.

'Not quite. Alex, there's something else I've got to tell you about, something serious that worries me. I never thought I'd have to talk to you – or anyone – about it but I don't have a choice anymore.'

Alex put her cup and saucer on the sheet of glass that covered the top of the carved trunk. 'Please just explain, Mum. I'm more than grown up so please don't try to hide anything from me. Anything at all.'

Lily didn't meet her eyes. 'I got a call from someone whose name I don't want to say. If I can, I'll forget it. I did that once and I can do it again, so don't ask me to tell you. She was a social worker when I was expecting you. The foster family I lived with then was lovely and they cared about me, but they were old-fashioned and they didn't know how to cope with the questions that started. They tried to carry on but the jabs got worse and they had children of their own to consider. Times were different, Alex. So, well . . . my social worker took me into her home. She was single with a nice house. There weren't any money worries for her and I suppose she got an allowance for my care, too. She kept me until you were born and took me back to her home afterward.'

Alex chewed her bottom lip and watched her mother's changing expressions, the way she swallowed awkwardly and looked away frequently.

'We were with her a long time, Alex. I thought she was wonderful. She was kind and she loved you so much.' Looking up she added, 'She loved you too much – too much. I felt funny sometimes because she did everything for you. And for me. We had everything.'

'What are you saying, Mum? Or what aren't you saying?'

'What she wanted was to set me up with a new start. I would get back into school, go to university, have all the things I'd always wanted. The catch was, you – she wanted you. She could give you a perfect life.'

Alex rubbed her face. 'A social worker. Where was all the money from?'

'Inherited. That's what she told me and I believed her. I still do. I don't know why she wasn't interested in having her own baby – perhaps she couldn't. I don't care. Perhaps she doesn't like men. It doesn't matter. She had made me an allowance, a generous one, and I saved almost all of it. I didn't need to spend the money. When I said I was taking you and leaving, I wanted to give all the money back but she wouldn't take it. Afterwards I was grateful for that because it got me through – that and the job at the Black Dog. And the kindness of strangers like the Burke sisters and Gladys Lymer. And you were a good little soul – I could have you at the pub when I had to and you were an angel.' Alex's mum smiled. 'What happened?'

Alex smiled back. 'That's an old joke, Mum.'

'Sweety, that woman went nuts on me. She tried to take you away anyway. She told me she could have me put in a home because I had endangered my child. The things she said were crazy. The people at the child protection services place were her friends and she insisted they would stand up for her.'

'What did you do?' Even trying to imagine what her mother had gone through was impossible. 'You were so young and she had all the power.'

Getting up, Lily flexed her shoulders and raised her chin. 'I went to the agency myself. I didn't accuse Beverly Irving of anything, just said I was ready to go out on my own and was there any reason why I shouldn't. They told me it was fine as long as I could prove I had a plan and you would be safe and well-cared for. I had the plan and that was it. I went back and packed. When I told that woman what I'd done she backed off as if I'd slapped her. Then she threatened me and said she'd find me and get you for herself in the end, but I left and never saw or heard from her again.'

Carefully watching her mother, Alex said, 'Sit down again, Mum. You said this person's name, Beverly Irving, but it doesn't matter if I know her name. She's gone from our lives and that's all that matters.'

Lily remained standing. 'She's not gone, Alex. And she wants to make us suffer for what she lost, what she still believes – all these years later – should have been hers. And she talked about how I intend to spoil the life she has now and how she won't allow it. I never did anything to hurt her and I never would.'

'Have you seen her again?'

'No, absolutely not.'

'Why are you afraid of her again? How could she have any idea where we are?'

'I think she does. And I think she's got a lot of misconceptions about us wanting to hurt her. She threatened us. She said she would hurt someone I love if I don't do what she asks.'

Alex swiped at her moist brow. 'That's senseless.' She shook her head and went over to hold her mother's shoulders. 'You're imagining things that won't happen. It's so far in the past it's never going to touch you again. Forget it.'

Her mother stroked Alex's cheek. 'Sweety, yesterday after I picked up my mother's things, I got a threatening call from that woman. She knew I'd been to the agency and picked up my mother's things. She's found us again.'

TWENTY

'Gather round,' Dan O'Reilly called, walking into the Folly parish hall, once again their makeshift squad room. 'Make it fast, if you please!'

Stewed coffee vied with fried radiator dust and damp woolen uniforms for 'smell of the day'. The windows, cranked open a measly half-inch, had lost any battle with the coating of hot air and thick, grimy steam that painted the glass. More falling snow closed away the scene outside, but they all knew it was as cold as hell wasn't, and sleet was starting to strafe the land.

Bill Lamb ducked around Dan to put a steaming mug of his personal brew on the nearest table. 'There you go, guv. The real stuff.'

Groans of envy went up as the other detectives in the room dragged folding chairs to make a half circle in front of Dan. All except newly minted Detective Constable Jillian Miller, just off the beat and into civvies. Miller managed to wear a beguiling smile – and fresh lipstick – and was perched on a desk with her long legs crossed.

Dan had a lot on his mind, more than he could stuff away for later consumption, but he made a mental note to make sure Jillian Miller didn't become any kind of a problem in the department and that her new status was not allowed to make her feel more powerful than she was.

'Anything from Harding and Trafford?'

'They called in earlier,' Miller said, heel swinging. 'They're at the Hill estate and they aren't ready to leave, or they weren't then. Said they had some information and they'd bring it in. Apparently, they didn't think they could trust me with it.'

Dan nodded and made no response. The usual barrier of whiteboards and screens had been erected across the hall but there were too few pieces of useful information on the boards.

'Where are the pictures of Lance Pullinger and Darla Crowley?' He and Lamb had decided not to divulge the possibility that these two had used the same name for reasons still awaiting final explanation.

Detective Constable 'Longlegs' Liberty all but levitated from his chair and hurried to shuffle through folders spread across a trestle table. Straight blond hair stood up at his crown while soft brown eyes missed nothing and kept him looking perpetually young. The leather jacket and blue jeans he favored added to the twenty-something misfit appearance. He pulled out photos of the two deceased victims and put them on a board.

'Good for you,' Dan said. 'There should be a chart of the

Hill development near Winchcombe with Arson's comments and information for the house in Winchcombe where the first victim was found.'

'Second,' Miller sang out.

'Darla Crowley died first,' Dan said flatly. 'The post-mortem reports are in and confirm this.'

Longlegs was already sliding out maps and charts. Tall, slim and with the look of a man who didn't eat enough, Liberty was an asset who covered bases before most of the crew knew they needed covering. But he steadfastly avoided the sergeant's exam and insisted he'd risen as far as he needed to go – to Dan's puzzled irritation. Dan never intended to give up on dragging some ambition to climb the ladder of advancement out of Liberty.

Fifteen minutes on and the whiteboards, although not crowded, took on the expected case-in-progress appearance. Dan started using markers to connect elements, slashing lines quickly from photos to other photos and from charts to maps.

'The burns on Crowley were definitely made by cigarettes?' Jillian Miller asked. 'How do they know that?'

'They know it from comparing them to photos of other established cigarette burns and because forensics – and the police surgeon – have seen hundreds of them.' Sometimes he thought Jillian talked just to hear her own voice. When he felt more charitable, he classified her as intelligent but over-eager.

Bill Lamb put his empty coffee mug down. 'You want to go through anything we got from house-to-house, guv?'

'Yes. I take it we're talking about Winchcombe.'

Detective Constable Ashton, young, dark and eager, raised a hand. 'It's not easy along the street there. Most of the people we spoke to are shopkeepers and they might as well have got together to decide what to say. If they saw anyone coming or going from the house in question they either didn't take any notice or thought it was people working on the place. A couple remember Darla Crowley but didn't know her or anything remarkable about her. Not one of them recalled seeing Lance Pullinger.'

Dan passed the marker from hand to hand. 'That doesn't

make any sense. Do the canvas again.' He thought for a moment. 'Pullinger could have been cautious enough to limit his visits to after dark. Let's find out how the neighborhood changes at night. And we need to take a good look at alternate entrances to the building. We know there's one from the back via an access road from Castle Street and from the yard behind for deliveries from when there was a shop on the ground floor. Find out how easy it is to get in and out from that yard. I'm expecting that it's very easy. Supposedly the sale of the shop floor is still not finalized. It was being sold separately from the rest of the house. That doesn't have to mean you can't get in that way.'

'I'll get on it,' Detective Constable Ashton volunteered.

'Good. Daily, you go with him. See if anyone remembers any vehicles parking repeatedly. Either at the back or in front.'

A commotion on the other side of the screens silenced them. Bill Lamb raised his eyebrows and Dan held up a silencing hand. A raised, garbled voice could be heard over all the noise.

Dan went around a hanging whiteboard and between the screens. He was confronted by one of his constables dodging back and forth to stop a brawny man from getting past him. Tightly curled dark hair, sharply memorable features and a hard-muscled body beneath a navy-blue pea coat and jeans made for a man not easy to forget – or to underestimate as an opponent if he ever chose that course.

'OK, OK, OK,' Dan said, loudly enough to be heard but without shouting. 'What's the problem here?'

'You O'Reilly?' the man asked in a London accent.

'Chief Inspector Dan O'Reilly,' he responded.

'Yeah. It's you I'm looking for, then. They said you would know where my wife is.'

Dan could feel the officers behind the screens holding their breath, listening hard and willing themselves not to interrupt. If he'd wanted their help he'd have let them know.

'Who told you to come here?' Dan asked. He didn't believe any police officer would send this man.

'Look,' the fellow said through his teeth, 'you don't get to ask me any questions, I—'

'Who sent you here?' Dan felt his constable move a step

closer. 'Come on, man. Speak up. I'll help you if I can, but be straight with me first.'

The man narrowed very dark eyes. 'A woman, if it matters. I don't know who she was. She came out of the back of that row of cottages in Winchcombe in a hurry and she wouldn't tell me what she was doing there. Cheeky bitch. None of my business, she said. It was the cottage where Darla was living.' He flexed his hands, opening and closing his fingers, turning the tips white. 'I can tell you she ran away. The snow didn't slow her down. A wiry one, she was. Had on one of those ski hats that only show the eyes and mouth. I think it was blue but I don't take notice of things like that. I followed her as far as the front of the buildings but it was too busy for me to stop her from leaving. She'd have kicked up—'

'All right, all right, I've got the picture.' What woman could have been in Winchcombe poking around the crime scene?

'Now I think of it, the hat could have been red.'

Dan made a mental note that the hat was probably blue. 'Take a seat over there.' He pointed out a row of seats against the front wall of the building and took out his notebook and pen. 'What's your name? What's your wife's name? Where did you last see her, and how long ago was that?'

'I've been away. I work the cruise lines – a decky. Haven't seen her in months and she stopped writing or calling – or picking up when I called her – but I know she's alive and well because she's cashed the checks I sent her.' He sneered. 'She would. *Women*. I'm Vince Crowley and she's Darla Crowley.'

TWENTY-ONE

'Come on, darling. The sooner we do this, the sooner we can put it behind us.' Tony looked back at Alex who pulled against his hand like a truculent kid. 'Come on! You said you wanted to come. You said you were up for this? We tell them what we know, which isn't much, and get home for an evening by the fire.'

'Grr,' she said. 'It's déjà vu all over again.'

'Aren't you the original one?' He knew when he'd better keep things light. 'We haven't been in the lovely parish hall for ages. We miss it, don't we?'

'No, and I wish Dan and Bill would find themselves a home away from home somewhere else. OK, I'll pull myself together. But only because I want to get out of here fast and your fire sounds OK.'

'Only OK? Thanks. Let's move before our boots freeze to the spot.'

They had walked the short distance from the Black Dog to the parish hall in increasing darkness. For now, the snow mixed with sleet had stopped but he didn't fool himself it wouldn't start again soon enough. Alex walked beside him up the driveway to the front doors of the hall.

'You looked pensive when I got to the Black Dog,' he said. 'Was it just this Gladys thing that had you down? You haven't said a word about how it went with your mum.'

At the bottom step, she paused. 'There's a lot more to say but I'd rather wait until we're at home to talk about it.'

She often talked about them being 'at home' as if they had somewhere they belonged together. Well, even while it got other thoughts going around in his head, he liked to hear her say it.

'At least tell me if the talk you had with Lily was OK?'

Alex nodded, yes, and took hold of the cold ring of metal to open the door. He helped her turn it then put a shoulder to the warped wood to meet the expected resistance as the door scraped open.

He shoved the door shut behind them. 'They can't all have gone home. There are cars outside, including the Jag.'

As they had the last time they'd been here, the police had set up a row of screens that cut off most of the hall from anyone coming in casually. In front of the screens a row of desks was empty.

Alex held up a finger. Voices reached them from the other side of the screens and almost immediately a uniformed police constable came from one side.

'Evening,' he said on seeing Alex and Tony. 'How can we help you?'

'We're looking for Detective Chief Inspector O'Reilly.' He didn't like interacting with these people any more than Alex did. 'Is he here?'

'Yes, sir,' the officer said. 'He's busy but if it's urgent I'll see if he can talk to you.'

'It's not urgent,' Alex said quickly. 'It'll keep.'

'What will keep?' Dan appeared with Bill Lamb. Other members of their team straggled out and began to leave the building.

'Buy you a pint at the Black Dog, guv?' a striking black man Tony remembered from the last time this crew took over the village asked. 'Unless you'd rather we stayed to finish going over what we were talking about. Better in the snug or the restaurant than here. You, too, Sergeant Lamb, if you haven't got other plans.' He gave what could only be called a sly smile.

'Good idea to deal with it there,' Dan said. 'I'll be along as soon as I can.'

'About time you called me Bill, Ball— LeJuan.' Bill Lamb's expression was too angelic. 'Can't make it until later tonight but it'll be my shout if you're still around when I get back. Don't forget to find out how Longlegs made out with that man he took to Gloucester. We need to double-check contact information for him, too.'

LeJuan gave an abbreviated salute and left with a blond man Tony also remembered.

But for one uniformed officer on a desk, the hall emptied out until the three of them had it to themselves.

'We'd better get our interview room together,' Dan said smiling and seeming relaxed. The man was a damn sight too good-looking for Tony's liking, and too charming, and that he had a thing for Alex didn't fade from the way he looked at her.

The three of them dragged grey metal chairs over to a corner they'd used on previous occasions. Next to a hissing radiator and beneath a snow-encrusted window, it felt too familiar even if the seasons had changed since the last time.

They sat, quietly considering gaps between parched and splitting floorboards. Tony looked sideways at Alex and felt guilty at the flush that swept up her neck and cheeks. She was a prisoner to her furious blushes.

Dan cleared his throat. 'So, what brings you here this evening?'

Tony felt no guilt over the scowl he sent the man. The least he could do was throw Alex a kinder lifeline.

She scooted to the back of the shiny metal chair and crossed her arms. 'Remember . . . you don't remember. You don't even know. I called Gloucester because Gladys Lymer was missing.'

'When was that?' Dan looked sincerely lost.

'Last night.'

Frowning, Dan considered, then took a breath and nodded. 'Yes. Of course. But there was a call back to say she wasn't missing. I got a note about that. Don't tell me she's done another runner.' The irregular scar along his jaw had grown paler but not much less noticeable than when Tony first met the detective.

'This probably doesn't mean a thing,' Alex said, sitting up straighter on the chair's slippery seat. 'In fact, I'm sure it doesn't but I'd feel awful if . . . and it isn't likely, but if it turned out to be some important piece of a puzzle.'

'It's always good to speak up about anything. I think that's something we've all learned, haven't we?'

'Yes.' She cleared her throat. 'It's very stuffy in here. It can't be good for all of you.'

'We're managing,' Dan said.

Tony wasn't managing very well. He laced his fingers together between his knees and willed Alex to spit out what she had to say. If he were inclined to turn red he might do it now.

'Good. Frank Lymer was at the Black Dog last night. To be honest I thought he'd gone home. Actually, I wasn't thinking about him at all. We all got a bit strung out by Grant Hill coming by about the pub name contest . . . That's not what I wanted to say to you. We were diverted. My mum had been gone. Well, you know about that. Anyway, I was upset about it and not taking proper notice. We were going to lock up but out comes Frank from a corner – like I said, I didn't see him there – and he said he was waiting for Gladys. Gladys is his wife. And she wasn't there. She hadn't been there since one in the afternoon, you see? She just started work cooking breakfasts for us and she's really good at it.'

Tony looked at Dan who either deserved applause for appearing interested and patient, or was just doing what came naturally because people made a habit of waffling on at him.

'I think I'm getting your drift,' Dan said but Tony didn't believe him. 'We'll get back to Frank and Gladys but I don't want to forget about . . . someone called Hill? What did you say his full name was?'

'Grant Hill.' Her sigh was audible.

'Any relation—'

'His son.' She cut Dan off. 'He and his mother brought entries for a contest to name a pub they're probably going to build in that new development. Or I think that's where it's planned for. It was the other day they came. Last night Grant came to find out how it was going with the entries. His mother – that's Esme – wasn't there.'

'I see.'

Again, Tony didn't see how Dan would make sense of the contest thing, but he'd been quick to pick up on the Hill name, darn it.

Alex tapped the floor with the toes of her boots and waited.

'Well, we may come back to that but let's deal with your Frank and Gladys. Frank was waiting in the bar because he thought Gladys was somewhere around but she wasn't.'

'Exactly. And he got furious when he found that out. He stomped off and I had to run after him. I was very worried – as anyone would be. I felt responsible.'

'Why would you feel responsible, Alex?'

Tony watched her raise her shoulders. 'I don't know. I wasn't responsible. But I employed her and I should have . . . no, that makes absolutely no sense. Why would I follow up employees all the time to find out their movements? Silly of me. I'm really rattled about this, Dan. Something isn't right but I seem to be the only one who thinks so. I called the Lymers' cottage several times later in the evening. At first Frank said they were private people. As if they had something monumentally secret they couldn't share. But that was after he'd told me I was to blame for Gladys going missing because I gave her a job! The second time I called him he more or less told me to mind my own business.'

Dan took out his bag of sticky sweets, the ones he always carried, and offered it to Alex. 'Have one. Sweet things are good when you feel a bit shocky.' *Damn that warm voice he could put on when he wanted Alex on his side.*

And she took one of his bloody *sweet treats*.

'Thank you,' she said quietly. 'That's nice of you. I used to love these when I was a kid.' And she put the sherbet lemon in her mouth.

'You carry on at your own pace,' Dan said. 'There's no hurry.'

No, no hurry at all . . .

'When I got to the Black Dog this morning, there was Gladys cooking breakfasts, wasn't she, Tony?' Her green eyes turned to him for support.

'Yes, darling.' He took her hand and rested it on his thigh. 'Damndest thing, Dan. There she was, large as life, cooking breakfast while Liz Hadley served.'

'That's not the point though,' Alex commented with a little frown. 'When I asked Gladys what had happened last night, she told me nothing had happened. And she said she'd ridden her bike home, only she hadn't – or I don't think she had. I found it under a layer of ice and snow around lunch time, I think it was. Hugh helped me get it out. He didn't seem to think there was anything strange about that, but I do.'

'OK,' Dan said gently. 'Tell me why you think it was strange. But remember she could have ridden it back today, not that I think it's likely in this weather. Was it standing where it's usually put?'

'No, I thought I said it was on its side. Perhaps I didn't, but it was. The thing is that Gladys said she rode home. Of course, she must have got home because Frank brought her back this morning. And he picked her up again when she was finished with work.'

Dan tapped a finger against his mouth. 'I'm very glad you came and told me this,' he said eventually. 'It sounds to me as if there may have been a domestic issue between the Lymers, but we'll keep an eye open just in case. You never know when a piece of seemingly disconnected information will turn the key to something of major importance.'

Dan stood up and Tony was quick to join him.

Alex remained where she was, frowning at the floor again.

'You ready to go, Alex?' Tony asked. 'It'll take a while to get up the hill.'

'Yes.' She got up slowly. 'Thank you, Dan. I think you'll remember what I've told you tonight – even if I did mess it up a bit. I hope you don't remember too late.'

Tony saw how Dan stiffened slightly and straightened his own spine. He didn't believe in hunches.

TWENTY-TWO

The sound of Tony's laughter stopped Alex. She'd reached the top stair and turned to sit and look down at him. 'What's funny?'

'You.' He stood in the hall unwinding his scarf. The dogs had already raced past her to find a bed for the night. 'Running upstairs without even taking off your coat – or boots. I thought we were going to sit by the fire.'

She plunked her elbows on her knees and propped her chin on her hands. 'I'm too cold to wait. I like looking down at you. Do you know we didn't say a word on the way up here? You only get better looking. I shall have to start thinking about Botox injections or you'll want to trade me in.'

He laughed again, shaking his head. 'I was afraid of this after tonight with Dan. You're stuck talking in non-sequiturs.'

'That is so mean. I'm going to sleep with Bogie and Katie.' She carried on to the landing but went to Tony's room rather than the one the dogs had made their own.

Alex shed her coat and sat down to work her boots off. If she and Tony ever had a baby, which room would make the best nursery? Slowly she set the second boot down and sat still.

Tony's bed was simple, a plain oak head and footboard. His sheets were white cotton covered by a puffy dark gray-and-white striped duvet. Light curtains hung in front of gray blinds and the rest of his furnishings were unobtrusive. Books ruined what would otherwise have been the tidy appearance of the room. Books overflowed two bookcases and made wobbly piles on chests of drawers and the floor.

This looking around at what she'd seen often enough before was a shield she'd pulled down between that errant thought of nurseries and the muddle it had made of her mind.

Tony had said he would like them to have children.

Did she want that – with him?

Perhaps she did, or would.

She wouldn't want children with anyone else.

Moving quickly, she went into the bathroom to brush her teeth, stripped off her clothes, left them in a pile on the floor and made a dash and a dive to the bed where she pulled the covers over her head. The only light in the room, beside the bed, shone through the sheet.

She kept nightgowns and underclothes, changes of outfits, here. She didn't go to bed naked – or she hadn't before.

The door opened and she could feel Tony looking at the bump she made in the bed. Soft carpet swallowed any footsteps but in moments she knew he stood beside her.

'I thought you were spending the night with our girls,' he said quietly.

Alex thought about her answer for a moment before saying, 'I changed my mind.'

'Because you want to be with me or because you don't want the dogs hogging your space?'

She smiled to herself. 'I'd rather have you hogging my space.'

Tony didn't say anything else and soon she heard water running in the bathroom and his electric toothbrush. How domestic it felt. Was that what she wanted – domesticity? Once she'd been sure she did, now she wasn't so sure. Sensual warmth suffused Alex's body and she shivered. She wanted carnal obsession. She would welcome lust.

And now she was shocking herself. Was this a way of closing out all the uncertainty in her life?

Tony pulled back the covers. He didn't smile while he looked down at her.

The urge to cover herself came quickly and left almost as quickly. Scooting onto her back, Alex put her arms over her head and turned her face away from him. The bed sank as Tony sat beside her thighs and stroked her slowly, watched his hands slide over her skin.

'I need to kiss you,' he said, turning her face up to his. He did kiss her, but not wildly as some men might have. The kiss was gentle, and when it eventually stopped, Alex wished it hadn't.

'We're going to have to do something about us,' he said, and still he didn't smile. 'You know that, don't you?'

She felt a hard pulse in her throat, a tightening in her belly. 'Yes.'

'Good.' Tony turned off the light and pulled her from the bed. 'I can't wait much longer – and I can't restrain what I really want to do with you any longer.'

Alex felt the cold wall against her back, the heat of his mouth between her breasts. She drove her fingertips into his shoulders, closed her eyes and let her head fall back.

Rose and deep lavender tinted the sky over distant white-covered hills. If he could, Tony thought, he would hold hard to this time, stop the clocks, keep away the storms that promised to return – and control the complicated bonds that held him to Alex, through incredible pleasure, through the certainty that they belonged together, and the hovering uncertainty that would not let them go.

Leaning sideways against a jamb in the open kitchen doorway, he was grateful for the little rushes of icy wind that whipped his hair and stung his face. The dogs romped in the snow, barking, their bodies rising and falling as they chased back and forth. They wouldn't wake Alex – he had heard the shower come on.

The coffee was made, the bacon ready to go, and the eggs cracked in a bowl for scrambling. He smiled slightly into another gust. After last night she could hardly talk about cholesterol and the need for more exercise.

Alex had surprised him, although not perhaps as much as she might have. She had given to him, to them, the power of the fervor he'd felt in her many times before, more often in the face of injustice and anger, but he had sensed she held back from being what she really wanted to be when they loved. And what they felt and did was love. Now he grinned. He might have to be patient before he decided it was time for a frank discussion about all the aspects of love, not that he was an expert.

But he wanted to learn!

He heard Alex come into the kitchen from the sitting room and looked over his shoulder. She wore leg-hugging black corduroy trousers and a green turtleneck jumper – and she rubbed her hands together, shivering as she came toward him.

'Good morning.' He held out an arm and pulled her in tight. 'You look cold. I'll warm you up.'

She pulled her bottom lip between her teeth, not quite smothering a grin, and raised her eyebrows.

'No, not again, Alex. It doesn't matter how much you beg me, I will not do it again right now, even to warm you up.' He rubbed her arm briskly.

They both laughed but were immediately sober, and pensive, and watchful. 'And I don't want to do this, but I think I'd better tell you what my mother talked to me about yesterday, or some of it. The parts I'm probably going to have to deal with for her, or talk her into doing for herself.'

'Of course. The dogs need to come in. They think they're both two years old.' He called Katie and Bogie inside and they arrived, shaking bits of frozen snow from their coats, and promptly went to lie together in front of the kitchen stove.

'They do know how to find the most comfortable spots available.' Alex took a couple of the towels kept there for the purpose and rubbed down both animals.

Tony had closed the outer door and now poured her a mug of fresh coffee. 'Sit. Breakfast is almost ready.'

'Let me finish the cooking.'

'No, thanks,' he told her. 'I like to do things for you and I don't get the chance often enough.'

She met his eyes over her coffee cup. Last night had changed some things – for them both, Tony decided. He could see and feel the difference in her; and sense that she was thinking about some of the same things that had been on his mind for a long time.

The bacon soon piled up on a plate kept warm in the oven and he started the toast. 'Butter.' He put the dish on the table and whisked the eggs by hand.

And throughout they glanced repeatedly at one another. 'You look as if you want to say something but you're not sure you can or maybe that you ought to. Am I right?' He gave her a plate of bacon and eggs and pulled cutlery from a drawer.

'You might be. Perhaps I should just say you're good for me, Tony, but I'm not sure how good I am for you.'

He rolled his eyes. 'Oh, really? Let me put your mind at rest. You are extremely good for me and I intend to make sure you stop questioning that. I won't get it done all at once. Not like a bulldozer. But bit by bit until you believe what I've been telling you. Now, eat.' He joined her with his own plate.

'I want to go back to last night and what I told Dan, but other things first. Mum was missing because she went into London, to Child Protection Services, and picked up the things her mother left for her. She talked about that with Harriet and Mary when we all sat together. You'll remember that. The photos are interesting and a lot of the notes about family. Even my mum's drawings from when she was a little girl. She used to draw pictures for her mother. Angela kept them. I've got all that to look at. There hasn't been time to get through much but what I have looked at makes me sad, Tony. I get sick of the damage people do to other people.'

'It seems to be part of the human condition, my love.'

She got up and went into the hall and returned with a small, bubble-wrapped package. 'This is my mum's. She's going to hang it on a wall at Corner Cottage.' After looking at it herself, Alex gave Tony a black and white photo in a silver frame that had taken some knocks.

He studied the faces and the clothes. 'They aren't getting married, are they? They're just kids. But there's the buttonhole and her rose.'

'Mum thinks they were about 18 and 20 and that is a wedding

photo. Those are my mum's parents, Angela and Simon Devoss. Four months after that Simon was killed by a bus and Angela was pregnant. Both of their families disowned her.'

He looked steadily at Alex. Breakfast didn't interest him so much anymore but he wanted her to eat, so he put a forkful of eggs in his mouth.

'It's a horrible story. She was sent away to Ireland, to a convent where they said she wasn't married because the ceremony hadn't been in a church. They wanted to take my mum away from her. The nuns sold the babies.'

Alex's cheeks lost their color. She repeatedly ran her fingers through her short, shiny dark curls. Tears welled up and ran down her face until she wiped them away, and then they did it all over again.

She showed him a silver medallion with her mother's name on it – her baby's name. Each time she tried to stop, he made her carry on. They had come this far and now he wanted it all out, or at least what she knew.

Bogie got up from his spot by the stove and went to put his front paws and chin on her knee. His liquid brown eyes watched intently, brows lifting, first one, then the other. If he could cry, too, he would. Alex rubbed him absently.

'When I hoped my mum would talk about my father and what happened to the two of them, she stopped and I couldn't bring myself to push her anymore. She was tired. But she told me something awful, Tony, about the woman who supposedly wanted to help her after I was born. This woman was a social worker and she'd taken Mum into her own home. It all turned out terribly wrong and now . . . we've got to do something. It's another thing I need police help for, but after last night I can't face going back yet.'

'Lily does seem to have an excuse to not keep going when she gets close to talking about the man who was your father,' Tony said. *Why keep pretending otherwise?*

Alex scraped back her chair and got more coffee to fill their mugs. 'That's true. It can't be easy and she has so much to cope with now. Tony, just listen to this. I don't blame Mum for being scared.'

With his elbows on the table, he drank coffee and watched

the play of emotions across Alex's face. And he realized how much she must have needed him to let her know he was there for her last night. She wasn't alone and never would be if he had his way.

She talked in spurts and he watched her confidence drain away. By the time she finished, he understood why. 'This Beverly Irving has to be found,' he told Alex. 'We can't make a major move without your mother's agreement, but this woman doesn't sound balanced. Where has she been all these years and why is she surfacing now?'

'Exactly. I've thought about it over and over and I think I know what we must do first. We need to find out what made Beverly search for my mother – and me – again. She couldn't just have woken up one morning and thought it was a good idea. Something triggered it.'

She made sense, of course. 'But what? What's happened that's different and could make Beverly feel threatened? She's desperate to protect her way of life – whatever that is. What can she think Lily could do to upset it?'

'It all brings us back where I started. We find Beverly Irving. I'm going to the Family Service Office, or wherever it was Mum went to. When Beverly made that bizarre telephone call, she talked about the things my mum had picked up, which means someone there talked to Beverly – they told her about Mum coming. Beverly was angry about that, not that she had any right. Those people know something about her and where she is, don't they? Or they have some ideas?'

For the first time in days, the sun shone through the windows. Tony glanced at light sparking off a row of crystal glasses. He knew what he needed to say but he avoided what he knew would cause contention.

'I'd better wait to go up to London. I need to catch up here first and make sure Mum's OK with the idea.' Alex crossed her arms. He heard her let out a shaky breath. 'What if that woman has known exactly where we were all these years? She did know Mum was away from home that day. And from when she talked to her she had to be aware that my mother hadn't come back home yet. The idea that she's keeping tabs on us makes me feel sick.'

'Lily's got to accept reality,' he said. He poked the table with a forefinger, emphasizing his points. 'This can't be controlled for anyone's comfort anymore. And if Lily thinks logically, she'll see that you don't avoid confrontation just because it's easier, not when there's no way to know exactly what this woman means or what she's capable of doing. It isn't as if she didn't try to manipulate Lily all those years ago. Now she's threatened to hurt someone Lily cares a lot about. Who could that be? To me, the top candidate is you, Alex.'

TWENTY-THREE

Silence on the phone made Alex wonder if she'd been forgotten by the woman at the Child Protection Services who had asked her to wait. She glanced at her watch. Almost lunchtime already. Too late to get to London today.

Lily held Kyle Gammage's gray tabby over her shoulder. She nuzzled the cat's head absently with her chin and gazed into space as if she hadn't heard Alex's phone conversation. They were in Doc James's study at his house, where Alex had finally caught up with her mother.

'Yes, I'm still here,' Alex said into the phone. At Doc's insistence, she'd taken over the chair behind his desk and held a pen over an empty pad of paper, hoping this wouldn't be as unproductive as she expected it to be.

'It's a busy place there,' Lily murmured, jiggling Naruto as if she were a baby. The cat purred loudly enough for Alex to hear. 'Do you think we should call back later?' her mum added.

Alex shook her head, no. She understood her mother's reluctance to follow up on the phone call she had received from Beverly, but they had already waited longer than they should, given the inference that had been made.

Doc James was seeing patients in his surgery and Tony had gone to his clinic. It had been Doc's idea for Alex to come to his house where Lily seemed more comfortable than anywhere else. The closeness between Lily and Doc was ever more obvious.

'Yes, hello,' Alex said. 'Thank you very much. Didn't I tell . . . I thought I'd explained why I was calling.' After explaining – again – that she wanted to find Beverly Irving, an old friend of her mother's, she listened to what the abrupt woman at the other end of the line had to say for some minutes, making a few notes as she did so. 'Very well, thanks,' she said finally and hung up.

Holding the cat even closer, Lily watched Alex's face.

'Do you remember signing for Beverly to be responsible for any correspondence that came in for you?' Alex asked.

Lily frowned and thought about it. 'Yes, but that was before you were born. It was when Beverly was a saint to me – she wanted to save me, or I thought she did.'

Clearing her throat, Alex thought about how to ask the next question. 'Did you ever cancel that order, Mum?'

Too long passed before Lily said, 'No. I never thought about it. I assumed they would get in touch with me once I was a certain age if there was anything they needed me for.'

'So, you made sure the agency had your address?'

Her mother put Naruto down slowly. 'No, I didn't. I didn't want Beverly to have a way to find me.' She stood still, looking into the fire. 'The letter I got about Angela dying was forwarded.'

'From where? I didn't see the envelope.'

'There wasn't a return address – at least I don't think so. It was typed. Beverly must have sent it to me. She would have been afraid of questions if the agency made a concerted effort to find me. And they might have asked her things she wouldn't want to talk about. She knows my address. She probably knows everything about me.'

'Now do you see why I'm going to London to push for information about Beverly?'

'No.' Lily closed her mouth firmly.

'We could just tell the police what we think and—'

'No!' Lily cut her off. She planted her hands on the edge of the desk, across from Alex and looked down at her. 'This is my life. I want it to stay the way it is.'

Alex stood up. 'And I don't have a right to my life, Mum?' she asked quietly. 'Don't you see what I've been trying to explain since I got here? Your Beverly is psychotic. She's spent more than thirty years spying on you – and me. There's nothing else to call it. And now she's really lost it and she's openly threatening us.'

'She's threatening me,' Lily said. 'If she's really threatening anyone at all.'

Alex came from behind the desk. She took her mother gently by the arms. 'Mum, she told you she would hurt someone you love. She didn't have to mean me but she may have. I think I know what you've suffered but we've got to be sensible.' *Sensible? Did that mean she should go to the police now, regardless of what Lily wanted?*

'I'll go and find out myself,' Lily said, one hand hovering in front of her mouth. 'I'll go tomorrow morning. I'm sorry I've done this to you but I didn't let myself think what it could all mean, not really. When I have Beverly's address, I'll go and see her and make her stop. She's not a bad person.'

No, just crazy.

TWENTY-FOUR

'We don't need a warrant, Mr Hill,' Dan said. 'Not unless you refuse to let us take a look at that carriage house. I'm sure you can see that wouldn't be a good idea unless you want to make it look as if you've got something to hide.'

'Come in,' Hill said. He walked stiffly but showed no sign of suffering pain. 'Make me understand what's going on first.'

From the outside, Knighton House was a large, austere, grey brick house with rubbed crimson brick arched over the many uniform sash windows flanking the front door. Palladian, very symmetrical. Massive chimneys clustered on the central bay were impossible to ignore. To Dan, a porte-cochère seemed an ostentatious afterthought, but what did he know about great houses?

Hill led them through a long hall, past large rooms to a decidedly masculine and comfortable library. 'Come in and take a seat. Will you have a drink? I imagine the morning is a bit early.' The man gave a short laugh. 'Coffee or tea?'

'Nothing, thank you,' Dan said and Bill Lamb also declined. 'We don't want to keep you, sir. You must still be recovering.'

'I'm doing well, thank you.'

Brown leather chairs, studded and used to a shiny patina, both flanked and faced a fireplace where logs burned, throwing out considerable heat. Large rugs, silk, Dan decided, were worn thin but held their softly blurred colors. He wouldn't say no to sitting in this room, alone, for hours. Books reached from floor to ceiling on all walls.

'Quite a house,' Dan said. 'Is it Georgian?'

'Close enough. It's around three hundred years old.'

Dan went to one of two French windows leading onto the grounds at the back of the house, working out where the carriage house and stables were in relation to the house. He had the chart of the property in the car and he had studied it again before coming to the door of Knighton. Unthinking, he held back a heavy green velvet drape and opened a door to step outside. Rainfall surprised him and he came back in.

'Make yourself at home, chief inspector,' Bob Hill said, sounding amused.

Dan smiled in response. 'What is it you want to know before we go to the carriage house?' he asked. LeJuan Harding and Barry Trafford's report from their poking around of the day before had surprised the team. Dan felt they might be moving firmly in the direction of a breakthrough.

'How is your investigation shaping up?' Hill asked. 'Do you have any suspects for the fire yet – and what exactly happened to Lance? Do you know if he tried to get out? And the woman in Winchcombe? You must have some thoughts about the motives behind all this by now. I take it the woman's death was a separate issue from Lance's, though? Just a coincidence of timing?'

'Is that all, Mr Hill?' It was Dan's turn to sound amused. 'Most of what you ask we still don't know. We do feel we're moving toward some breaks in the case but I really couldn't share any of that at this point.'

He watched the other man's face with interest. The impatience he'd expected wasn't there. Bob Hill looked puzzled and disconcerted.

'Why is it taking so long?' he asked. 'Did you find out who was driving that car?'

'Which car would that be?' Dan said, grateful he had enough control over his reactions to sound interested rather than surprised.

Hill frowned. He rubbed a hand over his jaw and glanced away. 'I think it was a Jeep 4x4. Dark green. Not new. I was too tied up with getting to the construction trailer. The Jeep was on its way to the gates, I presume, and I was on foot and running. I think I almost forgot it until now. Isn't that strange?'

Dan wasn't a psychiatrist but he supposed shock and injury could block things out – or not. 'This Jeep drove past a trailer fire, did it? Just drove by? I'd think that was pretty memorable but the mind does odd things.'

'The vehicle was already past the fire when I saw it,' Hill said. 'At least, I think it was. The fire was just starting to be visible then. There was smoke, of course.'

Bill wrote busily in his notebook. Whenever there was a pause, he turned his head to look at book titles. Usually Dan forgot what an avid reader his sergeant was and that he usually read large tomes with esoteric titles.

'Thank you for telling us about the Jeep,' Dan told Bob Hill. 'We'll look into it. It's too bad there aren't any cameras . . . there aren't, are there?'

'No, damn it. Well, there are but there's a glitch and it hasn't been fixed yet. It should have been by now but it hasn't happened. One of a number of things I wanted done immediately that fell by the wayside.' He turned away as if embarrassed and Dan wondered if Lance Pullinger was the one who had tended to fall down on the job. 'It's a good idea to have active cameras during construction to make theft more difficult,' Hill added.

'Or to catch an arsonist,' Bill said without looking up from his notebook. 'Did you happen to get the plate number for the Jeep?'

'Would you have, sergeant? Under the circumstances?' A phone rang on a small gilt table beside one of the leather chairs and Hill was quick to pick it up. Apparently no one else was expected to answer the call because he didn't announce himself, just listened and stared straight ahead. He frowned deeply and closed his eyes. At last he hung up, still without a word.

'I doubt I'm telling you anything you don't already know, gentlemen, but it appears both Lance and this Darla Crowley woman were murdered.' Scrubbing at his face, he seemed to bow over at the shoulders. 'Murdered. Lance. It doesn't make a single bit of sense. He was liked – well-liked by everyone who knew him. What could have happened?' His dark eyes settled on Dan's face.

So it was out. They had been given the gift of more time than he'd expected anyway, but he hated the thought of dealing with the media. 'Losing a good friend is always hard, sir. Death by murder is often impossible to accept at first. Please trust us to be on this and work for a satisfactory result as soon as we can. We can't bring Lance Pullinger back, but we can hope to find justice for him.' He decided not to press Hill for the identity of his caller or the source of the information. That would come soon enough.

Hill paused. 'Yes, well, go ahead and check out the carriage house, both of you, although I can't imagine what good that will do you. I'm told the renovation is getting along nicely – if slowly. Lance hadn't been there for some time before he died, but I'll give you a key.'

They returned to the hall that ran completely through the house to a conservatory that opened onto walled gardens.

'I added the conservatory,' Hill said. 'I've always been partial to them. Watch your step with all this slippery stuff on the ground. It was nice to see a bit of sun first thing, but thank God for some rain. Could be we'll finally see good reliable dirt again. There's a path over to your right that takes you through the wall and onto the rest of the estate. You'll see the outbuildings easily enough. Don't make a mistake and walk into the pool house – an indulgence for our children. We keep it going in winter so a wrong step in the dark could land you up to your neck. This is the key you need.' He unhooked one from a crowded board inside a door to the kitchens which, from a brief glance, looked like acres of green marble and stainless steel atop polished stone-tiled floors. Nothing Georgian about all that. Dan almost asked if the house was listed but stopped himself. If it was and Hill hadn't followed the tight requirements, he'd have to sort that out for himself.

Leaving Bob Hill behind with his thoughts, they set off in increasingly heavy rain. Before they reached the path they'd been promised, they both wished they'd worn wellies but it hadn't seemed appropriate to go into the Hill castle in rubber boots.

'Don't you wonder who called Hill?' Bill asked.

'I'm only human. Of course, I do. We're bound to know soon enough – and find out who got the information to spread. Damn the leakers, but they're always around.'

'This stinks,' Bill said, his feet squelching by the time they passed through the wall around the garden. 'I'm going to need a shoe allowance shortly.'

Dan chuckled. 'I want to hear you try that on the super.'

'I thought you'd arrange it for me.'

'Yeah, shoes and three months' paid vacation a year. Anything else?'

They snorted in unison.

'Like Hill said, at least this rain is starting a bit of a melt,' Dan commented, wiping rain from his eyes to see ahead. 'Bugger it. Where are these outbuildings?'

They trudged for what felt like miles in the slushy ground snow, following what they could find of the path as it led them through a heavy stand of mostly cedars. 'There.' Bill pointed ahead. 'That'll be them over there.'

When they reached the first building, Dan looked at it and said, 'Pool house. Must be nice.' The place was modern with a visible domed skylight.

Beyond this were what was probably the carriage house, built of the same gray brick as the house and which looked to be in very good repair, and several stone buildings in front of a stable with an empty paddock. Dan didn't care enough to get even more wet going to see if there were any stabled horses. There were no signs of life at all.

Dan used the key on a very solid-looking door to the side of the old carriage doors which had been left in place. The roof had a central apex and high windows were an obvious addition.

'Mess, is it?' Bill said when they stood in a large, open room that resembled a good barn conversion more than a carriage house in need of considerable repairs. 'Looks damn good to me. Ready for one of those magazine layouts like they have in the *Cotswold Journal*. I doubt Hill's been out here himself lately.'

'If ever,' Dan added, looking around at expensive russet colored suede furniture, multi-striped throw rugs on polished oak floors and a round stove in the middle of the room. 'Hill's too tied up with his own construction. Must just accept what he's told about what's going on around the estate. Let's put our phones on vibrate and keep things a bit quiet, just in case someone walks by and asks what we're doing. We probably need more time than Bob Hill imagines us to be out here.' Dan dealt with his own phone.

'Is Detective Chief Inspector O'Reilly available?' Alex asked of the first officer she saw inside the parish hall. She had only walked from the Range Rover parked at the lot entrance, but rainwater dripped from her hair and inside the neck of her jumper.

'I don't think he's back,' the constable said. He was an older man she had not seen before. 'Let me check.' He walked behind the screens.

She waited, fending off the desire to flee. If she had not come, she'd be an idiot and because she had come she felt like a traitor to her mother. And she felt sneaky for saying she was going home, but coming to the police instead.

LeJuan Harding appeared, his lovely smile lighting his face. 'Good to see you, Alex. The guv'nor's out for a bit. Can I help you?'

Giving him a smile that felt like a poor effort, Alex shook her head. 'No, thanks, Sergeant Harding. I really do have to talk to him.' That sounded too desperate but she couldn't take it back.

'Let me give him a call?' He produced his mobile and pressed the contact before Alex could think how to stop him – or if she wanted to.

'Thank you,' she said faintly.

Harding smiled, head on one side, and kept listening. At last he said, 'Would you mind waiting a minute?' to Alex and left her alone.

A desk phone started to ring, producing a tall blond woman from the zone-of-secrets behind the screens. She picked up the phone and looked at Alex. Cringing and hoping it didn't show, Alex remembered the last time she saw Constable Miller. It had been raining then, too, and Miller had made Alex feel a complete fool.

'Did you try Sergeant Lamb?' Miller asked over the phone, watching Alex as if making sure she didn't pinch the paperclips. 'Right. We'll follow up from here. Crowley? Who's Crowley – ah, Vince, the husband.' She listened with her mouth slightly open, waiting to break in. 'How the hell did you manage that? Wait till O'Reilly finds out you've lost him. You're toast.' More listening. 'You think he'll care if it was you or not? First one he sees will get it. Crowley had better be found and fast.' She hung up with a satisfied little smile on her attractive mouth.

'Excuse me,' Alex said to the woman's back.

'Wait if you want,' Miller said, walking away. 'But if I were you, I'd leave and call before you come back again. Chief Inspector O'Reilly's a busy man and he's not available.'

Miller wore street clothes, Alex noted as the other woman walked out of sight, which probably meant a change of job. A promotion? A perverse charge of dislike – which was pointless but empowering – had Alex making for one of the chairs under the windows. If nothing else, she might become invisible to the officers coming and going. Darla Crowley, that must be who Miller had alluded to on the phone. The police had taken Darla Crowley's husband in for some reason and the man had got away from them. If there was more to know about that, Alex wanted to hear it. Excitement made her breathe more rapidly and she'd like to call Tony only she couldn't risk drawing attention to herself.

The constable she'd seen when she arrived returned to his desk and his computer with only a brief glance in her direction.

She settled, wishing she'd brought a book – except that would interfere with watching the door for Dan and keeping her ears trained for more useful information. If the police had taken in Darla Crowley's husband and he had managed to get away from them, what did it mean? Why would they want him unless . . . unless Darla had been murdered. Could they be interested in him for Darla's murder, or even think he had something to do with what happened to Lance Pullinger? Alex didn't imagine for a moment that anyone would willingly answer any questions on those subjects.

LeJuan Harding reappeared at a run and pulling on his coat. Barry Trafford was beside him. Men intent on a mission. They didn't look at Alex.

It took only seconds, and no reluctance, for her to leave the parish hall and hurry to her Range Rover. She gave the two detectives a couple of minutes' head start and followed. Harding and Trafford had been alerted by the failure to get in touch with O'Reilly or Lamb. And the escape of Darla Crowley's husband was an emergency. She was sure of it. Alex wanted to see where the action was. Besides, what harm could there be in taking the same route as the detectives in front of her and driving rapidly through Folly?

'I don't think it will be long before Hill sends troops to find out what we're up to out here,' Dan said. 'This doesn't seem like a big deal but it could turn out to be. Someone's lying. Probably not Hill, but someone with something to hide.'

Bill squinted around. 'This is a lie for a start. They said they were renovating the place and they aren't.'

'Easy enough for them to explain away,' Dan responded. 'They didn't know how far the renovations had gone. Typical construction delay. It won't be hard for them to slide out of any questions we raise on that front.'

'Then we'd better come up with something else,' Bill said, his face set.

Dan liked his partner when he showed spine. 'You're right. We'd better do that.'

Stairs, or open stair treads anchored into the wall, rose to a loft room closed off with sliding panels of thick etched glass. Dan decided to start by looking up there and climbed the unsubstantial-feeling flight.

Behind the glass panels lay a simply furnished, comfortable bedroom with a slick bathroom. Over the windows, electric blinds of some fine metal mesh would close out the light on brighter days or retract to give views of the night sky from anywhere in either room.

Dan soon found the reasons for LeJuan and Barry's conclusions. A couple used this place all right. Expensive lingerie filled the top two drawers in a chest. Women's outdoor clothes consisted of a couple of pairs of trousers and some blouses in the closet together with a cardigan and jacket. A few items of underclothes and a jumper were in a bottom drawer. The rest of the closet and storage space was taken up with a man's clothing. In the bathroom, most of the toiletries were masculine except for a few feminine items.

Bedside drawers were empty but for condoms in one.

There was no paperwork.

He went over every space again and when he'd finished, stood with hands on hips, trying to make sense of what he now understood; the bed was newly made with new sheets fresh from their shop packaging. The lingerie appeared unworn, as did every item of clothing in the place. The box of condoms was unopened and toiletry items had yet to be used.

A set-up. Furious, he went back downstairs working on what it all meant. For a moment he watched Bill going through a shelf of books, taking out each volume and shaking it, searching for anything of interest.

'Is there a desk or anywhere to store bills and papers?' he asked Bill.

'Nope, guv. But if you want wine or champagne, or any kind of spirits you can think of, you've arrived at the right place. All you've got to do is take the seal off something. No glasses, though, which is strange.' He pointed to a table where limp chrysanthemums bent toward the sides of a tall glass jug.

'They're only just starting to go over. If I was trying to convince someone a place wasn't used, I'd get rid of those.'

'Right,' Dan agreed. 'And I'd get everything else packed up in here. Unless I had another agenda in mind, in case people like you and me showed up. Upstairs is just the way LeJuan said. A nest built for two only our eagle-eyed pair didn't notice no one's moved in yet, could be no one ever has spent time here. Is that what we're supposed to assume. We're going to figure out what they really want us to think and why. Dammit, Bill, I think they're sinking themselves, or I hope they are. Everything upstairs is new, untouched. We need to find out who staged this. They don't expect us to swallow the scene they've arranged here – they can't. But they could think they're making it impossible for us to get at the truth.

'Hill thinks Pullinger's been away from the place for some time. He believes that. And I believe him when he says it. And I don't think he'd send us down here to look if he knew it was kitted out like this. If Pullinger was here with a close friend, it couldn't have been too recently, but I'm damned if I've got the faintest who decided to gussy this up for anyone who got in here before they could do a complete clean-out and get renovation work going. And I do think if we'd been a couple of days later, this would have looked like a demolition site.'

Bill narrowed his eyes. 'It's only days since Pullinger's death, but if Hill knew what the man used this for when he was here – essentially sex and general good times – he could have arranged to get any stuff that was here bagged up and disposed of just in case. If Hill wanted to save his friend, Lance's, reputation for some reason, it would be easier to explain a failure to start construction work than having nothing at all in here. I just don't get why it would be a big deal for a single man to entertain women. They've made too much out of it.'

Thoughtful, Dan rubbed a thumb back and forth over his mouth. Then he said, 'You're on the ball today, Bill. What someone's done is overkill. These people are so used to getting their own way they didn't think we'd actually insist on coming out here. But they covered their arses anyway. Not that they really needed to unless we can connect this cover-up to the murders. That's my take. Still, I can't imagine anyone with a brain could have known it had been left like this. It's like some practical joke. No, no, I can't figure Hill for this effort.'

Bill rubbed at his crew cut, sandy-colored hair, sending little drops of water flying. 'I wouldn't mind these digs myself, guv. One of these days I'll find the time to look for something better than that miserable flat.' Bill was divorced and hadn't tried to find a good place to live.

'Right.' Dan had heard about the house Radhika was having renovated but thought better than to mention it. 'Any other ideas about why we were discouraged from coming here?'

'I'm still in the mulling phase, guv,' Bill said. 'Things could be getting close to gelling, but you know me, not one for rushing in till I think I'm sure.'

'For now I'm sticking with the idea of protecting Pullinger. Not because of the affair with Crowley, though,' Dan said thoughtfully. He paced. There was no scene to protect for forensics. 'Could be Pullinger had more than one lady friend. That is another thought. Or why couldn't there have been someone else using this – someone other than Pullinger?'

Bill's pale blue eyes moved in Dan's direction and his face took on the strangely passive appearance that went with his brain being in top gear.

Dan made 'give-it-to-me' motions with his right hand.

'Well, I could be grabbing for straws. But how about the son, Grant? I've only seen him a couple of times but he's got a big ego, that one. And he's mouthy. Too sure of himself. He obviously thinks he's the brightest bulb around.'

'And you know all this, how? Just from watching him?'

Bill's wince suggested he recognized how thin his deduction might be. 'You've got me there but I'd pit my visual observation against a lot of so-called evidence.'

'So would I,' Dan agreed, only slightly grudgingly. 'I suggest we get out of here with a minimum of chit-chat – at least until we know more about the son, or anyone else who could have been shacking up here. If he's the one using it, there would be no shortage of people around ready to cover for him. But I'm still sure his father didn't know. Again, though, we're looking at pointless overkill.

'The staff seem strangely absent – did you notice that? You can be certain there's plenty of them in a place this size and they've been told to stay out of our way. Less risk of a careless comment that way. You've got to keep wondering where that phone call Hill got came from. For all we know it was someone in another room in the house.'

Bill nodded. 'Could be.'

'But the staff would run interference for their employer's son to protect their jobs,' Dan continued. 'Or maybe that's not fair to some. A lot would.'

'Wouldn't be the first offspring to take advantage of a parent they didn't trust, or a parent they were afraid of.'

'Have you been reading those damn psychology books again, Lamb?'

Bill grinned. 'Could be. And by the way, my butler has orders to get lost when company calls.'

'Mine, too.' They both snorted.

The door at the back of the building crashed open.

Dan swung around to confront Barry Trafford with a pistol in his right hand.

'What the hell are you doing?' Bill snapped, keeping his voice down. 'Get in here quietly and put that damn thing away. What made you think you'd need a firearm?'

With a sheepish expression on his Nordic features, Trafford holstered the gun beneath his jacket. Through the front door, quieter than Trafford but a deal more threatening, came LeJuan Harding, firearm in hand.

'Good grief,' Dan said through his teeth. 'What's the matter with you two? You knew we were here and why we were here. If you had a problem, you should have called.'

He met Bill's eyes and grimaced. 'Yes, well, sorry about that. We turned off our ringers to avoid attracting attention before we were ready to leave. We didn't expect to be so long.'

'We decided we'd better be prepared for an ambush,' LeJuan said. 'That's why we checked out firearms.'

Dan crumpled up his forehead. He massaged the scar on his jaw, something he rarely did these days unless he was stressed – big time. 'Tell me you got permission from someone other than the super.'

The blank expression on LeJuan's face gave way to the smirk he was trying to hide. 'Why would we do that? You authorized them, boss.'

Dan moaned. 'You'll get us all fired yet, Balls.'

'We had to find you, boss,' Barry Trafford said, surprising everyone. 'There was a call from Gloucester. Vince Crowley took off – well, he wasn't officially under arrest, of course – but he went to the men's room and they think he got out of a window.'

'Why the hell wasn't someone keeping a close eye on him?' Dan exploded. 'That man may have murdered his wife and you know what he's been doing to her for years. Seems likely he was the one giving her cigarette burns anyway, doesn't it? Even if we can't prove it. He could be out there finding another victim to punish – especially if he's in a rage, which he is.'

'Guv,' Bill said quietly, 'we'd better get moving.'

'Longlegs Liberty is organizing the search, boss,' Harding said, completely serious now. 'That man's a peach and he's wasted, but we might as well make the best use of him.'

Dan gave him a thoughtful look. Harding would go far. He had an eye for sizing people up and he wasn't threatened by competition. He summed up people as well as the best . . . 'Harding,' he said, remembering. 'How come you and Trafford didn't notice everything in this place is new. The clothes are unworn, everything else is unused. This is just a set-up meant for us, or so Bill and I believe. What we don't know yet, but we will, is why someone went to so much trouble. If you two had kept your eyes open yesterday, we wouldn't have lost a day getting started on a new angle. And in case you haven't noticed, we aren't exactly buried in good leads.'

Both sergeant and constable had the sense to stay silent.

'We're looking at Grant Hill for the set-up. Bill's idea. We don't know why he'd do it, but he's convenient. For all we know some of Pullinger's things were here and now they've been disposed of. We don't think Robert Hill would be foolish enough to pull a stunt like that and expect to get away with it. Let's get back to Gloucester and find out how Crowley got away.'

The rain had all but stopped but an evil wind tore at them while they made their way back toward the stand of cedars. They held their collars around their chins and went in silence – until Dan made a sudden stop.

'What?' Bill said.

The two younger men followed Dan's close attention to the ground. 'Stay where you are. All of you.' He turned, bent over, and retraced their steps to a side wall of the carriage house. Then he walked carefully almost to the corner that turned to the front door.

Back he came again, passing the others. 'Watch where you put your feet. Don't move until I say.' On he went until he stopped again, looking ahead. 'OK,' he called. 'To the right of the path there's a row of footprints with wet mud in the bottoms from the rain. They're a mess but clear enough to tell me what happened. I think someone followed us to the carriage house and listened until they were afraid of getting caught. We don't have an excuse for forensics and I doubt we'd find out who knows entirely too much about what we know. And they'd realized the footprints would be a trail that could lead us to them, so the footsteps stop. Too bad he had the sense to get to the path. We won't catch up now, not that we had much chance anyway. Who knows when he left? What we do know is that eavesdropping on us was a risk worth taking.'

'If this whole thing is just about no harm no foul, boss,' Trafford said, 'why run away?'

'Because there is a connection here somewhere, at least to the Pullinger murder. Having us see who was here would put them in the picture.'

'Tosser,' Bill said flatly. 'If I get hold of him, or her, they'll wish they'd stayed away. Do you still think Hill's clean, Dan?'

'I think someone could be setting him up to take a big fall.'

TWENTY-FIVE

What harm have I done them? I've tried my best to make sure they never suffered, and even if they didn't need help, I've had their backs, just in case.

If they keep digging, it could be all over for me. But I won't be caught just to keep their cushy lives safe, not now, not anymore. OK, so I've made some mistakes, mostly because I've trusted people. And I thought, in time, the good I've managed to do for them would be obvious and they'd thank me for it.

That makes me a fool, but I never thought it would come to this.

I've warned them, given them time to see that if they keep trying to turn what I've done into a crime . . . What then? Don't be a fool again. Think about yourself for once. If it looks as if I'm going down, they must go down, too. Not with me, but first. I will get rid of them and save myself. I have no choice.

Why should I be afraid now? There's no justice and it makes me very, very angry. I warned that fool to do as she was told, but she was too weak to keep her mouth shut. I can't risk waiting to see if they come for me. The time to get this rolling is now.

TWENTY-SIX

Kev Winslet had taken to smoking a pipe, or carrying one and assuming the country gentleman's crossed arms, bowl of pipe between finger and thumb posture.

'Good thing you can't smoke that in here, old chap,' Major Stroud said, as he'd said at least once or twice every time he'd seen Kev with his latest accoutrement. 'Probably choke yourself to death and I'd miss you.' Stroud guffawed.

Tapping the end of the pipe stem against his teeth, Kev gave the major a dismissive shrug that surprised Tony, who always expected fireworks when the two long-time sparring partners got going.

The bar wasn't full. Hugh managed nicely on his own behind the counter. He folded his arms to lean and nurse a half pint of bitter. 'Tell me to shut my mouth if you don't like the question,' he said, 'but any idea what's keeping Alex?'

'She was up at her house. Probably trying to catch up with some of the stuff that never gets done when you've got several places to call . . . home.'

Hugh grinned. 'There is that. Since I'm in a mood to get my block knocked off, when are you two at least going to get down to one house up there in the Dimple?'

Facing the man and lowering his voice, Tony said, 'I'm working on it. I've been working on it a long time. Could be we're getting closer. Could be that's a dangerous statement to make. We're both one-time losers and Alex is particularly skittish about trying again, I think. Not that I blame her.'

'Only one-time losers?' Hugh lifted his glass and slipped the beer to and fro inside. 'Just don't give up. You two make a natural pair – if you can ever figure out a way to keep her out of trouble.'

'Yeah, I know. I notice the Hill family seem to have made us their local. Given the reason they found us, I'd prefer they stay away. It's a long way from Knighton House, especially if you like to have a couple.'

'Whoops, the sisters are giving subtle signals,' Hugh said. 'Excuse me.'

'I'll go.' Tony enjoyed the ladies. 'I need to check on those renegade dogs.'

'Thanks. Should I get out the Harvey's Bristol Cream?'

'Do that. They do enjoy their sherry. I don't think I could ever separate Katie and Bogie now, y'know. They think they're related.' The dogs curled up on their blanket before the fire and beside the Burke sisters. They ignored Max the cat who enjoyed taking occasional swipes at them.

'Might be a bargaining chip, that,' Hugh said. 'No real difference from being brought together by children, I'd say.' His Scottish accent never faded and the dichotomy of his Welsh name and Scottish background remained a mystery.

Making his way around the edge of the room, beer glass in hand, Tony made sure to pass by the Hills, Esme and her offspring, in case he heard something interesting. Grant sat sideways as if wishing he didn't have to be seen with his mother and sister, Carmen.

'Dr Harrison, isn't it?' Grant said as Tony drew level. The younger man stood up and shot out a hand. 'Grant Hill. I know you're cozy with Alex. I was hoping to have a word with her.'

Smart-mouthed, arrogant, little bastard. 'She'll be along eventually,' Tony said, looking into Grant's vaguely insolent eyes. 'If you're still here I'm sure she'll be glad to talk to you. Excuse me.'

A chair waited for him at the sisters' table. Before he sat down he said, 'Harvey's, ladies? Hugh has the bottle ready for you and he's pouring me another Windrush Ale.' The latter wasn't true but it would be.

'We won't say no to a nice sherry,' Mary said for both of them and Tony signaled Hugh, holding up his own almost empty glass. 'Is Alex doing well. We've been worried about her – and dear Lily. Has anything more happened?'

For moments, Tony considered, then he decided that at least where Lily was concerned, it was up to her to share as much as made her comfortable.

'It has, ladies,' he said. 'I do expect Alex to come in at any time and she may have something to share. I know she thinks of you as family. Lily does, too, but she has a lot to deal with.'

'I know,' Harriet said, looking troubled. For once Max, the one-eyed orange tabby who definitely belonged to Mary, was on Harriet's lap with his back firmly turned to Mary.

'What's Max's issue?' Tony said, smiling and stroking the cat who gave him an evil stare with his remaining eye.

'Mary had Oliver on her lap this afternoon. He hasn't been feeling well. But Max has taken offence and now he's giving her the cold shoulder.'

'Spoiled boy,' Tony told Max. 'Anything I should take a look at for Oliver?'

'We'll see in the morning. Scratch caught his ear and might be infected. I wonder how that happened.' Mary turned her mouth down.

Hugh arrived with a tray of drinks and a large dish of popcorn. He put everything on the table. 'Alex just came in. I'd let her make her way in here. She seems a bit quiet – unusually so.'

Tony looked across the bar and Alex appeared, straight-faced. To customer greetings she responded with a nod but she waved at Tony and Hugh and the sisters.

Before she could pass the Hill's table, Grant got up again and turned a determined smile on her. He had a sheaf of papers in his hand.

'Must want to tell her the result of the naming contest,' Hugh said.

Tony didn't like what he was seeing. 'So why does she look as if he just hit her with a cricket bat?'

'Cheeky fellow,' Harriet said, hefting the increasingly chunky Max higher on her lap.

Without another glance at Tony, Alex went ahead of Grant toward the restaurant but they let themselves out of the front door instead.

'Bloody hell,' Tony said. 'I'm going to let him know he's out of bounds with his demands.'

Hugh bent near. 'I wouldn't if I were you. Make up your own mind, but she'll not thank you for letting that upstart know you don't think she can handle herself.'

'It's too cold out here without a coat,' Alex said. Getting away from this strange man was more important than being cold. 'I suggest you come back during the day tomorrow.'

Grant placed himself between her and the door. With the light from inside behind him, she couldn't see his face but he lifted an arm and she flinched.

'Jumpy, aren't we?' he said, tapping her lightly on the shoulder. 'Is there anything you'd like to discuss with me?'

'Not a thing.' He made her skin crawl and prickling scaled her back and neck, a sure sign she expected trouble.

'We've got a winner,' he said, flapping papers in front of her face. 'When we've finished here we'll make an announcement. We Hills know how to make ourselves popular.'

Alex decided she couldn't bear this young man. Far from being attractive, his self-confidence had a similar effect on her as fingernails scraped on a blackboard.

'You're quiet, Alex. Is there something on your mind? A guilty conscience perhaps?'

'Why don't you make your announcement now? We'll hope the winner is in the house.'

'I don't think so. Not yet. You and I have things to discuss first.'

She was hesitant about trying to walk around him to the door. If he stopped her physically, even by cutting her off, there would be a scene, besides, he was obviously strong and who knew what excuse he might come up with for hurting her.

'Do you remember the suggestion I made to you that first night I came here?'

Alex wasn't sure what to say. He sounded threatening but in a normal, even enough voice. Every word was a warning.

'Come on, Alex. You know what I'm talking about. I came back for my gloves, remember that?'

'You already had them,' she said, and wished she hadn't.

'Really? That would be your word against mine, wouldn't it? Like most things. I told you it would be a good idea if you stayed away from my father. Does that ring any bells?'

'You've said enough. Now move aside so I can go in. I'm freezing.'

He lowered his voice close to a whisper. 'And frightened? Why are you frightened, Alex? Not of me, surely. I'm a pussycat. Ask anyone and they'll tell you what a nice chap I am. Ask Carmen. My sister thinks I'm her teddy bear.'

This time she held her tongue.

'It's time you learned to do as you're told,' Grant said, still with his voice lowered. 'Sneaking around my father's house today was a bad idea. You didn't think anyone saw you, did you? Wrong again, you little opportunist. What have you got in that devious mind of yours? Blackmail? Or are you trying to find a way to worm yourself into his affections. It's obvious he's grateful to you for what you did at the building site, but that doesn't translate into his being attracted to you.' He tapped her shoulder, harder this time. 'The mind boggles, my dear. Pa has a wife – she's sitting in there with my sister. Or is it an affair you're after?'

'That's enough.' She made to walk past him. Despite the cold, she felt sweat along her hairline.

'Ah, ah, ah.' That hand clamped her shoulder this time. 'You asked me out here to talk, now you're getting shirty.'

'I did no such thing. You're mad. And I have no interest in your father beyond wishing him well . . . and a speedy recovery.'

Shouting for help might be a bad idea but she'd do it if she had to.

'You sneaked up to the carriage house on Knighton land. I saw you outside. Lucky. If I'd been a bit later I'd have missed you, but I didn't. Something spooked you. You lost your nerve. Were you going to poke around inside to see what you could find out about Lance Pullinger? Do you think my father had a reason to set that trailer on fire? Were you planning to look for something that would implicate him so you could see what it would be worth to keep you quiet?'

Abruptly, anger tore through Alex and she shrugged away from his hand. 'Listen to yourself. You're dreaming up an entire imaginary story and it is rubbish. It's rubbish and what I don't know is what your problem is. You saw me, so I was there. But you don't know why and you couldn't be more wrong about the reason.' He hadn't mentioned the police. Did that mean he didn't know they were in the building at the time?

'I wish I hadn't gone there, but I didn't mean any harm to anyone. Why didn't you confront me . . . something to hide yourself?' Baiting him was a dangerous idea.

'No.' His voice returned to normal. 'But we aren't done with this subject, not if you try to make any trouble.'

'I must have looked suspicious. Of course, I did. But it wasn't what you're thinking, so can we just forget it?' She needed time to decide what to do. It wasn't necessary to be a genius to work out that Grant must be the one with something to hide. 'You're uptight, and I don't blame you. We feel protective toward our parents. There's nothing to worry about from me. I . . .'

'You what? Other than think you can treat me like a kid?'

'I was curious about Knighton. I've always loved old estates and it's beautiful. You're lucky to have grown up around wonderful houses.'

'Rather than in cheap rents with an unmarried barmaid mother? And even when you managed to reel in a rich husband you screwed it up. I know all about you.'

She didn't like his tone or his angle but she couldn't get upset over the nastiness. He didn't seem to know about the police being at his father's estate or if he did, he was deliberately avoiding talking about it.

'Could be this isn't the right time to announce the contest winner,' she told him. 'Let's do it when we're both thinking more clearly.'

The front door opened behind him and Tony emerged carrying a coat which he put around her shoulders. 'What's going on here, Hill?' he said in the voice Alex rarely heard, the one that would and had sobered up belligerent drunks.

'Evening again, Harrison. Alex and I have been talking about the contest. She's wondering if there should be runners-up for the main prize and honorable mentions. I think she's right, don't you?'

'Alex has good instincts,' Tony said. 'Whatever she thinks usually works out best.'

'I bow to your opinion,' Grant said to Alex, inclining his head. 'I'll put this announcement off for a day or two while I discuss the best course with my father. Excuse me.' He returned to the building and Alex saw his silhouette through the windows, walking smartly back to the bar.

'What the hell, Alex?' Tony said, putting an arm around her shoulders and looking down into her face. 'You've been out here for ages. It can't have been just about this ridiculous contest.'

She stiffened her spine, locked her knees. If she told him what she'd stupidly done, he would have plenty of reason to wonder what else she hadn't told him – or what else she was hiding.

'Sweetheart?' He massaged her back, stroked her hair away from her face. 'You're sweating, honey. He did something to upset you – badly. You can tell me anything, you know. I'm on your side and whatever's going on, I'll help you.'

'I know you will if you can.' With a sigh, she leaned against him and reached up to put her hands inside his collar. 'This time I think I may get into trouble. There's spontaneous, and there's reckless. I've been reckless, and stupid.'

TWENTY-SEVEN

Apart from the low lights always on behind the bar and inside wall sconces on the way upstairs to the inn, the Black Dog had the gloomy closed-up look Alex disliked. She might be quiet herself but she enjoyed feeling the place come alive with customers and their chatter, their laughter.

She put her head to the open service window into the snug where Tony sat on a banquette with the dogs at his feet. 'Anything to eat with that brandy, Tony? Crisps? Nuts? There are sausage rolls still warm.'

He got up to fetch the glasses she pushed through. The brandies were doubles. 'A sausage roll would be good. I didn't have time for dinner. Coleman's mustard, too, if it's handy.'

She smiled at him, a little sheepishly. 'Coming up. I'll bring them around.'

The hot case hadn't been off long and the sausage rolls were quite warm. Together with one remaining steak and kidney pie, she put half a dozen rolls on top, anticipating the return of Dan and Bill who were so late she could only do her best not to invent some of the scenarios that could be keeping them, including the discovery of her Miss Marple act of the afternoon.

She pulled several bags of crisps from their display and

hurried to join Tony and the dogs. 'This should fill a hole,' she said although it didn't sound as chirpy as she'd hoped. 'The kids can share one of the rolls. I did fill their water dish.'

Tony watched her scurry but didn't say anything. He was a controlled man, she'd give him that – among a lot of other things – although the expressions that had crossed his face when she told him about her escapade to the Knighton estate had done nothing for her confidence. At least he'd confined himself to nothing more than nods and looking bewildered, or sometimes impatient.

He took a swallow of his brandy. Alex slid into a barrel chair facing him and did the same. 'I'm not a real brandy lover but it is a restorative in some situations,' she said.

'I want to be sure what you intend to talk to Dan and Bill about,' he said while he unscrewed the yellow cap from the Coleman's mustard. 'And what you expect from me. You went to the parish hall to find Dan and intended to tell him about this Beverly?'

'Yes.'

With a knife, he ran a layer of the mustard along the length of a sausage roll. 'And now you still don't want to tell him anything else? Not about the threats you got from Grant Hill, the story he invented about you, or the way you followed Harding and Trafford to the Knighton estate?'

'We've already gone over this.'

'We have. But I'm making sure you haven't changed your mind. I don't want to put a foot wrong.'

'What do you think Grant was doing watching the carriage house?'

He said, 'I don't know,' and took a bite of the sausage roll. Katie and Bogie sat at his feet, staring up. Tony took another roll, broke it into four pieces and dropped them into waiting mouths. 'Now go lie down. Now!'

She wasn't the only one who recognized The Voice. Bogie and Katie swallowed and retreated to a corner.

'You shouldn't have followed the way you did,' Tony said, eating but she doubted tasting. 'You could have got in a horrible fix if you'd been caught. They would have been merciless and you know it. You did get caught in a different way and look what we're up to our necks in now. If Grant wasn't watching the police, too, what was he doing out there?'

'I don't know. I didn't see him, did I? He could have been coming from the stables and seen me by accident. Or he could just have been checking around. I heard what was said in that carriage house and they had some theories about him being involved in a cover-up. It's hard to think he saw the police or heard a thing they said. If he had I don't think he'd be so cool. I'm not even sure he wouldn't be keeping his distance from me, and from anyone else involved in the case. There weren't any cars there. Harding and Trafford parked in a layby half a mile away. I was farther than that. I don't know where Dan and Bill's vehicle was but Harding and Trafford obviously knew where to find them. They left the parish hall and went directly to Knighton House. Or to the grounds. They knew how to bypass the house and gardens on foot and go directly to the carriage house.'

'And you followed them.' Tony opened a bag of crisps and ate them with absent-minded precision. 'I don't think the murders have anything to do with us. How could they? Not with what's going on with Lily and you. It's all coincidence and it's making it more than messy to figure out. You're not a witness to a murder in the normal way. You were there for the fire. Who knows how the death happened – we don't.'

Their friends in Serious Crimes knew, Alex thought. She didn't say as much. 'I think it makes sense to push all that out of our minds – at least as much as we can, and tell Dan everything about Beverly. But, Tony, don't you think I should mention that Grant was threatening toward me the first night he came to the Dog? I think that's relevant enough that I owe it to them.'

He sighed. 'Yes, I agree. But there's more and that you've been involved in that could be relevant to the police on this murder case. Are you OK with keeping our options open on sharing more with Dan and Bill if we decide we should? After we deal with the charming Beverly, that is?'

Sipping her brandy, Alex thought carefully. 'I think so. My mum's been through some horrible stuff. I've got to protect her first. Whatever I tell the police won't bring Lance back to life.'

Tony sat back and hiked an ankle onto the opposite knee. He stared into space.

'What?' Alex said. 'What are you thinking?'

'That I hope there's never a point when you and I disagree on the right thing to do.'

The sound of a key turning in the front door lock jarred Alex. She gave Tony a desperate look and leaned toward him. 'Is it a bad idea to talk to him tonight?'

He shook his head. 'We'll be OK. We'll both know what's right.'

Alex hoped they would agree on that. 'I'll let them know we're here.' She got up and went out of the snug in time to meet the two detectives coming in. Neither of them looked thrilled to see her.

'I'm sorry to ask you this,' Alex said. 'Would you come and have a few words with Tony and me, please?'

Bill looked at his watch.

'It can't wait?' Dan said. 'We're both whacked.'

'I'm sorry,' she said, feeling like a recording. 'Really. I've been trying to get hold of you for hours. I don't want to sound panicked, but Mum and I are . . . we're not sure what we should do about something.'

Windows in the restaurant rattled, startling Alex. The wind was revving up for another good blow. 'It's about when I was born, really.'

Dan squeezed the bridge of his nose. 'I see.' The way he said it made plain he didn't see anything and didn't want to unless it was on his own terms and time frame.

'OK.' She looked at the floor, trying to decide how to disengage gracefully. There was nothing to be gained by pushing this now.

A hand holding her elbow brought her face up fast.

Bill Lamb smiled at her. It happened so rarely she hadn't realized what a nice smile he had, or how it changed his usually expressionless eyes. They shone with something approaching humor and the skin at the corners crinkled very nicely.

She was tired, too, and losing all objectivity. 'Yes?' she said to Bill. You were in a bad state when the slightest sign of kindness turned you into a jellyfish.

'Why don't we get my fearless leader a drink and go into the snug like you suggest? Let's all have drinks and you can get whatever's worrying you off your chest.' He frowned slightly. 'Unless you'd rather I not be there. I understand that, of course. Wasn't thinking.'

'Tony and I would appreciate having your opinion, too,' she said before she could decide if she was getting sucked in by a little charm.

'Off we go then,' Bill said and they joined Tony with Dan, apparently slightly mollified at the prospect of a drink, bringing up the rear.

This time Tony insisted on getting their drinks and left Alex alone with Dan and Bill. 'Let's get started,' Dan said. He shed his coat but not his suit jacket and still managed to look disheveled with his tie askew and his shirt collar wrinkled. Not at all his usual appearance.

'You have had a long day, haven't you?' Alex said, feeling guilty.

Dan glanced down at his clothes and raised one brow. 'It shows, hm? Yes, but sitting here in the warm and looking forward to a brandy makes me feel better by the second. How about you, Bill?'

'Just ducky, guv.' Bill took off his trench coat and his dark grey suit jacket. He was of average height but powerfully built. No fat on that trim body.

Alex almost suffered a pang of guilt for noticing Bill Lamb the man – almost. She smiled to herself.

'I hope you got started, darling,' Tony said pushing the door open with a shoulder and coming into the snug with a tray of brandies.

Tony, you are the real standout. And he was, but she was definitely not concentrating on the reason they were all here. 'I'm going to keep this short and sweet, Dan,' she said, all business. 'No waffling all over the place. Sorry I did that to you the last time. Nerves make a mess of me sometimes.'

Accepting his glass, Dan took a hefty swig and looked at

her. 'Don't you worry about the other night. We all have difficult moments.' He helped himself to a sausage roll and Bill captured the steak and kidney pie, a plate, and silverware from a caddy on the bar.

The brandy warmed Alex and did a good job relaxing her. 'There's a woman called Beverly Irving who took my mother in when she was expecting me and had no place to go. You know . . . I think you know my mum has never been married. She spent a lot of years just holding things together for the two of us. I've got to stay focused.' For a moment she paused and mentally rearranged what she had to say. 'Beverly Irving tried to take me away from Lily. She said she wanted her to go back to school and finish her education but the price was for Beverly to adopt me. It was all supposed to be altruistic, but it got a bit sick.'

She sketched in the story, glancing from time to time at Tony who gave her encouraging nods and smiles or said an occasional, 'That's right.'

Dan and Bill listened intently, each of them leaning forward in their chairs, drinks forgotten.

At last Dan said, 'So this woman threatened to hurt someone Lily loves. What do you think she meant by that? What does Lily think she meant?'

'All I think is that it's ominous coming from someone who was supposedly out of the picture years ago,' Alex said. 'My mother had forgotten she signed to have any mail redirected to Beverly. This happened over a lot of years and Mum put it behind her. I think the only reason the last effects of Mum's mother reached her was because someone got scared there would be trouble if they didn't. The people in Child Protection Services are so busy. Mum said you should see their offices. Mad, she said. They just let anything meant for Mum slip through their fingers. I don't even know if there was anything before my grandmother died and left those few things. Beverly was furious my mum had them. She must have found out from the office and she called Mum. It's as if she's known everything about us all these years. It's sickening.'

They sat in silence, thinking, before Dan said, 'This isn't a

Serious Crimes incident – not at this point and I hope it won't be.'

'No,' Bill said, giving Alex another of his smiles. 'But we won't just let you dangle. Gosh, I wouldn't want to face Radhika if she found out we'd done that.'

Dan gave an explosive laugh. 'The little lady has my partner wrapped around her fingers, folks. But Bill's right. I don't like the sound of this. We stopped any surveillance of you but perhaps we'd better have someone keep a look out again – unofficially, of course. We can always tie it to your being a witness to the Hill fire – if we have to.'

'I think you should watch Grant Hill, too.' Alex let the statement pour out and put a hand over her mouth. 'I shouldn't have said that.'

If there had been any doubt about her having their attention, there wasn't anymore.

'Good for you,' Tony said. He got up, came around the table and planted a less than chaste kiss on her lips. 'Good girl. You made the right decision. Listen to her, Dan and Bill. There's something whacky there.'

The detectives looked at each other.

Tony disappeared for a couple of minutes to return with the brandy bottle. He topped up the glasses, pausing at Alex's; she nodded emphatically.

'We may need this,' Tony said.

Alex tried to be concise. She tried not to embellish, and didn't, but the facts were the facts and Grant had threatened her.

Falling back in his chair, Dan regarded Alex with a mixture of respect and amazement. 'You followed LeJuan and Barry to the Knighton estate.'

'Yes,' she said quietly. 'I didn't know that's where they were going. I only thought about getting to see you and it was obvious – or I thought it was – that they knew where you were. So I followed.' She felt miserable.

'The footsteps were yours,' Dan said. 'That saves some work. What if it hadn't been us in the carriage house? What if Harding and Trafford were going after criminals – desperate men who would stop at nothing – and you got in the way.'

Tears in her eyes embarrassed her. 'I believed it was you two there.'

'This is bizarre,' Bill said.

Tony jumped in. 'It was a poor decision but it worked well for your purposes. You've got to admit that.'

'You've got to swear you won't repeat a word of this,' Dan said. 'Nothing you overheard. You may well have to talk about it on the stand in court but we'll cross that bridge when we come to it. Can you keep your mouth shut? You, too, Tony.'

'I would never jeopardize a case,' Alex said.

'Of course not,' Tony agreed. 'What about this Beverly Irving.'

'We have to think about it,' Dan said. 'Don't worry, we'll set the wheels in motion to find her and figure out what she wants and why. You say you never met her?'

Alex shook her head, no.

'And Lily hasn't seen her since she got away?' He didn't wait for Alex's answer. 'She's been hanging around in the shadows, that's for sure. And she's been getting information about you. She couldn't get everything from a sporadic communication by letter. Let me see if we can get someone we know assigned to the case.'

A great rush of gratitude overwhelmed Alex. She gulped and since she heard it she assumed everyone else must, too.

Dan's phone rang and he patted pockets until he found it. 'O'Reilly,' he said. 'No, I haven't. Should I know her . . . all right. Had anyone spoken to the husband? Oh. That doesn't help . . . does she now? That's the place to start, then. You're sure of the identification?'

All but slopping her drink, Alex moved hastily to sit beside Tony. He held her hand and turned up the corners of his mouth. 'Take it easy,' he said.

'Yes,' Dan said. 'We'll be right there.'

He put his phone away. Dan was already on his feet replacing jacket and coat.

Dan sighed and looked from one to the other of them, ending with Alex. 'I hope I don't regret asking this but I'd do it in an interview if that becomes where we're headed.'

'What do you mean by that?' Tony said.

'I'm talking to Alex. Do you know a Winifred Sibley?'

Staring at him, uncomprehending but with a sinking sense of doom, she said, 'I do.'

'She doesn't have a family?'

'I think she has a husband who travels with his work. He's away a lot. I can't remember ever seeing him really. Gladys Lymer is her best friend. She works at Leaves of Comfort.'

Dan sniffed. 'A neighbor told one of our officers she didn't think Winifred was married.'

'I'm probably wrong then,' she swallowed.

'Something's happened to Winifred. What? Just tell us now. We can get to what we know about her after that.'

'You're going to know anyway,' Dan said, on his feet and gathering his overcoat. 'She's dead. In a shed workroom behind her house. Blunt force trauma to the head.'

TWENTY-EIGHT

Winifred Sibley's pretty cottage was at the edge of the village green, several doors from Lily Duggins' home. Lights each side of the front door picked up a coat of fresh powder green paint.

A SOCO van was parked at the curb of a narrow pavement and LeJuan Harding parked between that and the nondescript vehicle he recognized as the police surgeon's.

At the windows of every little home, lights shone cheerfully through the darkness. At first glance, it was an almost magical scene that belied the violence LeJuan expected to find shortly. As soon as he got out of his car he heard quiet conversation. Just past the SOCO vehicle, people had gathered on the pavement. Their tones were horrified, disbelieving.

He approached quickly, beckoning a young woman constable to accompany him. 'Evening all. Please move back. The officer here will place tape so you'll know the area we need to keep clear. Thank you all for your cooperation.'

'Make sure no one gets past the tape,' he said to the constable quietly. 'Patrol until you're relieved. Eyes open for media. No one gets past. No details given out.'

'Yessir,' she said smartly. 'These people will already know the name of the victim. They may know more. They're likely to talk.'

'Nothing we can do about that. With any luck we've got a bit of time before the press get here.'

The front door was closed and an officer had been stationed there. Silently, he indicated a path around the cottage and LeJuan quickly reached the back garden, cast in odd gray and white shapes by the glaring lights that had been erected. The temperature had plummeted again and iced-over puddles of melt shone glassy black.

A tiny white dog, his fur standing up all over, had parked himself a few feet from a surprisingly large shed with an open door and constant movement inside. The dog gave an unearthly whine that broke into bursts of frantic yips before sinking back to the whine. LeJuan gave the dog a quick stroke on his way past. Dog, or oversized white mouse? He stopped to scratch the creature's neck before moving on.

Dr Lewis's was the first voice he heard, strident as usual. DCI O'Reilly's face turned to him the instant he stepped through the door.

'Good for you, LeJuan,' O'Reilly said. 'That was quick.'

LeJuan didn't volunteer any information about where he'd been when the call came in. 'Dispatch said one victim. An older woman. Is it murder then, guv?' He could see the victim and already knew the answer.

'Yes, poor woman.' O'Reilly screwed up his eyes. 'What's that bloody racket out there?'

'I'd say a mourning dog, guv,' LeJuan told him. 'Be a disaster if someone trod on it. Might weigh a couple of pounds soaking wet. I don't like to call Animal Control. Could be someone else it's close to will take it in.'

The dog cried out again and then didn't stop. 'Of course. I already knew about him. Have someone take him across the road to the pub and keep him warm in a coat pocket or something,' O'Reilly said. 'Tony Harrison's there. He might as well do something we ask him to do for once and quiet the dog down.'

Another uniform dealt with removing the dog but the sound it had made stayed in LeJuan's head. 'Poor little beggar,' O'Reilly muttered and LeJuan liked him for it.

The dead woman, wrapped in several old sweaters and with a scarf around her neck, was slumped sideways in a wooden rocking chair beside an electric bar fire. Her right hand rested in her lap, a long length of white material beneath her fingers. The left arm hung beside the chair.

On the right side of the head was a terrible wound. Blood was stuck thickly in her hair and made spidery blackish rivulets across her face.

'Furious force there,' O'Reilly said. 'Hit her twice, although I'd say the second blow was unnecessary. She would probably already have been dead.'

'Don't see why I had to come at all,' Dr Molly Lewis said, but with humor. 'I'd say you were right, Dan. But the second hit was responsible for a lot of the mess. Took out the eye and socket, the cheekbone and most of the nose. Crazy bastard whoever he is.'

LeJuan winced.

'I don't suppose you've got any hunches about whether this is our man from Darla Crowley?' Dan asked.

'Hunches?' She looked around. 'Just making sure you aren't talking to someone else, my friend. I don't work on bloody hunches. This doesn't have to be the same perpetrator, but I wouldn't be amazed if it was.'

'Is this as pointless as it looks?' LeJuan heard himself say. 'What was she doing? Making lace? God, I didn't know anyone still made the stuff. There's blood on it.' He rubbed a hand across his eyes. There were times when he wavered, times when he wasn't sure this was his life's work the way he'd once been so convinced – when he was younger and thought he was needed to help avenge the cruelly treated.

'Bastard,' O'Reilly said. 'I don't know who he is but I hate his guts. Still, this is our job, stopping the crazies. I think I've got everything I'll get here, Molly. I'll be there when you do this one. When do you think you'll get to it?'

'In the morning,' Molly said and her voice was as flat as LeJuan felt. 'I'll get to her first thing. Shall we say eight?'

'Eight it is.'

LeJuan stood with O'Reilly who said, 'I should mention we've had a break about Darla. She was Lance Pullinger's sister. Looks like he bought the cottage as a place to keep her safe. Not sure from what yet. Now we'll go to the kitchen and talk to the woman who called in. Bill was dead on his feet so I told him to turn in. You can fill in for him, not that there'll be much to deal with until later when we line up more interviews.

'The neighbor who found the deceased came to check because of the dog. A lot of neighbors will have heard him so checking the times should be easy enough. House-to-house with the usual patience. Follow-up on Winifred Sibley's close contacts and her movements over the past day or so. Emphasis on last night, of course. I doubt she went out to her workroom to make lace after midnight but we'll know more when we get an idea of the time of death.'

'Right,' LeJuan said. 'Should I put someone on making a list of family, friends, neighbors and such?'

'Yes. You'll have plenty of help with that. She worked for Mary and Harriet Burke at Leaves of Comfort.'

LeJuan watched the photographer work. 'That will be a good source of information. The ladies know what goes on locally, don't they?'

'They do. Now let's get this initial interview over with fast and move on. Lily Duggins called in the death. She's the one who found the victim.'

'The police are out there in the shed now,' Lily said into her phone, looking along Winifred Sibley's back path toward her shed. 'All kinds of them. No, Alex, I'm not a wreck, I'm more-or-less OK. Shaken up, naturally, and sad but I haven't fallen apart. The shock will come later.'

She listened to Alex worrying and trying to plan for what Lily should do next and interrupted, 'James is on his way here now. Nothing for you to worry about. Yes, I know they took the little dog over to Tony. Nice little girl. Her name's Lillie Belle . . . yes, it does suit her. I think she's a Maltese. She's so upset.' Lily was also upset, sick to her stomach and frightened, but she wasn't going to tell Alex or anyone else just how frightened.

'Alex, I think we're going to find ourselves more in the middle of whatever's going on around here. It's different, isn't it . . . yes, I know murder's always different, of course I do, but, well, you're a bit more involved than usual. I hate to say murder is usual but you do seem to get yourself dragged into these awful cases.

'You do know Gladys has been close friends with Winifred forever, don't you?' The younger generations didn't tend to take a lot of notice of what older people did. 'Well, she was and she's going to take this very hard. So are Harriet and Mary.'

'Winifred? No, not married, or not officially. She did have a close friend for some years but that must have ended and we never spoke of it. She doesn't have any close family, just an ancient aunt somewhere up north.'

She listened to Alex trying to decide how the Burke sisters should be told about Winifred. 'The police are going to ask me questions soon, sweety. Don't worry, I'll mention Harriet and Mary and find out if James can be the one to tell them. He isn't just their doctor, he's their good friend. He'll make sure they're all right – not that I don't think they're stronger than the lot of us. Try to get some sleep yourselves. I expect Tony can give Lillie Belle something to calm her down. Tell him his dad's coming to me . . . yes, all right, I'll let you know what the police say. Now I'd better hang up. I see Dan and LeJuan coming along the path.'

She turned the kettle on and stood at the door while they picked their way over uneven crazy paving.

Dan looked up and raised a hand in greeting. 'Hello, Lily,' he said. 'Bad night all around. We're sorry to keep you hanging around like this.'

'I understand. Coffee or tea? The kettle's on.'

'Tea,' the men said in unison.

Were there things she should avoid saying, Lily wondered, if only for selfish reasons. Winifred had been Gladys's close friend and they must have talked about so many things. Sometimes she couldn't decide how much Gladys remembered of Lily's early days in Underhill and Folly but she'd rather they were not brought up with strangers like Dan and his people. She had a disturbing thought that it no longer mattered what Gladys might have told Winifred.

The men came in looking tired. Dan sat immediately and rubbed his hands over his face. She had kept the kettle close to a boil while she waited for them so the tea was quickly made. Again, using Winifred's things while she lay dead at the bottom of the garden caused a nasty sensation. Lily couldn't bring herself to look for biscuits.

'Just routine questions for now,' Dan said.

It was LeJuan who took out his notebook and began to write. He gave her a reassuring smile.

'The dog woke me,' she said. 'Poor girl howling like that must have woken up the village. I thought she'd got locked outside. The light was on in here so I knocked. When Winifred didn't come, I opened the door but she . . . she wasn't in here, was she? Lillie Belle ran back and forth on the path and that's when I saw another light in the shed window – there's a window in the door – and I found her.'

'That's all very clear, Lily,' Dan said while LeJuan scribbled rapidly.

Tears shocked Lily, first stinging her eyes, then pouring. Her throat burned and she coughed, couldn't stop coughing.

LeJuan steered her into a chair and brought her some water. She heard the two of them murmuring but not what they said to her. With tissues pressed to her eyes and face, she gradually caught her breath. The tears took longer to stop.

'Hey, there, Lily.' She looked up into James's face. He rubbed the back of her neck and her shoulders. 'Take your time. These things are shocking.'

'She's a trooper,' Dan said.

'We want James to tell Harriet and Mary,' Lily said. If she sounded odd, so what? 'I told Alex I'd ask. She's worried the upset will be too much for them.'

'Understood,' Dan said. 'But you accept we'll have to be there, too. First reactions are important.'

Lily nodded, yes.

They went through all the simple questions she'd expected

and her muscles began to relax a little. James stood beside her. She had never needed anyone to help her get through, even if she might have liked stronger support sometimes, but she needed this man now.

'We're finished for now, then?' she asked.

Dan helped himself to more tea. 'Not quite. What time did you come over?'

'Well before midnight. Lillie Belle had been barking a long time.'

'Make sure Molly knows that,' Dan told LeJuan.

'Switching gears a bit. I'm told Gladys Lymer was her best friend.'

TWENTY-NINE

Doc James knelt on one knee before the fireplace in Lily's tiny sitting room to set chips of wood and logs on top of firelighters. Alex and Tony sat on the couch, Alex with Lillie Belle in her arms while the dog drowsed from the sedative Tony had given her.

In one of the chairs near her Chinese chest, Lily huddled into a corner with her face averted from all of them. 'Mum?' Alex said.

Lily didn't respond or even register she'd heard.

After so many years, her mother was still shamed by the thought of people talking about her being a teenaged single mother. Despite how little that meant now, it had the power to embarrass her. And although they had agreed that the police had to know about their history, Alex was sure Lily blamed her for telling them. She hadn't said as much, but Alex knew it was so.

'We came because you said you wanted to talk about this evening,' Alex said to her mother. 'I know it's been horrible but we can help each other.'

'You don't understand,' Lily said. 'How could you? You told the police about me and our history, but it wasn't as if you were talking about yourself. It's different when you tell someone else's story.'

'I'm sorry you feel like that. I thought it was my story, too. I'm sure Dan wouldn't try to make you uncomfortable. I'm not sure why your past came up tonight anyway. You had the horrible experience of finding Winifred's body. I'd assumed they'd only be asking you about that.'

'I thought so, too. We were both wrong. They've been digging around into Beverly Irving already. I knew she should never be mentioned. I tried to hide that but you kept pushing for information, Alex. Now look what's happening.'

The fire sent lively flames up the chimney and Doc James stood before it, dusting off his hands and looking directly at Alex. If he was trying to send her a message, she couldn't tell what it might be.

'We're all very tired,' Tony said. 'Do you think we should call this a night and talk about it all later?'

'You can if you want to,' Lily said. She chewed a fingernail. 'I can't stop you but I won't sleep until I know where they're going with all these questions. Dan talked about Beverly and Gladys and how Gladys was Winifred's best friend. He asked me if I knew Esme Hill and her family before the night you were there at the fire, Alex. I feel as if I'm losing my mind. What is he thinking, and how do I come into all that?' She shook her head repeatedly.

'Let's talk it out, Lily,' Doc James said. 'As much as you can, anyway. Why don't you tell me everything that was said? It may come clearer that way.'

'I'm not leaving either,' Alex said, knowing Tony would also stay. 'But I've got an idea about all this. It's not fair to leave you or any of us hanging like this and I don't believe Dan would do it deliberately. He started this, he should finish it. At least he should explain where he's going with these questions.'

'Oh, sweetheart,' Tony said, scratching the now sleeping Lillie Belle's head. 'Dan doesn't have to explain anything unless he wants to. This is an official investigation.'

'Why did he ask Mum if she knew Esme Hill and her family before the fire? What possible connection could Mum have to any of that?'

'None, I should think. Only that all of this, the approaches by Beverly, Gladys's odd behavior at the Black Dog and now the death of Gladys's best friend started coming to light around the time of the fire. He's just trying to connect the dots the same as we are.'

Lily leaned toward Tony. 'I just want it all to go away again. We were fine before it started to happen.'

'People are always fine before things happen,' Doc murmured.

'Don't be so reasonable, James.' Lily's voice rose. 'I did my best to carry on and build a fresh life and I don't want to look back. I don't want anyone poking around or finding things out about me. That's why I took the plate with my name on it . . . Alex's baby's name . . .'

Tears stood in her eyes and she looked at her hands in her lap.

Alex saw Tony shake his head at his father, warning him not to ask what Lily had just meant.

'I'll tell you why,' Lily said. 'Then you won't have to ask. Alex had the bench put in the churchyard as a remembrance to her baby, Lily Mary Edwina. That was the name on the plaque, so I took it. I didn't want anyone else to find it and make a connection to us – find us. Silly of me. Beverly wasn't likely to stumble over it even if she went to the churchyard, and she has no way of knowing your baby's name or why you used it. Neither does . . . well, I don't think anyone else knew the name really. Not all of it.'

Alex tensed. 'Neither does who, Mum? Neither does who? You were going to mention someone else who might find it, weren't you? Someone else you didn't want to know about the name and its connection to you.'

'No! Now leave it alone. I've told you all about it, stupid as it was.'

A firm rap at the front door silenced them all and they looked at one another. 'Who can it be at this hour?' Tony said. He glanced toward the windows. 'With all the lights on down here they know we're awake.'

He got up and went into the hall. A few moments later he returned with Dan O'Reilly and LeJuan Harding.

Neither detective smiled. Both appeared tired and drawn.

Doc went to Lily and said something quietly. She nodded and said, 'Please sit down. Bring over that bench.'

While Doc James went into the kitchen, Tony and LeJuan shifted Lily's heavy, dark, wood bench from beneath the window. By the time they had the long cushion replaced on top, Doc had returned with a bottle of Glenmorangie and a fistful of scotch glasses, their stubby stems threaded through his fingers.

Clacking his handfuls on the glass-topped chest, Doc dispensed more than suitably substantial doses of the whisky and handed it around. 'Doctor's orders,' he said, his expression dour. 'I'm too tired myself to minster to the fading – or fainting.'

They accepted their glasses and found seats, all in silence while they took their first tastes.

'Good idea, Dr Harrison,' Dan O'Reilly said. 'If we don't need it now, we may later. Lily, does everyone here know something of the woman we discussed earlier? The one from your earlier years.'

Alex noted how carefully he chose his words. She swallowed more whisky.

Lily said, 'Yes,' in an even voice, her eyes on the detective. 'Beverly Irving, if that's who you mean. They all know now.'

'You said she called you recently. How did you know it was her?'

'She told me who she was and knew everything about me. Right down to my movements on the day she made the call. She seems to have been watching me all this time.'

'You haven't seen her, though, so you don't know where she's been or how she found out all this information about you.'

Lily frowned. She put her hands beneath her thighs and rocked back and forth. 'I told you I haven't seen her, and I don't know how she's found out so much.'

'This is very important or I wouldn't ask,' Dan said. 'Do you have any photos, anything at all of Beverly?'

'I could have an old one somewhere. I'm not sure though.

Do I have to look for something? The idea of seeing her face truly bothers me.'

'Please start looking, Lily. We need to have a police artist work on an age progression sketch and do some potential disguise pieces. The artist will need to talk to you and to Gladys. I'm sure she'll be delighted to help.' Sarcasm wasn't his usual thing. 'These sketches have to be circulated. Also, we might flush out someone else who knows Beverly although I doubt it.

'We've had a number of our people tracing her since Alex came to me. They're very good at their jobs. You both have a considerable amount of clear information. We do know that any correspondence sent to you was forwarded to Beverly Irving at a post office box and picked up. There was a request for your mother's effects to be sent there. That request was denied. Evidently it must have struck someone in Child Protection Services that they ought to actually see you and that it wasn't appropriate to continue the arrangement they'd had with this Beverly.'

'They should have figured that out years ago,' Alex said. 'It's disgraceful they never checked after such a long time.'

'So it is,' Dan said. 'Lily, I think you believed the story you told me. What I don't understand is why you didn't check it out sooner.'

'I had no reason to,' she said, her face set.

'I'm afraid you did,' Dan told her. 'This doesn't go beyond these walls, but so far the only Beverly Irving who fits your description, the age she would be, and so forth, died almost eleven years ago.'

THIRTY

'Aye, aye, look what we've got here,' Longlegs Liberty said, sotto voce. 'Mr Crowley in the flesh. Slimy bastard.'

Four hours sleep followed by a busy morning so far had left Dan bleary-eyed and in a foul humor. 'Bugger,' he muttered. He stayed behind his battered desk in Folly's parish hall and flicked a biro back and forth between his fingers. 'Good morning, Mr Crowley. Nice of you to join us again.'

Longlegs got up and wandered toward Dan, murmuring, 'Do I cuff him?' as he passed.

'Wish you could. Can't – no reason to yet,' Dan said, equally nonchalantly, while Vince Crowley watched him from the doorway. 'Come and join us,' Dan called.

'Thought I'd stop in on my way by,' Crowley said, shoving away from the door jamb with a shoulder. 'I've got business to attend to in Winchcombe.'

'That so?' Dan said. He pulled a lined yellow pad toward him and made a couple of notes. 'I didn't think it went well the last time you were there. Scared you so badly you started jumping out of bathroom windows. Would you like to explain that one?'

'Didn't know where I stood then, did I? I'd had a run-in with the silly moo in Darla's place and I expect I was a bit shook up.'

Dan bit back a comment about the ease of burning female adversaries with cigarettes. 'I expect that was it.'

'You thought you could pin Darla's murder on me, didn't you?'

Looking into the man's dark eyes, Dan decided this wasn't a fool who came out with comments that might lead him into trouble, but a sly manipulator with a plan designed to benefit himself. 'Did you hear that, Liberty?' Dan said loudly and laughed. 'A man who hasn't been accused of anything suggesting he might be linked to a potential murder charge.'

'Is that supposed to make me nervous?' Crowley said. 'I haven't done anything so I don't have to be nervous. Darla and me were still married, see. We used to have our little spats, mostly because she couldn't keep her legs together. Sure, that upset me but I still loved her and she loved me. One of the reasons I stuck with working the cruise lines was because the long trips agreed with me. When we got back together, it was a honeymoon and by the time she started getting bored and looking around, I was off again. It wouldn't have suited a lot of men but it suited me. And the money's really good.'

'Why are you telling me all this?' Dan genuinely wanted to know but doubted he'd ever get a straight answer.

'I don't know why. Just getting it off my chest, I suppose.'

They'd left the front door open to flood the place with fresh air. It got stuffy from being closed off most of the time. Coming out of the light and into the hall – Mary with her cane rather than the walker – were the Burke sisters. They entered the hall without saying a word and sat on two of the seats by the front wall.

For an instant that quickly passed, Dan thought of taking Vince Crowley into the storage room at the other end of the parish hall where interviews were occasionally conducted. There was nothing going on that had to be private.

'I'm glad you and your wife had such an agreeable marriage,' he told Vince.

'Yeah, well we did. Now, what I want to know is, what happened to all of Darla's papers and her other things? I expect they're evidence till you catch her murderer but I need to look through the papers.'

Longlegs coughed and said, 'Sorry about that. I'm getting the winter crud.'

Dan thought Crowley's request had caught Longlegs as much off-guard as it had him. 'What papers would those be?' he said.

'All of them,' Crowley said, managing to sound innocent. 'I want to make sure all her bills are paid and her affairs are taken care of. She didn't have anyone but me. Darla was particular about not having any outstanding debts. And then there's the house payments. They can't be allowed to fall behind.'

Well, well, if he wasn't the slow one today, Dan thought. Finally, the reason for this chummy little visit began to make sense. He was aware of Harriet and Mary but avoided looking at them. 'You're an honorable man, Mr Crowley,' he said, trying for sincerity. 'I'm afraid case evidence isn't something I can discuss. You can be sure you'll be hearing from the appropriate department in due course.'

'Not good enough.' Vince Crowley planted his hands on the desk and glowered into Dan's face. 'Don't give me that crap. I wasn't born yesterday and when I say I want to see my wife's papers now, I want to see them now. There are things that need to be taken care of. And while you're at it, you can tell me who she was seeing when she died. I haven't seen anything about you taking someone into custody. About time you did and it seems to me her latest fancy man would be number one on the list of suspects. Who is he, tell me that!'

The man really didn't know. Pullinger's name hadn't been officially linked with Darla's but leaks were getting ever more commonplace in all cases.

'This is an officially open investigation. There's nothing I can do to help you. And surely you know her family. Have you contacted them?'

'I don't know if she had any family and if she did they didn't do anything for her.' Crowley made a fist with his right hand and his face reddened. 'Who was her solicitor then? Tell me that. You can't say I don't have a right to know who dealt with her affairs.'

'But you were married to the victim, Mr Crowley. Did you go to the solicitor you had before you left to get your last ship? He might well be able to help you.'

'I'm Darla's next of kin. I need the deeds to that house. And her will if she made one and I doubt she did that.'

Dan pushed his chair back a bit. 'Surely you bought the house together? Didn't you make sure you knew all the details? Did you keep a copy of the deed in the house, perhaps, and you've forgotten?'

'I've never been in the place . . . The, er, sale was still being seen to after I left.'

'You, sir, are a disgrace. A disgrace.' Harriet Burke marched her sensible lace-ups, encased in sturdy plastic drizzle boots, across the dusty floorboards. 'How dare you heckle a fine man like Detective Chief Inspector Dan O'Reilly. And you're a liar, my man. You are here about the possessions of that poor young woman, Darla Crowley. And if she was your wife, I'm sorry for her – even more sorry than I was before I set eyes on you.'

Dan cleared his throat. He smiled, very slightly, at Harriet and held up a hand to calm her.

The effect she had on Vince was startling. He had

straightened away from the desk, stepped back, and regarded the woman with his mouth open.

Mary Burke, thumping the rubber tip on her cane onto the floor, approached more slowly to join her sister. 'Every word Harriet says is true, you reprobate. It's because of so-called men like you that we're watching a generation of sloppy, pot-smoking, thieving, bottom-crack displaying hoodlums grow up. With their hands held out for what they're not prepared to work for, may I add.'

'Bravo, Mary,' Harriet said and put the gloved fingers of one hand over her mouth.

'This one wants his dead wife's possessions,' Mary said. 'And look at him. A strapping fellow who shouldn't need anything from anyone. *And*, he was a wife-beater, mind you. Worse than that – he burned his wife with cigarettes!'

Dan shot from his chair. 'Ladies, we need a private chat. Detective Constable Liberty, kindly take the Misses Burke to our interview room and get them a cup of tea.'

'I don't think you murdered your wife, Mr Crowley,' Mary said, undaunted. 'You'd probably be too afraid to do something to her that couldn't be kept hidden.'

Crowley seemed to shrink inside his pea coat. He pulled up his collar and went to the door. 'I'll be back, mind you,' he said before walking out. 'I've got a right to get information about my wife.'

'Oh, dear,' Mary said. 'I didn't know I had it in me but I'm glad I did. That man is a toad. We'd love that cup of tea, please, but we don't need an interview. We only came to find out where Winifred's Lillie Belle is and if we can have her to take care of. It's the least we can do for dear Winifred.'

THIRTY-ONE

The drive to Gloucester had been made in near silence. Gladys had asked Alex and Lily to take her and Alex, although deeply sad and sickened at the thought of going to the morgue for Winifred Sibley's identification, had not expected quite such a miserable journey.

They entered the building she wished she could forget, and immediately saw Dan O'Reilly and Bill Lamb hovering ahead of them.

'I'm not talking to them.' Gladys broke the silence, her voice a weak squeal. 'You came with me. There's no need for them to be here. I don't want anyone to see me with them. If they stay, I'll leave now.'

Lily raised her brows at Alex who sucked in the corners of her mouth and said nothing. She didn't know what to say.

'If they try to leave here with me, I won't have it.' Gladys grasped Alex's arm with a shaking hand. 'Tell them to stay away from me. All they bring is trouble. They're dangerous.'

'I'll have a word,' Alex said, completely bemused by Gladys's outburst. 'Stay here.'

She left her mother with Gladys and walked rapidly ahead to the two detectives. 'Don't ask me what the deal is, but Gladys is having a fit just at the sight of you. She says she won't stay unless you leave and if you try to be with her when she's ready to leave, well, I don't know. But it might be better to do as she asks. What you do later is something I can't control. I don't want to control that or anything else about this fiasco. It's awful.'

Dan's hand on her shoulder was unexpected but she didn't let herself stiffen. 'OK, Alex. Thank you for doing this. Could you do something else for us?'

'I will if I can.' *Anything – just let this be over.*

He smiled, reminding her of how charming he could be. 'Please would you listen to what's said and let us know? I doubt if there'll be anything, but just in case. And remind me to tell you about the visit we got from Harriet and Mary a couple of hours ago. It was something else. Vince Crowley, Darla's husband, came into the parish hall with demands and the ladies let him know why he had no right to ask for anything. And one of the reasons they gave was something they should not have known. He couldn't get out of there fast enough.'

Alex grinned, she couldn't help it. 'I think I feel sorry for him.'

'We'll be in touch later then,' Dan said, patting that shoulder.

'Thank you, Alex,' Bill said sincerely, and the two of them walked away in the opposite direction.

For a minute or two Alex stood still. She had the feeling she'd just been bamboozled by two of the best bamboozlers.

When she turned around, Lily was walking Gladys toward her and a mortuary attendant appeared from one of the rooms. She approached, her green boots squeaking on the linoleum floor, pulling off long rubber gloves as she came.

'Mrs Lymer?' she asked. 'One of you is Mrs Lymer?'

'I am,' Gladys said, fiddling with a button on her blue wool overcoat. 'I think I need to wait a minute. I'm all sixes and sevens.'

'Take your time,' the attendant said. 'Would you like to sit down?'

Gladys shook her head, no. 'Nothing to be gained by that. I'm ready.'

Through the door the woman had used, then past a pair of swinging doors and they were immediately upon a gurney carrying an unmistakable sheet-draped form. Gladys let out a high-pitched, 'Oh,' and stood still.

Alex couldn't move, but at least Lily seemed calm and rubbed Gladys's back, murmuring softly to her.

'Are you ready to do this?' the attendant asked.

Gladys nodded but didn't move closer. The sheet was lowered, revealing Winifred's head held up on an autopsy neck prop. There was no way to lessen the impact of the damage to her head and face.

'Winnie!' was the only sound Gladys made. She nodded again in response to the attendant's question about the identity, but suddenly moved to the dead woman's side.

Alex made a move to join her but Lily held her back.

'Winnie, it's my fault,' Gladys said, making a choking sound between each word. 'It's because of me. I should be there, not you. Oh, Winnie, I didn't know they'd do this.'

She touched her dead friend's cheek, turned, and collapsed.

Tony took off his oilskin coat and threw it across a chair in one of the hospital's family waiting rooms. 'You have to be knackered,' he told Alex. 'When was the last time you slept?'

'The last time you slept,' she said, eyes closed, legs stretched out in front of her on a chair in the corner.

His dad had taken Lily home and Tony was glad. He wanted to concentrate on Alex.

'Do you know what's happening now, sweetheart?' he asked her.

She opened those very green eyes, a bit bloodshot now. 'They put Gladys in a bed and she slept for a couple of hours. Frank came to be with her. I know Dan was going to question her. I've also known there was something strange going on with Gladys but not how strange. I still don't, but I know I was right. Now we're just supposed to wait. You should be at home sleeping.'

'Not without you.'

She smiled and closed her eyes again. 'It's ugly and getting uglier. I wish I could figure out how it all goes together – if it does.'

'Why can't I take you home? They can get in touch later.'

'The pace is picking up. They were adamant I had to wait here. Gladys said some troubling things and I had no choice but to pass them on to the police. Bill Lamb came and said something about arranging for Gladys and me to talk again. I hate it all.'

A tap on the door preceded LeJuan Harding. He showed no sign of being stressed but he was serious when he came into the room. 'Lily left?'

'She went home with Doc Harrison,' Alex said, sitting upright in her chair. 'Why?'

LeJuan appeared to consider what to say next. He looked at the windows where rain was striking the panes again, blurring the dark and laden skies outside. 'We've got issues with Mrs Lymer,' he said after a long pause. 'Why do they paint these rooms puke green? Is it supposed to calm people?'

'Probably.' Tony smiled and didn't comment on the change in subject.

'It makes me jumpy, or it would if I got jumpy.' They were treated to a LeJuan grin. 'Gladys Lymer is not going to talk to a detective unless we slip her a truth serum. She won't even look at any of us. Either we stayed out of her room or she was leaving, with or without permission. She wants you and Lily. End of story. Are you up for it if she'll talk to you on your own?'

'I suppose so. Yes, yes, of course I am, but won't you eventually need to get a statement out of her somehow?'

'It would be easier but there are ways around these things.'

Alex got up. Even as a skinny kid the mean kids had picked on, she had been composed. She looked composed now but Tony questioned how she felt inside. She was looking at him as if she wanted to ask a question she wasn't sure how to word.

'Gladys will be glad to have you with her,' he told her, partly to move things along. 'If she wants Lily here before she says whatever's on her mind, I can run in and get your mum. Or Dad will bring her back.'

Alex nodded and said, 'Let's get on with it. Gladys probably wants to talk about Winifred again. That was a horrible thing – seeing Winifred, and watching Gladys's meltdown.' She closed her eyes briefly, then went to the door. 'If we have to get Mum I'll send a message.'

LeJuan followed her out and Tony took a chair into the corridor. From there he could see the entrance to Gladys's room. Given the bed shortage, keeping her there was a stretch and probably Dan O'Reilly's doing.

LeJuan hovered until Alex went into the room before returning to Tony. 'My boss wanted me to ask you exactly what Alex said about going over to the Knighton estate. Is there something else he ought to know?'

'You've got to be kidding.' Tony stood up. 'You're not really asking if I'd be prepared to repeat something Alex told me in confidence.'

'If it related to something she heard said in the carriage house while she was lurking about outside, I am.'

'Lurking?' He gave the word a moment to hang. 'Do you see Alex as the type to lurk, sergeant? If you want to pursue that line of questioning you'll have to talk to the lady yourself. Good luck with that.'

* * *

'My Frank says I should be able to go home if I want to.'

'Do you want to?' Alex said. 'Before they're sure you're well enough. You were unconscious for a bit, Gladys.'

Fully dressed, Gladys sat in a chair beside a bed. 'I did ask for Lily to come as well. I need to talk to both of you.'

'Doc took her home but we can get her back if that's what you want. I'm glad to be here with you, though.'

'We had a shock,' the woman said. 'All of us. Let Lily be. You can tell her what I'm going to say. I'm going to try not to ramble but it's a long story, Alex. I haven't done right by you and Lily and being sorry isn't going to make it any better.'

'Say what you think matters. I don't mind how long it takes. We've got to get whatever it is cleared up.'

Gladys pushed her hair back from her eyes. 'I suppose the first thing is the night someone took me out of the parking lot behind the Black Dog. If I had told you the truth right afterward and something was done about it, maybe Winifred would still be alive.' Tears welled. 'They gagged me with something and put a bag over my head. I heard something crash down which I realized the next day was my bike. Off I went in the dark. Couldn't make a sound. I banged myself up when I was put in the car, I can tell you.' She pushed up a cardigan sleeve to display bruises turning from black to green and yellow. 'I struggled but it didn't make any difference. Hurt my knees, too. It was high off the ground – the car or truck or whatever was high off the ground, I mean. I hit my knees when they pushed me in.'

Alex's hand went to her mouth. 'What did the nurses say about those bruises?'

'I wouldn't take my clothes off. Not me. Not when they'd ask all sorts of questions. There's more bruises on my hip and ribs. And a big blood blister on my side. I couldn't do anything to help myself. Not that I should be complaining when Winifred's lying dead down there.' The tears slid down her cheeks now. 'We drove but I didn't know where – or I didn't until they pushed me out of the car. I went down on my hands and knees and I heard them drive off. Then I managed to get the bag off and I was only a little way from home, but I've never been terrified before I was in that car, not like that. She said I wasn't doing what we'd agreed and she wasn't putting up with it.'

'She? You said, she. This was a woman who did this?'

'I think so. And she was strong. They say if you're mad enough you're strong enough and I suppose that's what it was. She didn't make any bones about it. She was going to make sure I did as I was supposed to and that meant I wasn't to talk to anyone about the things she'd had me do for her.'

'Did you know her voice?'

'She sort of whispered. A loud whisper. But I would know that voice now. You won't know who I mean but it was Beverly Irving. Your mum was staying with her when she was expecting you and afterwards for quite a bit. But something happened between them, at least I decided that's what it was. They fell out. Lily had been to the Folly and Underhill area while she was in school still. The year before she hoped to go to university. For a summer camp, she told me, that's why she was here. She liked it and decided she'd take you to Underhill and see if she could find somewhere cheap enough to live. I don't have to tell you it's a lot cheaper than Folly itself. And she got a flat in a little house next to where we were then. It was lovely having a young person and a baby nearby, I can tell you. Lily got a job at the Black Dog. But that's when I met Beverly Irving.'

'She went to Underhill?' Lily had never suggested Beverly had been there.

'No. Oh, no. She must have had help finding out about the people who lived near Lily and settled on me. Which doesn't make me feel good if it was because she decided I was easy to control. I went to Burford each Thursday for a meeting with some other women. We just drank coffee and chatted really. That was something else she found out. Then she made sure she ran into me in the street there, and started talking like we were old friends. I thought I must have forgotten her or something. But she said she knew about me, that's how she put it, and she said she had something important to say about Lily and you and would I go in for a cup of tea with her. I thought I'd better do it in case Lily might need to know about her. And she did need to, but Beverly made sure she sucked me in and then I was afraid to tell Lily because I was in the wrong, see.'

Responses weren't coming easily to Alex. 'We all do things we aren't proud of.'

'We didn't have much money,' Gladys said, rubbing her palms together until they squeaked. 'Frank didn't have a trade. Neither did I, really. But I kept working for other people. Cleaning, that sort of thing. Beverly knew that. One time when we met – she would make sure she saw me about once a month – she gave me some money. It was more than I could earn in a month. She insisted she knew we were having a hard time and said she could afford it. It was to help because I looked after you sometimes so Lily could do what she needed to do, that's what she said. Beverly knew I wouldn't take money from Lily for babysitting because she was struggling. Anyway, I never had babies of my own so I loved it when Lily let me have you for a bit. Why did I take that money? It was so wrong and look what it's done.'

'When was the last time you saw Beverly?' Alex hoped Gladys gave the right answer.

'Years and years ago. She started just calling instead of visiting.'

'I did know about Beverly,' Alex said, aware that she was deliberately avoiding mentioning the woman's death in case Gladys stopped talking. 'Mum told me.' And that much was true.

'Ah.' Gladys looked away. 'Beverly asked questions about you and your mum. She pushed and it made me anxious, but I thought when you were a bit older Beverly wouldn't ask me anymore, but she kept on and sometimes I knew what she wanted to know was too personal. But I didn't expect her to turn crazy on me like she did. Telling me to get a job at the Black Dog and let her know everything you and Lily did, or as much as I could. It made me feel sick.'

Why hadn't Gladys refused? 'Were you always afraid of her?'

'Once before I tried to stop doing it and a dead crow was left on our front step. I knew what it meant. I'd get punished if I stopped telling Beverly things. Then, after she made me go to your place to work and I told her a few things, I asked if I could stop. Now you know what happened to me after that. It was so horrible.'

'You knew how dangerous she was after that.'

Gladys looked close to tears again. She nodded and blotted her face with tissues.

'You could have gone to the police—'

'No! She told me she'd know if I did that and I'd be sorry for the rest of my life. Like I'm sorry now because of Winifred.'

'You went to the police?'

'I told Winifred. That woman must have found out—seen me talking to Winifred, I expect. So she killed her to punish me.'

THIRTY-TWO

Once more they followed in the wake of fire engines blaring and flashing through the graying of early evening. This time the only remaining snow was caught in crevices along drystone walls and covered with black grime thrown by vehicle wheels.

Bill drove. He had slept more than Dan who propped his jaw with an elbow precariously juddering on the rim of a closed car window.

The radio emitted signals and voices, one after another. 'Guv?' It was Sergeant Miller's speaking.

'Here, Miller,' Dan said.

'The fire's on the east side of Trap Hill. Vehicle driven between rocky outcroppings and set there. Or that's what they're saying happened. It's well under way.'

'Was Robert Hill the only one to call it in?'

'No, guv. His wife did, too. Mrs Esme Hill. She was out riding and saw it.'

'Do we know if the vehicle was occupied?'

'Not yet, sir.'

'Right. There shortly. Make sure the scene is protected.

There could be no connection to anything we're interested in but just in case . . . extra caution.' He signed off.

'Ashton's at the parish hall in Folly and he's been over the maps,' Bill said. 'That seems like a fair distance away from Knighton itself, but that land still belongs to Hill. He owns a bloody country over there.'

Following the fire vehicles, they started making a wide circle around what Dan had assumed, incorrectly, was the entire Knighton estate. The wind picked up, buffeting the car and slapping the odd broken branch across the road. A rumble set up, long and low. 'Thunder,' Dan said, glancing at his partner. It was a little while before lightning flared along distant hills, swelling and fading like a reflected firestorm.

Dan rolled down his window an inch in time to hear the crackle and then a muffled boom. 'Nothing like some well-timed sound effects.'

'The engines are turning here,' Bill said, making a left and climbing what must be Trap Hill. Mud sprayed in fans from the tires.

Half a mile and a fireman flagged them down. Bill opened his window and the man bent to look at him. 'Police,' Bill said, holding up his warrant card.

'No point trying to get closer,' the man said. Water dripped from his helmet. 'One of your lot already tried to put in a perimeter but everything's shifting with the fire and the weather. The vehicle is about gone. I'd say it's burned out completely.'

A tall figure flapped downhill toward them, dark hair plastered to his head, mud covering his boots and a good deal of his heavy coat.

'Robert Hill,' Dan said.

'He called us in,' the fireman commented. 'He'll have been sent down, too. Best wait for our chief to give you the go ahead before you carry on up there. We won't be letting anyone get closer yet.'

Bob Hill went to Dan's side of the car. 'I'm no expert,' he said, 'but from the shape of what's left, I'm just about sure that was a Jeep. Don't ask me what kind. If it's the one I saw at the site, I couldn't tell you much about that, either.'

'Get in,' Dan said, unlocking the back door and relocking after Hill was in the seat. 'How did you know what was happening?'

'My wife called me. She was riding back to Knighton and saw the flames. She said she'd called for police and fire but wanted me to do it as well to make sure. Her signal wasn't sounding good. She didn't have a clear connection. When she mentioned she'd got close enough to see a green vehicle it seemed too much of a coincidence so that's why I tried to get hold of you, but I couldn't get through. You do remember me telling you I thought it might be a green Jeep I saw.'

'I remember.'

Tony's clinic assistant, Radhika, had made them tea but Gladys still looked frozen. With the news that Beverly was dead and couldn't be hanging around that area, her spirits had lifted, but a message from Dan suggesting she shouldn't go home yet had clearly frightened her again. She would not try to think who her attacker had actually been.

They sat together in the small office that doubled as an overflow for caged and recovering animals. The cages were all empty but Milkshake, a long-haired tortoiseshell Radhika had acquired as the clinic cat by what Tony called nefarious means – the excuse for adopting the cat was that she would, in extreme situations, make blood donations – Milkshake slunk past Gladys giving her the stink-eye she reserved for strangers.

'Nice cup of tea,' Gladys said into the silence.

'Good.' Radhika, strikingly framed by the deep green of her sari showing at the neck of her white coat, smiled at Gladys. 'Sergeant Lamb promised to get back to you soon and he always does as he says he will.'

Alex caught Tony's eye and he grinned. They continued to have an oddly matched and strangely fascinating love story evolving before them.

The phone rang and Alex doubted she was the only one who jumped. Radhika picked up. 'Folly Animal Hospital.' Tony had renamed his small animal clinic. 'Oh, yes, yes indeed. Would you like to speak with her? Oh, very well then. Mr Frank Lymer will come for her. I shall tell her. But the rest of us should wait here. Yes, thank you. I will, I promise. And so should you. Goodbye.'

Radhika looked around. 'Not very remarkable, but Sergeant Lamb said your husband is coming for you, Gladys. They are no longer concerned about you going home.'

'But why *were* they concerned?' Gladys frowned around the room. 'Don't you think it's funny not to say why I shouldn't go home then say I can, but not tell me why about any of it?'

'It is a bit,' Alex said. Honesty couldn't hurt in this case. It was funny, as Gladys put it. 'But look on the bright side. If they aren't worried about you, neither should you be.'

'The rest of us should wait here but what was it you promised Sergeant Lamb, Radhika?' Alex asked innocently.

'To take care of myself,' Radhika announced, sounding defiant. 'We are concerned for one another always. I think you know that. I am very lucky.'

'And so is he,' Tony said; tritely, Alex thought.

They heard the bell at the back door of the clinic and Gladys jumped up. Tony walked out behind her, leaving Alex and Radhika alone – except for Milkshake who now curled up on Radhika's lap, spreading black and golden hairs on her white coat.

Tony returned and let out a sigh. 'That's some of the tension gone but I'm still concerned about that long loose end. Who took up where Beverly left off?'

'Let's not worry about it tonight,' Alex said. 'I wish Dan and Bill would come and ask or say what's on their minds, so we could go home.'

The doorbell rang again and all three of them laughed, if nervously. 'I hope this is a case of saved by the bell,' Tony said. He got up again. 'We could move into the sitting room.'

'It's warmer in here,' Radhika said. 'And I don't want to wake Milkshake up.'

Tony grunted and left the room once more to return only minutes later with the two detectives.

'Oh, my,' Alex said before she could stop herself. 'I'm sorry but you both look awful. I thought I was tired but—'

'We're buckling,' Dan said, interrupting her. 'But we haven't fallen yet. Question, Alex. When you were at the Hill site on the night of the trailer fire, did you see a vehicle driving out?'

She shook her head, no.

'You're absolutely sure? Think about it.'

Alex looked aside, trying to remember being among the new houses and seeing the start of the fire, the black, oily smoke. 'No – except, yes I did, but not right there. I was driving up that rough road toward the new village. A utility vehicle came at me like the proverbial bat. Nearly hit me then shot past. I was shaken up and sat there for a minute before carrying on.'

Dan looked dubious. 'First you say you didn't see a moving vehicle then you talk about almost being hit.'

His manner irritated her. 'That's right. When I was focused on a trailer fire and a man in trouble, I didn't think about *almost* being hit. I've had a lot on my mind since then.'

'So you have,' Dan agreed. 'A utility vehicle perhaps. That's what you're suggesting. Any idea of the make.'

'No.'

'Large, small, new, old, color, license plates?'

'Not large. Not small. Could be new or old because the mud on it made it camouflage color – or that's as close as I can come. And license plates? You've got to be joking.'

Dan whistled tunelessly.

'We're all tired and irritable,' Bill said. He grabbed a straight back chair, pushed it toward Dan and got a second one for himself. 'Some camouflage is sandy and brown, some is green and beige and brown. Roughly.'

'Mostly mud in this case,' Alex said. 'With some green, I suppose. But I wouldn't swear to it.'

'You don't have to, me darlin',' Dan said with a grin that surprised Alex. His Irish brogue was usually reserved for humorous moments so she assumed he was at least pleased with her response.

'Does that mean we can all go home?' Tony asked. He didn't look amused. 'And could you let us know if you have any suspects for the woman who took over from Beverly Irving to watch Lily and Alex. I don't know what makes you so sure everything's sewn up safely because Beverly died.'

'Nothing's sewn up safely. Would you say, Bill?'

'Yes indeed, guv. I would say so. We're a murderer – or two – short for a start. Frank Lymer's in the clear which is why Gladys needed to wait with you until we were sure. He knows they need to be vigilant. Thank you for the report on what Gladys told you, by the way, Alex. Very, very helpful. It's cleared up a lot of questions. Unfortunately, our band of clever elves in Gloucester has turned up information that puts us back where we were with one aspect of these cases but does in fact simplify another.'

Bill went to Radhika and held out his hands. She deposited the cat in his arms and it crawled to drape over his shoulder where it had obviously spent time on other occasions.

'I take it you'd like me to finish up here, Bill?' Dan said but he sounded even enough. 'Evidently Beverly Irving found a means of getting herself on someone else's death certificate.'

'Oh, no,' Alex exclaimed. 'I don't believe it.'

'Believe it. And now logic would suggest she'd be walking around in the identity of the person buried as Beverly but that didn't happen. Her ashes were interred with all the right official steps – with her name and details supplanting those of a woman who had really died and been cremated. The deceased's identity can't be released yet, not that she has any interested family apparently. Our Beverly thought of everything until she must have undergone a brain-change and brought attention to herself. I think she really believed Lily and Alex and Gladys would keep quiet because she could control them.'

'But who is she and where is she?' Alex said. 'I mean who is she pretending to be and where is she?'

'Hey ho,' Dan said, pushing to his feet. 'It's off to bed we go. Maybe the answers to the questions will come to us in dreams.'

THIRTY-THREE

'Do you see anything different? With the sisters?' Hugh studiously made a point of not looking toward the fireplace. The night was bitter and a stout fire roared up the chimney.

'They've complained about being cold so you built an extra big fire for them?' Alex suggested.

'Dopey answer, Alex,' Hugh said. 'Look again.'

She stared for a few moments. 'Oh, no. Two covered grocery wheelies. Tell me the second one has their shopping in it. Max is on the table, as usual.'

Hugh pulled a beer for Kev Winslet and poured a glass of Cinzano for his lovely little wife, Fay, who rarely accompanied her big, often loud, husband. If his bluster bothered her, she showed no sign, rather Fay looked at him with undisguised fondness.

'Well,' Alex said when Hugh turned back to her. 'Is there another cat in the Burke family?'

'No. At least I'm told there isn't.'

'This is a ploy to take my mind off the current nastiness, isn't it? You're not funny, Hugh, and it isn't working. Not a word from O'Reilly and Lamb since last night. I'm choking on my own nerves.'

'A ploy? I'd use a ploy lightly? Never. It's a dog, I think.'

Alex shook her head. 'No, it's not. That's silly. Can you imagine those cats with a new dog in their house?'

'I'm just passing along some news, that's all. If you want to abuse me for it, I'm a big boy.' His grin was shark-like.

Leaving the counter and walking quickly to the sisters' table, Alex asked, more abruptly than she'd intended, 'Have you got a dog?'

The red tartan blanket across Harriet's knees moved and a tiny white dog pushed out its head. Bright black eyes regarded Alex, sadly she thought, and a long, very pink tongue protruded from the side of a closed mouth.

Alex leaned over and scratched the dog's nose, rubbed between her ears and finally planted a kiss on her head. 'You took in Lillie Belle. Thank you, ladies, but aren't the cats having fits?'

'Oliver ignores her and Max thinks she's a kitten that barks. She barks and he taps her with one paw, like an irritated mother, and Lillie Belle stops barking. It's really working very well.'

'You're the kindest, nicest people I know. I didn't even think about where she was.'

'That glamorous Mrs Hill and her son just came in,' Harriet

said in a low voice. 'I wonder if they've picked a winner for the contest. If they have, someone will be very happy.'

'I'll be glad when it's over. Talk to you later.' With a sinking stomach, Alex turned around to see Esme and Grant Hill talking expansively at the counter while Hugh listened politely. When he saw Alex coming, he gave a wave. He didn't deal well with overpowering people and was ready for her to take over.

'Good evening,' she said. 'Lovely to see you. I hope you had an easier drive tonight. At least we're only getting rain, not snow.' She came close to wincing. Her heritage was showing. The British could always use weather to make empty conversation.

Esme threw her arms around Alex in a smothering hug, murmuring how thrilled she was to see her. Over the woman's shoulder, she met the cold eyes of Grant Hill who would never make an actor if it meant covering his real feelings. He detested Alex.

She untangled herself from Esme, smiling as she did so. She was saved from welcoming Grant. He turned his back to her and ordered drinks.

'Bob,' Alex heard Esme exclaim.

Bob Hill joined his family. He looked at Alex. 'My poor family isn't used to me turning up like this,' he said. 'Workaholics like me get bad reputations for being no-shows but I'm working on improving, aren't I?' He gave his wife's shoulders a squeeze.

Esme rested her head on his shoulder and smiled at him.

'Audra changed her mind about having a night in and came with me,' Bob said, searching around. 'Where did she go? Oh, might have known. She's persuading people they wanted to move so we can have the biggest table.' He cast his eyes upward.

Audra, Lady Mekins, was indeed pouring the charm onto a couple at the largest table in the bar and they were in the process of moving to share a smaller table with another couple. Inwardly, Alex cringed but the new tablemates seemed quite happy with the arrangement.

'What'll you have, Dad?' Grant asked and Alex took in a sharp breath.

The delight on the son's face at the sight of his father almost hurt to watch.

'Orange juice and tonic,' Bob said. 'It'll be gin and tonic time for Audra. How are you, Alex?'

'Well, thank you.' She didn't belong with this group. 'We're having a busy night but that's how we like it.'

'It's the atmosphere and the way you treat people that brings in the folks. You make them want to come. That's a gift.'

He embarrassed her. 'Thank you. Please make yourselves comfortable.'

'We've picked a winner for our pub name,' Grant said, still not cracking a smile at her. 'Would you like to make the announcement?'

'Why not let your father do it. Everyone would like to put a face to his name.'

Bob accepted a piece of paper from Grant, and some envelopes, and said, 'Hello, everybody. I'm Bob Hill. For my sins, the new village near Winchcombe is being built by my company. I won't bore you by going on about how good it's going to be for the area. Now, what are we going to call the new pub there when it's built?' He waved the envelopes. 'And who wins a thousand pounds? From this, I see there's a second place of four hundred and an honorable mention good for a hundred. Sounds very nice. Let's see what we've got.'

He looked at the paper and chuckled.

Alex noticed her mother slip through the archway leading to the restaurant and inn. She stood against the wall, her head on one side. It did Alex good to see Lily interested again.

'The first prize goes to The Cock and Bull, submitted by Alfred Short. Is Alfred here?'

A red-faced local farmer got up amid shouts and cheers. He came forward to accept his prize. 'A round on me,' he announced to the bar. 'Nothing over a pound apiece, mind you.'

Everyone laughed.

Kev Winslet got second for Bottoms Up and the honorable mention went to new incomer, Basil Lloyd-Edwards with Heads It Was Queenie, which Alex decided was a stretch for most imaginations.

Alfred Short bought drinks for all who wanted them and the atmosphere rose to a roaring pitch.

Smiling, Bob put an arm around Alex's shoulders. 'This is something,' he said over the din.

What Alex felt was Grant's eyes boring into her. She looked away and he walked rapidly to Lady Mekins' table where he stood behind the woman and leaned down to talk into her ear. Grant raised his face to stare at Alex but Lady Mekins frowned at him and shook his head. What Alex wouldn't give to be able to hear what he was saying about her. Whatever it was, he didn't seem to be getting a positive reaction.

Taking advantage of the diversion he'd caused, Bob Hill urged Alex aside. 'I've wanted to talk to you again,' he said. 'Have you given any more thought to expanding your business?'

She decided he had a face she liked very much. He had the look of a man you could trust. 'Not really, Bob. It's been busy around here and I don't think I took the suggestion seriously.'

'I want you to,' he said. 'You know what you're doing and I want you to put in a manager and run the Cock and Bull for me. Whenever you're comfortable with taking it on as a partner, we'll work that out.'

Alex didn't know what to say. Was she interested in expanding? She was only human, so the thought of doing well enough to grow the business appealed to her, but she was happy as she was. Then there was Tony and she could no longer even pretend she didn't want to consider him in her long-term plans.

'Alex?' Bob prompted her.

Before she could think of a response, her mother took her by the arm and whispered, 'Come into the kitchens with me.' Lily's head was purposefully down and she kept on walking.

The tug was insistent and Alex barely had time to catch Bob Hill's eyes before Lily hurried her away. 'What is it, Mum?' They faced each other in the middle of the kitchen. 'What? Something's happened.'

'Nothing's happened. Nothing is going to happen. Please, just this once, do as I ask you to do.'

'Just this once? What are you talking about?'

'Please come with me. We can't be interrupted. We'll go upstairs to your room. No one will expect that.'

Alex absorbed the desperation in her mother's eyes and took off along the back passageway leading to the restaurant and the stairs to the inn. The room she kept for times when it was easier not to drive up the hill to her house was just to the left at the top of the staircase. Lily had the key and let them in.

'Mum, will you put me out of my misery, please?' Alex asked as Lily closed the door. 'You're frightening me.'

Lily closed and locked the door. 'I'm sorry to do this to you. I haven't managed things very well. Liz Hadley can take over my work for as long as necessary. She's very good.'

'You're not managing whatever this is well, Mum.' That wasn't how she'd meant to sound. 'I mean . . . just tell me what you mean.'

Her mother's hands went to her neck. 'As soon as I saw Bob Hill's name in the papers with all the fuss about the development, I wondered if he was the Bob Hill I knew a long time ago. The pictures were grainy and I wouldn't let myself try to find out for sure. I didn't want it to be him and for as long as I didn't have proof I could tell myself this was a different man with the same ordinary name. It isn't. He's more than thirty years older than when I last saw him but it's the same face. A man, not a teenager, but it's the same person.

'Alex, Bob Hill is your father. He doesn't know that, although he's obviously drawn to you and the fact that you helped him the way you did has given him a reason to stay close to you. At least, that's what he thinks. He must feel an affinity he can't understand. If you get to know him better you may have to win his son over. He doesn't like you although he probably doesn't know why either. And Rob's wife – I called him Rob – could be overdoing how much fussy attention she pays you. And I may be automatically jealous of anyone else who could come into your life and share you. Other than Tony.'

Too much. Was this what freefall from a plane felt like while you waited for your chute to open? Alex swallowed with difficulty. She couldn't explain the sensation.

'You do believe what I'm telling you?'

She nodded.

'He has his own life and I have mine. I wouldn't have it any differently now. At the time, I loved him and I thought he loved me, but we were too young.

'I'm going to stay out of the way, probably at James's. It's secluded there and I want to explain this to him. He deserves that and much more.'

'You don't want Bob Hill to know the truth, do you?' Alex said. She felt shivery. 'At least not yet. He doesn't have to.'

'Thank you. Let me have time to work out how to deal with it all. That's a lot to ask, I know, when you must be very confused.'

'I'll be all right.' Would she? 'You come first with me. Can I tell Tony?'

Her mother's smile was a surprise – and puzzling. 'I want you to. Once James knows. And I will find a way to deal with it.'

'You've got guts.' Alex hugged her mother, held her for a long time.

THIRTY-FOUR

They all gathered around the series of computer screens ranged in front of Bill Lamb. On one screen, he pointed to a face wedged into a gap between the shoulders of two taller women. They were part of a group in front of an anonymous building. 'That's Beverly Irving. According to Lily Duggins.' He began to enlarge the picture, stopping and pulling back each time the image blurred completely. 'Dark hair, dark eyes, a bit chunky by the look of the face. Lily is here this morning, working with a sketch artist. They're trying for something that might be current together with another showing some age progression between this—' he pointed to the screen – 'and now. And since we're convinced this woman went into some sort of disguise, they'll be altering her appearance by different means. Subtle stuff mostly. Hair style and color – that sort of thing.'

The Gloucester digs gave access to all the equipment possible. And being back in their own quarters, the squad had the interview rooms and extra bodies Dan and Bill had decided they were going to need as they poured their all into assembling everything they had on three cases with one common element: violent death. Twice by blunt force head trauma and once, well, once by some exhibition of rage when a bottle was driven down Lance Pullinger's throat while he was too drunk to fight off his assailant.

'Gladys Lymer was here yesterday afternoon,' LeJuan put in. They're going to compare what each of them come up with. We're looking for similarities in what they say. The artist interprets witness comments in the sketches. Don't ask me how.'

'I saw Gladys Lymer downstairs,' Detective Constable Miller said. 'She looked scared out of her mind – if she's got one.'

'Nice, Miller,' Longlegs said. He wasn't one for snide jabs.

Bill wasn't in the mood for sniping between the troops and was about to say so when Dan walked in. He had several rolls of paper with him and began opening them up and tacking them to the boards. 'This is the one in the photo,' he said. 'With help from Lily.'

'Will you look at that,' Bill said. 'I know he had the photo as a guide but I still don't know how you bring a face to life the way these people do.'

'The artist is a woman,' Dan said, sounding distracted. 'Delia Stroud.' He unrolled a second picture, this one showing an older version of Beverly.

'Forties in this, do you think?' LeJuan asked. 'Good looking but I don't like her eyes. Something strange there.'

'Like she's pretending not to be angry, but she's mad as hell,' Ashton suggested.

'Yeah,' LeJuan said, hands on hips. 'Exactly. Doesn't matter a damn, though. Who knows what she looks like now?'

'More like this, according to the artist. See. Older. Eyes show it, and jaw. Thinner. The gray in the hair is window-dressing for now. At least a couple of these will be in tonight's papers and on the tele.'

Several phones, including Dan's, rang at the same time. Bill reached for the one on the desk where he sat. 'Bill Lamb. Yes. Go for it.' He listened and couldn't help smiling. Propping the phone between ear and shoulder, he jotted notes.

When he hung up he was in the middle of an expectant silence. He pointed to himself and Dan nodded, yes. 'The burned-out vehicle was a Jeep all right. Someone made a good attempt to destroy the VIN but didn't do a good job. In a hurry, I'd say. Enough left to make a stab at the identification number. Stolen about two years ago in Hull. Most recent trace to a used-car dealer with form for various reasons. He hasn't done much time. He's in London – Southwark. He'll be getting visitors shortly.'

Dan sang, '"Nine green bottles . . ."' and added, 'almost anyway. Now the bloody rest had better fall. What else?' He looked around for other reports from calls.

Silence told that story.

'Mustn't be greedy,' Dan said with a faint smile.

Miller stood up at her desk. 'Vince Crowley called Lost Property asking if they had his wife's papers.'

This was delivered with a straight face and it was several seconds before laughter broke out and Miller sat down again, looking pleased with herself.

Barry Trafford came into the room. He struggled out of his jacket, moving his mobile from hand to hand. 'Did you see the news alert on the tele? They're quick. I haven't even seen those recreations yet.' He glanced at the boards, saw the sketches and shrugged. 'How long have we had them?'

'I got these an hour or so ago,' Dan said. 'Buggered if I know who makes these decisions. But there's nothing to be lost by getting them out there.'

'I've got something on the carriage house clothing at Knighton,' LeJuan said. 'This is a strange one. The women's stuff is all different sizes and came from different shops in London. The men's clothing was all bought at the same shop in Burford and it's in the same size, but it wouldn't have fitted Lance Pullinger. Too small.'

'We know one thing for sure,' Bill said. 'We aren't dealing with professionals. Did they think we wouldn't check?'

'I talked to Lily this morning,' LeJuan said.

'He talks to everyone,' Bill muttered. 'Women, that is. Regular ladies' man, our LeJuan.'

'As I was saying.' LeJuan grinned. 'Lily mentioned she doesn't like the way Grant Hill looks at Alex. Like he hates her guts. I think it worries Lily. We might want to look deeper into what's got his knickers in a twist about Alex.'

'As you say, not deeply enough if he's still giving her the evil eye.' His phone rang and he took it from the breast pocket of his shirt. 'O'Reilly.' He listened for so long that the room gradually fell silent. Some worked. Most watched him and waited. His lips parted and he stared straight ahead. Finally, he said, 'You're fucking pulling my leg,' and listened some more. 'Right. I'm on it. That's one fox who never crossed my mind. All we have to do is get it in the henhouse and shut the door.'

Dan slid the mobile back in his pocket and crossed his arms. 'We've had an anonymous informant. Female, from what they could tell. Thinks we might like to know that Esme Hill was having an affair with Lance Pullinger. A long-standing affair.'

THIRTY-FIVE

'Let's go somewhere and talk,' Alex said, taking Tony by the hand and pulling him away from the pond on Folly's village green. 'You must have turned your mobile off again. I couldn't find you. What are you doing, wandering around out here anyway? It's the middle of the afternoon. Aren't there any animals you should be saving?'

'Not wandering – walking Katie,' Tony said. 'And I'm between patients. Anything else you want to know, Ms Duggins.' He caught her around the waist and kissed her. 'We don't have to talk, do we,' he added against her mouth. 'How are you doing? I was coming to dig you out soon.'

She pushed back and looked at him. 'I'm very confused.

Probably more confused than I was last night. And this morning before we left home. I don't know what to do next.'

'I like it when you call my house home, Alex.'

'We spend a lot of time there.' She wouldn't let herself look away. 'If we'd been at my house I'd have called that home.'

'We don't need two houses, do we?'

Katie returned from the edge of the pond with mud all over her graying beige muzzle. Tony sat on his heels and wiped her off with a glove from his pocket.

'That was a loaded question,' Alex said. 'But not as loaded as it used to be. We will have to do something about us one of these days. And we are going to. I'm going to make a list of questions, for myself and for you. You can do the same, if you want to.'

He smiled up at her, squinting into pale sunlight that had found a thin patch in almost solid white cloud cover. 'Right. A list. I don't usually make them without including a few things I can cross off immediately, just to make myself feel good. That wouldn't be cheating for this list, would it?'

Alex tapped her chin thoughtfully. 'No. It wouldn't. Go for it then, put the list somewhere safe and think about it. I'll do the same. I mean this. I'm not joking.'

'Right you are.' A little of the light went out of his smile. She knew he'd like her to go ahead and tell him when they'd go over those lists but the light moments had to be over for now. 'I'm scared, Tony. For my mother. And for some other people. I've spent hours putting together some of the bits I know, or I've observed, or heard, about the case. Or should I say cases, plural. Mum overheard something in Gloucester this morning. Dan would be furious but it wasn't her fault if the Serious Crimes people shout at each other when they're working.'

Tony bounced to his feet and pulled her hand beneath his elbow. 'Do you want to tell me about the things you've been putting together first, or what Lily overheard?' He bent to slip on Katie's leash.

'Beverly's alive so I'm worried about Gladys's safety.'

'So are the police and I don't doubt they're taking precautions.'

'I don't think Winifred Sibley was killed to scare Gladys.

Winifred had been told what Gladys knew so that's why she was killed – so she couldn't repeat what she knew. Why wouldn't Gladys be in just as much danger now?'

'We just covered that,' Tony said, walking them slowly in the direction of the road. 'I believe you're probably right on both of those counts but we have to trust the police to know, too, and do what they have to do. Something could have gone wrong that brought about Winifred's death. But I can't get past the idea that there was an element of trying to control Gladys without killing her. Doing that would have been a very direct connection to the past.'

'Ive to get to the bottom of it all. Grant Hill detests me, but not because we share the same father . . .' Alex turned away from him. 'Please don't make a big thing out of it. I'm not ready. Mum finally told me Bob Hill is my father and I haven't processed it yet. My mother won't say more about it. I know it has to be a shock to you, Tony, but it's more of a shock to me.'

'Oh, Alex. I'm sorry if you're taking it hard but I think he's a good man. Let it settle in your mind, love. Please.'

'Thank you,' she said quietly. He was always so reasonable and she loved him for it. 'I don't think Grant knows about it, any more than Bob does. But Grant has decided Bob is romantically interested in me and it's driving him crackers. Bob's kind to me and has made reasons to do nice things for me. Grant probably knows all of that, even the offer of a partnership in the new pub perhaps. Bob's very open. I can't blame Grant for coming to conclusions that are way out of line.'

Tony stood still. 'But Dan knows Grant threatened you. He'll have figured out what's going on in Grant's head by now.'

'They showed sketches of Beverly on TV today. I know you won't have seen them.'

He shook his head, no. 'What does Lily say?'

'I don't think I mentioned she's staying at your dad's. More secluded, she says, and she doesn't want to run into Bob Hill. I called her and she'd just got back from Gloucester and working with the artist – and trying to talk to Dan. I could tell she'd been crying. Of course, with what the artist has done so far, it just brought everything back but it didn't move her any closer to really knowing what Beverly looks like now. And she's sure she hasn't seen her because she says even in the later sketch it's still the Beverly she knew.'

'Are you going to let me in on what Lily overheard in Gloucester.'

'Let's sit on a bench. Keep your eyes open for anyone coming near us.'

Katie noted their change of direction and pulled toward the bench. She jumped up and seated herself in the center, making it plain she wanted one of them on either side of her. Tony and Alex obliged.

'Let me just say that I think Grant Hill has some plan to work everything out to the Hills' advantage. Like I mentioned, I overheard that Grant could be involved in sort of staging the carriage house. I'm not sure what that means exactly, but I do know Lance Pullinger used to live there some of the time and it sounded as if he might have had a female friend there quite often.'

'I got that, I think.'

'The most damning thing my mum heard today was Dan announcing that they'd had an anonymous call to the station from a woman – probably a woman – who said it was Esme Hill who was having an affair with Lance.'

Turning toward her, Tony hitched up a knee and held it. 'I didn't see that coming. Who would make a call like that? Someone with their eye on Bob Hill, perhaps? Stirring up doubt about Esme Hill's fidelity?'

'Could be,' Alex agreed. 'He's in a business where he's around a lot of people, women as well as men. And they must have a social life. I know you'll pooh-pooh this but I wonder about Lady Mekins. If her husband and son are the center of her existence – and I've heard her say they are – why is she always hanging around the Hills?'

'I think I heard how Audra and Esme met at the gym and they've been fast friends ever since.' Tony followed the flight of a pigeon for a moment. 'Have you noticed Audra hanging around Bob?'

'I've only seen them in the same place once but no, I haven't. And the two women are close friends, you can tell that.'

'So, is someone jealous of them both?'

'I've been invited to Knighton late tomorrow afternoon. For tea or something. Esme called me and asked if I'd like to go. She said she wanted to get to know me better, which creeps me out a little. Not because I don't like her, but, well, you know.'

Tony said, 'Yes, I do. You're not going, are you?'

'I said I would. It seemed a bit offhand to just refuse and I couldn't explain why, if I did say, no. And I might find out something useful.'

'Alex, Alex. You never switch off that nose of yours.'

Tony heard the door to the clinic open. Radhika had the afternoon off, so he went through the passage – and walked into Grant Hill.

'You won't like this,' Grant said, shoving past and into the sitting room with its old-fashioned and worn chintz armchairs and ancient electric bar fire. 'Is there anyone else here?'

Tony followed him and stood just inside the door. 'Do you have a sick animal?'

'Don't be funny. I'm sick. Sick and tired of your lady friend playing games with my family. I bet you don't know what she's getting up to with my father, do you.'

'I advise you to watch your mouth.'

'Or you'll what? What will you do? Tell the very small world you live in that the woman you sleep with is into hooking up with men old enough to be her father if she thinks they'll make her rich?'

Pity rapidly replaced anger. Throwing the idiot out on his arse would feel good for a minute or so, then he'd remember how it felt to fear the loss of a parent, the complete collapse of your family as you knew it. Tony's mother had been ill for a long time before she died and when she'd been slipping away faster and faster, he'd panicked and made things even harder for his father by blaming him for not being able to cure her. After she was gone it was as if everything Tony had thought he could trust had turned on him. For different reasons than Tony's, this young man was starting through the same tunnel filled with jeering mind games.

'Answer me,' Grant shouted. 'You need to show her up for what she is. Don't you have what it takes to save your self-respect and stop her from ruining a man who's at a certain age when his ego needs stroking? He's making a fool of himself and doesn't know it. You should see him fawning over her. It would make you sick. It makes me sick.'

'Are you finished?' The pity Tony had felt was waning. Grant Hill could simply be a nasty young man afraid of someone else getting any part of what he considered his – and possibly his sister's. 'Alex is kind to everyone. You're mistaking that kindness for something else and it's insulting.'

'I came here to give you a chance,' Grant said. He ran fingers through his hair and it stood on end, making him look like a panicky teen. 'Warn her off. That'll be the last you hear of it – either of you. Tell her I mean it when I ask her to stay away from my father, completely.'

The tone was unpleasant, threatening. 'Is that some sort of warning? If so, it's a bad idea. What Alex decides to do is her business. I'm not her keeper.'

Grant shoved his hands in his pockets as if he wanted to make sure he didn't do something with them that he'd later regret. 'Don't say I didn't come to you and try to make peace.'

'Is that what this was?' Tony laughed. 'You'd better go before you make an even bigger fool of yourself. Let grown-ups work out their own issues. They won't admire you for interfering.'

Shoving into Tony as he left the room, Grant said in a voice with an hysterical edge, 'You're all the same. You're jealous people. You aren't happy and you can't stand to see anyone else happy. You want what's ours. For all I know, you're encouraging her. You'll find out what I can do about that.'

He hurried from the building, slamming a shoulder against the doorjamb as he went.

THIRTY-SIX

efore six the next morning, a call from Harriet Burke catapulted Alex and Tony from sleep. Tony swung his legs over the side of the bed and grabbed his mobile.

'Tony?' Harriet all but whispered. 'I've never done a thing like this before but you gave me this number and I had to make sure you knew. You'll have to go to Alex and tell her. She'll need a lot of comforting. We think it's important for you to decide how to deal with it before people start babbling and asking all sorts of questions. You know how they are. Then they'll talk about so-called remembering this and that and how they can't imagine why they didn't notice at the time. You—'

'Harriet,' Tony interrupted, as gently as he could. 'Please, take a big breath and explain what's upsetting you.'

Alex scrambled to sit beside him and put her face by his, trying to hear the conversation. He moved the phone closer to her ear.

'Do you take the morning paper?' Harriet said.

'At the clinic, yes,' Tony said.

'Well, we get two copies and we each read one in bed,' Harriet announced. 'The murders are all over the thing. Of course, there aren't many other things of interest, are there? No. But, and it's hard to say this, but there's an unsavory piece written in that unpleasant secret-sharing way these people have sometimes. A source who can't be named for their own safety, that's what it says.'

Tony closed his eyes. 'What else does it say?' He thought he knew what was coming.

'It's one of those local interest pieces – at least I suppose it is. Just a sidebar but on the front page. About how some women can't be trusted with other women's husbands. A well-known local woman who owns one of the most successful businesses in Folly-on-Weir likes multiple men in her life. Lately she's been seen in rather questionable situations with a very prosperous businessman who is much older than she is. This isn't the first time this woman has caused heartbreak. She ruined her first husband's life with her demands during a messy divorce in which many consider her the unreasonable party.'

'That little shit,' Tony muttered.

'Excuse me?' Harriet said. 'What did you say? What can we do to help? You see, everyone will know who this is talking about, don't you think?' The sound of rustling paper was clear. 'And Mary says to tell you there's another artist's sketch of this Beverly woman – in a different article, of course – it shows her with more gray in her hair and older again than the first pictures. The police have had a lot of calls but it doesn't say anything about finding this person.'

'Thank you very much, Harriet,' Tony said. 'And thank Mary for me, please. I'll talk to Alex and we'll see you soon. Meanwhile, the only thing you can do to help is be noncommittal. The truth will come out eventually and we'll hope it doesn't take long.'

Alex held his arm and rested her head against his shoulder. 'I'm beginning to wonder if we will see all this cleared up.'

'I think we will but I don't think it's a good idea for you to go to Knighton today, do you? Under the circumstances?'

'If I don't and Grant finds out I was coming but changed my mind, he'll use that as proof that his nasty tales have frightened me because they're true and now they're in the open. Let me think about it.'

Yesterday's struggling sun was a memory. Lashings of rain slanted out of gunmetal gray skies and a vicious wind drove the rain harder while it made creaking monsters of the trees.

Dan ran from the car to the parish hall and cranked the door handle until he all but fell inside the building. Bill followed, cursing aloud at the infidelities of nature.

'Morning, guv, sergeant.' Ashton and Longlegs stared at their superiors. 'Early, aren't you? Good thing LeJuan got the coffee here. No pastries yet, though.' That was Longlegs' contribution. Ashton continued to stare.

'All right, all right,' Dan said. 'This isn't the first time you've seen either of us early in the morning. I'm glad you got the message to be back here today. I hope you also heard you'd better be on your toes. My temper is very short. You'll have seen what's in the papers and there will be an early news conference on the tele. Where's LeJuan?'

'He said he'll be back in half an hour,' Longlegs said. 'That was, well, it was a little while ago.'

'Does he have a romantic interest in Folly?' Bill asked. 'Someone he's romantically interested in, I mean?'

'I wouldn't know about that,' Ashton said, deadpan.

The constable answered a phone and frowned while he listened. 'I think he knows but I'll tell him. Yes, I'm listening.' There was a pause. 'Is that so? Any confirmed contact for that. Let me ask Detective Chief Inspector O'Reilly and one of us will get right back to you.'

Dan waited while Ashton hung up. 'Well?'

'Response to one of yesterday's sketches that sounds promising, guv. Woman says she's a retired nurse who worked for a plastic surgeon in London. They're asking what you want to do about it.'

Crossing his arms, Dan did his best to keep his tone level. 'What about the retired nurse who worked for the plastic surgeon?'

'Oh, sorry, guv. She thinks she remembers a patient who looked like the second sketch of Beverly Irving. That name doesn't ring a bell. She says if the woman in the sketch is the one she's thinking of, she doesn't look anything like that anymore.'

THIRTY-SEVEN

The mews flat where Joan Sperry lived was in St John's Wood. Regency villas surrounded Hamilton Mews, its cobbles slick and wet today. Lords Cricket Ground was a short walk away.

Dan and Bill had arranged to interview Ms Sperry themselves and driven from the Cotswolds to London.

'Evidently plastic surgery pays well,' Dan commented. 'Even the trusted nurses. This place must be worth a bomb.' They parked against a high stone wall at the back of the house where former owners would once have kept a horse and carriage stabled beneath Ms Sperry's flat.

'We're a few minutes early,' Dan said. 'The best way to do this is with a lot of respect and gratitude. You agree?'

Bill clicked his tongue. He hadn't been keen on doing this interview but Dan had rushed them out of Folly without discussion. 'You know how I feel about not being in the driver's seat. I do agree with you but I hope she's not a talker. And I hope she isn't eating up a chance at some fame or what she thinks could be fame.'

'We won't know till we get in there,' Dan said. 'It'll be obvious if that's the story. Did someone get back to us on Carmen Hill?'

'Back at some fancy school she goes to. She did go early but some of the girls do that to settle in. That's the school's story and I don't think they'll budge. I think the parents wanted her out of the way, though.'

'Let's go.' Dan pushed open his door. 'Keep your mobile on so you can step out if you need to.'

The door in the left lower part of the property, 2A, opened before Dan and Bill got there. Joan Sperry must have been watching from one of her upstairs flat windows and run downstairs to greet them.

'Good morning,' she said.

They took out their warrant cards and Dan made the introductions.

'In you go then,' Ms Sperry said, standing aside to let them precede her up the stairs. 'To the right past the kitchen. The sitting room is at the end. Make yourselves comfortable. Will you have tea or coffee?'

'Tea would be good, thank you,' Bill said although Dan's preference was for getting on with interviews minus the almost inevitable wait for refreshments.

'I'll also have tea,' he said.

The sitting room, long and narrow with a small marine style stove set into a red brick fireplace and radiating heat, was a room any reader would love. Dark green leather armchairs, footstools, strategically placed tables supporting books and magazines, a window seat upholstered in green and red tartan and partially hidden by heavy curtains in matching fabric, hung from a brass rod and looped back on either side.

An open book and a pair of glasses lay on the slightly sagging seat of a single fabric-covered wingback. Joan Sperry's chair, no doubt. She was reading short stories by someone named Flannery O'Connor, a vaguely familiar name to Dan.

'Do sit down,' Ms Sperry said, entering the room behind them. 'Just move anything in your way, please.'

She poured tea, added milk as requested, and left the mugs on the brass coffee table she'd used. Dan was glad not to be presented with fiddly china cups and saucers.

'I'll let you take the lead,' the woman said, sitting on the edge of a chair that threw her face in the shade and left Dan and Bill squinting toward the window. 'So, fire away and I'll answer what I can.'

From her tone, she was used to being in charge, even when she was telling someone else they were in charge.

'You recognized artist's sketches of Beverly Irving,' Dan began.

'I believe so.'

'Did you work at a busy practice?'

'That depends on what you mean by busy. We were an exclusive practice but there were never any open appointments.'

Dan glanced at Bill who hadn't written anything in his notebook yet. He stirred and said, 'Roughly how many patients did the doctor see in a day?'

'Surgeon,' she corrected Bill. 'That varied. He operated in the morning so there were no consultations until the afternoon. Clients required different lengths of consultation.'

'Depending on how much they were having done?' Bill said, finally jotting something down.

'Depending on the procedure being considered,' Ms Sperry said.

Dan barely stopped himself from remarking that she'd repeated Bill's question.

'On average?' Dan said. 'Four, perhaps?'

'Rarely. Two or three.'

'Still, two or three new people an afternoon. That's a lot of people to remember over the years since you think you saw this woman. I congratulate you on your recall.' Dan smiled at her.

'I have a better memory for faces than names.'

Apparently she wasn't a talker, nor easily flattered.

He picked up the file he'd carried in and slid out copies of the police artist's sketches. 'These are as clear as they get,' he said, passing them to her.

She put on her glasses and looked at each one carefully. 'I've seen her and I'm sure she was a client. Yes, she was definitely a client.'

'When a client came for a consultation, photographs were taken?'

'Yes. Always.'

'How long did it usually take between that appointment and surgery?'

'That depended.' The skies darkened and Ms Sperry turned on a lamp beside her.

'On what?' Bill asked bluntly.

She didn't smile even a little. 'On whether the case was for medical reasons, as in post-surgical reconstruction or perhaps a child born with an issue. Those were done quickly.'

'And then?' Bill kept his eyes on his notebook.

'Then the importance of the procedure or procedures.'

'Importance?' Still Bill didn't look up.

'I think you can work that out, sergeant. One doesn't like to mention money, does one?'

'This one is perfectly happy mentioning money, Ms Sperry,' Dan said. 'You're saying that if the patient is going to spend enough money, that buys a better place in the line?'

'As I said, you can work out these things.'

'And did Beverly Irving get treated quickly?'

'As far as I remember, she did. It really was a wonderful job. Eyes, nose, mouth, cheeks, jawline. Reconstruction, that is. There was a complete facelift of course. Naturally we didn't do the teeth. She was sent elsewhere for that.'

Bill glanced up and around the room. 'What did you say was the name of the surgeon you worked for?'

'I didn't.'

'May we have his address?'

'That won't be possible.'

Dan sighed. 'Impeding the law can be a very serious thing, Ms Sperry.' They could find out the details without her help.

'I'm not impeding the law. I remember this woman because she was transformed. It was amazing. I had never seen anything like it and I've seen many, many extensive plastic surgeries.'

'What we need most are the photos taken after the surgery.

As Beverly looked when all the work was finished and as she presumably looks now.'

'Full healing takes longer than just "after surgery" as you put it. I think you mean after full recovery.'

'Yes, Ms Sperry, I do.' Dan gave her another smile.

'There aren't any photographs.'

The desire to groan overwhelmed him. He clamped his teeth together.

'What does that mean?' Bill asked.

'If memory serves, the patient would not be photographed after recovery. When the transformation is that extensive, patients quite often refuse to be photographed.'

Dan considered his next move. 'In that case and since this could well become a most serious crime case, I must insist on contacting the surgeon.'

'He wouldn't be able to give you as good a description as I can. His magic was a rare one – seeing the before and after and how to get there in his mind. He died seven years ago. Only the records of medical cases were retained. I shouldn't even be telling you that but I'm doing my duty as best I can.'

'You're an extraordinary woman, Ms Sperry, and I'm grateful for all the help you're giving us.' *And why didn't you tell us these things before?*

'I'm glad to be of any help I can. The patient underwent an impressive number of procedures. I think I could do better if I wrote down everything I can think of. If I'd had more time before you came, I would have tried to get it ready.'

Dan took a card from his inside pocket. 'Please contact me the moment you're ready with your description. Call me at any time if you have a question.'

Joan Sperry studied the card. 'I can say she had liposuction – a lot of it. And breast augmentation – also extensive. She wanted to be unrecognizable and that was an accomplishment.'

This time Bill drove and Dan gave directions. 'The Duke of York,' he said, 'Queen Anne's Terrace, I think. Find the St John's Wood tube station and we've got it made. The station is on the corner with Acacia Road. If I'm remembering it correctly, you take the first right off Acacia.'

'When did you get to be an expert on London pubs?'

'When I lived here for a couple of years. I had a friend with a flat somewhere around here. Wonder what happened to her.'

Bill saw the tube station in question ahead. 'Her? Another one let you get away, you clever dog.'

'She was the one who got away.'

Bill looked sideways at him. Perhaps Dan O'Reilly of the granite heart looked a bit sad. But anyone who knew how much he regretted his divorce, and the constant struggle to get more time with his son, Calum, knew that O'Reilly's brittle shell was just that, a shell that could be cracked.

'I used to go to Lords for cricket with a couple of the other young constables. We'd go to this pub afterwards. Go down here. It's on the corner of St John's Wood Terrace. There you go. Painted green with green awnings. Great to sit outside but not on days like this.'

They parked and went inside for a full-bodied pint apiece and servings of roast beef and potatoes with vegetables. 'Knives are optional for this beef,' Dan said.

Hungry and tired, they treated themselves to another half each with the reminder that they didn't have to hurry back to the car.

A call came in on Dan's mobile followed by a series of short answers on Dan's end. 'Go ahead,' he said, almost at the end. 'Get the results to me as quickly as you can.'

Bill gave him a questioning look.

'Joan Sperry,' Dan said. 'Says she knows a sketch artist who could give us a picture of the new Beverly Irving. The artist works very fast, as the witness speaks. Joan says she has a clear picture of her in her mind now. Apparently, that's unusual for her. She sounded excited. We won't hold our breath.'

Dan drove this time and for streets he hadn't seen in years he made the route seem very familiar.

'Are we going to let this Beverly issue hang for a day or two?' Bill asked. 'Clearing up three murders—'

'Yes. That's what we're going to do. So far we've got to follow up Bob Hill, Grant Hill, and whoever placed the call trying to finger Esme Hill as Lance Pullinger's lady – the three of them with more than casual connections to Lance and probably Darla. The thorn in my side is Winifred Sibley. Nothing about her fits in with the other two – not really.'

'What about Gladys Lymer and Frank?'

'Yes,' Dan said. 'They belong on the pile, too. And much as I don't like saying so, Lily does as well.'

'But not Alex?'

Bill enjoyed irritating the people he liked best – something Dan didn't understand. 'Sure,' he said. 'Put her on the list, too.'

Bill mumbled to himself and shut up. The drive became very silent.

They were passing Bourton-on-the-Water when the sound of Dan's mobile ringing startled Bill. Dan answered, waited, and said, 'You wouldn't call me if you weren't worried, Tony. Look at it like this. At Knighton, they'll know Alex is visiting because Esme invited her over. So, they'll also know there's no mystery about her being there. Relax. Spay an extra dog or cat. Or do a crossword puzzle. She's been there about half an hour, right? Right, so let it be. You have no reason to make a fuss because Alex is at Knighton. But thank you for letting me know. We'll be back in Folly shortly. I'll check in with you when we get there.'

THIRTY-EIGHT

Following the directions of the maid who let her into the house, Alex walked out into a winter-sad kitchen garden at the back of the house.

'Go right. Then walk on the path through an opening in the big wall,' the maid had said. Alex got to the path and looked back. This was her father's house, his family's house for a long time. How strange she felt standing there.

She didn't belong and that was fine with her, but how could she not get goosebumps from connecting with a past she might have shared?

Through an opening in the wall, she went, and across mushy brown grass until the path became solid again. Eventually she was among familiar trees and the feeling this time was guilt. She smiled at herself. The previous visit had yielded interesting information but she had been sneaky – sneaky in a righteous cause. Or so she still hoped.

The big building with a domed skylight must be the pool house where she would find Esme. Fascinated as she was with Knighton, when she got to the entrance, Alex wished she hadn't come. In Esme's place, she wouldn't have chosen to take a swim when she expected a guest, someone she hardly knew.

Should she bag this and go home? Tony had tried to persuade her not to come.

'Are you looking for me?' Grant reached over her shoulder and pushed open one of the doors to the pool house. 'I'm touched. Welcome.'

Alex's heart beat a staccato rhythm. She felt sick. 'Hello,' she said. 'I'm meeting your mother. She was kind enough to invite me so we could get to know one another better.'

Trapped between his body and the open space between the doors, Alex went forward into the humid inside of the building. The only light was from sconces that threw muted yellowish fans upward against the walls, and a gray-white illumination through the sky dome. The pool gave off white mist that wafted above the water.

'There's mother. Sitting on the wall at the other end. She's waving at one of us. That's probably Audra swimming laps. That woman is a fitness fanatic. Excuse me, I'll change.' He walked away and disappeared into what Alex assumed was a changing room.

'Come on over, darling.' Esme's voice echoed through the towering space. 'Where are your swim things?'

'I didn't know you had swimming in mind,' Alex called back. She tried never to admit that she couldn't swim, or not effectively. 'I'll be happy watching and relaxing.' A row of chaises stood close to the edge of the pool at Esme's end.

Audra, in a white swim cap and goggles, continued to stroke the length of the pool, turn, and repeat the process.

Alex reached Esme. 'Carry on. It's warm in here and that can't be bad, can it? I'll sit and enjoy myself.' She took off her coat, pulled a chaise even closer to the pool and sat down.

There had been no reply from Esme who watched her over a shoulder.

A dull drone, muffled but steady, settled in the center of Alex's brain. The sound had to come from air conditioning, or pumps. This place must have all sorts of equipment in operation. Feeling claustrophobic in so big a space made no sense, but she did.

'Do you swim every day?' Alex asked, growing very uncomfortable.

'Just two or three times a week when I'm not in London,' Esme said. 'You're very pretty, you know. It's too bad you're not the right age for that naughty son of mine. He needs a good woman to settle him down.'

'It's too soon for that,' Alex said, swallowing the disgust she felt. 'Give him time to be young and enjoy himself.'

'Grant is troublesome. He's always been troublesome. Sometimes I think he's jealous of my love for his father. You know how some sons are. They don't like sharing their mothers.'

Alex didn't know, didn't want to know. 'Swim, Esme. You'll cool off too much sitting there like that.'

Esme climbed to stand at the very edge of the pool and took a long, clean dive into the water. She swam the crawl cleanly, making very little wake, made a professional looking turn and did the breast stroke back. Alex was in awe of the woman's strength. Every inch of her was smooth muscle and her shoulders and arms propelled her through the water with enviable efficiency.

In front of Alex once more, she remained in the water, her forearms crossed on top of the end wall. 'I'm sorry for not greeting you properly, Alex,' she said. 'I think I'm in a terrible mess and I don't know what to do. I came out here to think. I wish Audra hadn't come – her timing is awfully bad sometimes.'

Alex scooted all the way to the foot of the chaise and leaned forward. 'Can I do anything to help you?'

'I don't think so but you're very sweet to ask. Tell me, in the paper today, did they mean you in that nasty little article on the front page.'

How to answer that without causing more of a problem? 'Someone made a point of telling me it was about me,' she said. At least she wasn't lying; the hushed lunchtime conversation at the Black Dog had been unmistakable. 'But I don't see how it could have been. Tony and I are very close. We have been for a long time and everyone knows it. They didn't mention names.'

'Isn't that always the way it is?' Esme said. 'Audra felt she had to suggest it was referring to you and Bob, which is ridiculous.'

'Oh! That's horrible.' And coming from Esme's lips even the suggestion was appalling. 'Why would she say that to you?'

'Audra is the best friend I've ever had. I know she didn't mean to hurt me. She just wants to make sure nothing unpleasant happens to me. In a way, it's the same with Grant. He wants to help me. But why does the boy do such dangerous things? He burned up that vehicle, you know. I think he must have anyway. Please don't mention anything I tell you in confidence. I just feel so strongly I can trust you. Grant's been angry all the time lately and he thought that Jeep was mine and it had been used in ways that would get me into trouble. It wasn't mine. I never saw it until it was burned out on Trap Hill.'

Alex noticed Grant in the doorway to the changing rooms, still dressed, watching them in the pool. He turned sharply toward the building exit and hurried out, not saying a word to anyone.

She returned her attention to Esme. 'You're trying to carry too much on your own.' Alex thought about what Esme had said. 'Bob is a man with a cool head. The two of you should work things out together before something really terrible happens.'

'How sensible you are,' Esme said. She shot an arm around Alex's neck and hauled her into the water. 'Silly girl,' she said as Alex came up sputtering. 'What sensible person sits beside a swimming pool with all their clothes and their shoes on? Now you've fallen in and who knows what kind of trouble you could get into?'

Trying to kick, her boots weighing her down, Alex grappled with Esme, pushing away as hard as she could and trying to turn toward the wall. She pulled in gulps of air – but Esme grabbed her hair and shoved her under again.

Water hammered at her eardrums. It was the only sound she heard while she held her breath and fought.

With hands under Alex's arms, Esme pushed her to the surface again, behind her this time where there was less danger of the woman getting kicked or clutched, Alex thought, vaguely.

Alex coughed and gasped. She couldn't reach her eyes and shook her head trying to clear her vision.

Esme put her mouth near Alex's ear. 'Listen to me, darling. Be very still and quiet and who knows, I may let you go. Think how sad you'll make those lovely people who care about you if you drown in a silly accident. Are you listening?'

'Yes,' Alex whispered past a raw throat.

'Good. This was a bad time for you to come fawning all over my husband. I need him now and I can't afford to lose him to you. That article was the final straw. I knew I had to do something about you. You see, I was deeply in love with another man, Lance Pullinger. Then I found out he was cheating on me with a colorless little nobody. Darla something. I have a temper, I admit it. I went to talk to the woman, to ask her to stay away, but she laughed at me. Laughed, mind you. And I hit her. I didn't mean to do it, but I killed her. And then I went to Lance who was mine, not hers, and he was too drunk to listen. I . . . he died and if anyone found out about my being there with him, they'd blame me. But I got away with both of those deaths. Until the police started poking around. And you thought you should interfere.'

A rush of heat engulfed Alex. She jerked her elbows back at Esme, and shouted, 'You fool. You greedy fool. What you had wasn't enough. A good husband and family wasn't enough. You wanted everything, and more, and look what you did – for nothing.'

'Shut up,' Esme screamed.

Alex twisted, and twisted, desperate to reach the woman's eyes, to scratch until she let go. Nothing worked. 'Darla Crowley was Lance Pullinger's sister,' she cried, spitting out water, gagging. 'He wasn't having an affair with her. He was looking after her because she was going through bad times. But you were too blindly jealous to find out the truth, so you killed them both. For nothing, Esme. Do you hear me? You killed them for nothing!'

Esme's breath came loud and fast. 'Liar. You're lying. I don't believe you.' But she made a choking sound and Alex knew the woman was crying, sobbing through her rage. 'Did you think Bob cared a damn about you?' Esme half-shrieked. 'You little idiot. I'm the kind of woman he's always wanted, not you. But it doesn't matter what you think. I'm alone now and I need him. There's no room for you and your meddling.'

'Didn't you hear what I just told you?' Alex said, gasping for air.

Esme had no intention of letting her go. This outpouring came from a sick need to confess to someone she didn't intend to keep alive once she'd finished talking. She had heard the futility of her own actions, she raged in her mind, but she couldn't let go of what she'd planned, the way out of her crimes she intended to claim.

Alex didn't allow herself to start trying to escape again. The more still she was, the more she breathed normally, the stronger she'd become and the more distracted Esme would be.

Where was Audra? Still swimming laps and oblivious of what was going on? Would she try to stop Esme if she realized?

'Winifred was a mistake,' Esme said, crying with every word. 'It was Audra's fault. Gladys heard Audra talk to me about it outside your damned pub, about how it might get out that I was involved with the murders. I had to make sure Gladys hadn't told Winifred. Gladys was Audra's problem. If the dog hadn't made all that noise in the garden, I might not have killed the woman, but I was afraid someone would hear the dog and call the police.'

Why did you kill Winifred? She never harmed anyone. Esme changed her grip, held Alex by the back of the neck and pushed her under. The move was unexpected and Alex swallowed water. She tried to catch some breath but blackness billowed in at her. Both arms swung out in helpless arcs. Down, she went, farther, deeper, blacker.

Fingers threaded through hers. Fingers, or something wet and solid. Her mind wavered in and out, and then panic wiped everything.

Her face cleared the surface once more. Water gurgled up through her throat. She retched and spat.

Screams poked through the thick blanket over Alex's brain. 'Stop it, Esme!' Audra, her goggles around her neck, fought with her 'best friend'.

Alex made to pull up her knees. She wanted her feet free of the boots and to get away from this pool and these women. One boot came off, then the other while she kept slipping beneath the water with every struggling move she made.

The drag lessened. The surface roiled around her and Audra's face, deep red, with the mouth stretched open, sank backward into the pool. Esme held onto the goggles, the straps twisted tightly around the other woman's neck.

'No,' Alex yelled. Why had she allowed herself to remain a lousy swimmer, almost a non-swimmer. 'Let her go. She's dying.'

Esme didn't answer. She snatched a handful of Alex's curls and pulled her beside the still-flailing Audra. Esme held them both underwater.

Then Alex was free. She spun toward the other women and reached for Esme, but someone else was already there, hauling her off while she kept fighting to get away.

Grant had his mother in a paralyzing grip, his arms under hers from behind and his hands clasped backward, around her neck. All she could do was rage as he towed her to the edge of the pool.

Alex heard running feet but she didn't see Audra. When she was a girl, Lily said – each time swimming lessons failed – if she ever had to swim, she would. Alex swam now and caught an arm as it rose from the water. She pulled as hard as she could until she saw Audra's chin and mouth on the surface.

'Got you,' a voice yelled. 'Relax, Alex. Hold the other one, Dan. Tony, help him. Ambulance is on its way.'

Alex went limp. Her eyes wanted to close but she forced them open. The pool house seethed with movement. LeJuan Harding's very muscular body turned to sidestroke with her toward the poolside. He raised her up until another man could lift her to safety.

'Get out of there, LeJuan,' she said, puffing at each word. 'It's not safe.'

'Somebody hold a towel up and I will,' LeJuan said. 'Got a bit carried away with the strip down. This man isn't swimming in his shoes – or anything else but his skin.'

THIRTY-NINE

'Why would you want to sit in the corridor?' Tony asked Alex. 'It's quieter in here.'

'It feels as if the only news we'll get is bad news.'

'Sweetheart.' He sat beside her on a small couch in one of the Gloucester Hospital waiting rooms. 'What exactly is the news you want? Esme Hill is a murderer and she's alive and going to be well. She's under police surveillance while she recovers. But she's the strongest woman any of us have seen – she'll do fine.'

'She'll be in prison where she should be,' Alex said. 'Don't imagine for a moment that I'm upset about her getting punished.'

'What then?'

Alex laced her fingers between her knees. Dan and Bill and the rest of the squad were going about the business of winding down a case that had left no benefits in its wake. Lily had made it clear she had no intention of talking to Bob Hill about the past they shared, which meant Alex was left with a decision she didn't know if she'd ever make; would she go to her father with the truth or let that truth die?

'I don't know really, Tony. Perhaps I'd like to think some small good thing had come out of all this. I don't think it has, do you?'

He put an arm around her. 'Not unless I can count feeling that you and I have moved closer together. Have we?'

'I think so.' Was that so much to give him?

'Then we got a lot, or I certainly did.'

There was a tap at the door. Dan entered, clearly taking in the picture of closeness Tony and Alex must make. 'I wanted you to see this,' he said. 'The London plastic surgery nurse had this done by a friend of hers. It's her remembered image of what Beverly Irving looked like following all the plastic surgery. When it was healed.' He gave Alex a sheet of heavy paper. 'The artist is amazingly fast. She draws almost entirely from the witness's spoken comments.'

She and Tony looked at the sketch together. 'How extraordinary,' Alex said. 'There's no doubt this was done only by using Ms Sperry's comments about the way this woman looked?'

'No doubt,' Dan said. 'The artist is well known and trusted. She would have had no way of knowing anything other than what Joan Sperry told her.'

'Audra Lady Mekins,' Alex said quietly. 'That's who Beverly Irving is. It's so strange.'

'Only there isn't a Sir Hillary Mekins, surgeon, or a Winston Mekins, son of Sir Hillary and Lady Mekins,' Dan said. 'Beverly fabricated the whole thing. She made sure she met and became friends with Esme because she wanted to stay close to Bob Hill and keep an eye on you and Lily.'

'Why?' Alex murmured.

'Because she was afraid you and Lily would link up with Bob and the life she had invented for herself would blow up in her face. What she had no way of expecting was Esme's convoluted life – what it would become. And the more she tried to keep the Hills away from you, the more you became entangled with them. I almost feel sorry for her. But not quite. She didn't kill anyone, or do any real harm but accept Esme's help and then kidnap Gladys for an hour or two to frighten her. Audra did carry on threatening Gladys and she frightened Lily, but, left to her own devices, I don't think she would ever have hurt anyone. Her sin was wanting you as her own child so badly she lost all objectivity. Then anger and frustration took over. She couldn't believe her very clever manipulations didn't work.'

'I'd like to talk to her,' Alex said. 'She tried to stop Esme in that pool.'

'Could we talk to her?' Tony asked. 'If there's any chance of saving her from her own behavior, someone has to reach out, don't you think?'

Dan put his hands on his thighs and pressed himself to stand. 'You're generous people. I fell in love with Folly and the whole area because of the people.' Briefly, he rested his eyes on Alex and she felt his longing. Sometimes what wasn't to be could be painful. 'I'll have someone come and let you know when you can see Audra. If she wants to see you.' He started to leave but turned back. 'You do realize it was Grant Hill who really alerted us?'

Alex shook her head, no.

'He did. We were already on our way to Knighton or we might not have made it. We'd had a contact from LeJuan who had tried to reach you, Alex. That wasn't long after Tony phoned me. Hugh Rhys told LeJuan where you'd gone and he wouldn't set it aside, had one of his famous intuitions. But then Grant phoned and said he thought his mother was going over the top and he was afraid of what would happen next. That clinched it. The ambulance was called just in case. Good thing because we needed it.'

'Poor man,' Alex said. 'And poor Bob. They have terrible times ahead and Grant will have to deal with wondering if he should have blown the whistle on his mother – which he should. He did the right thing.'

'A personal question for you,' Tony said when they were alone again. 'Would you consider living with me permanently? We know we don't need two houses. We like one another. I think we love one another. But I'm not pushing too far. I'll settle for shared groceries as a start.'

She stood up and pulled him to his feet. 'Did you make that list?'

'No. Did you?'

'No, but I intend to. After we decide which house we're going to sell. Is that enough to make you happy?'

He wrinkled his nose but broke into a grin. 'You can choose the house. How's that for showing how reasonable I am?'

'Tony, I already know that. We'll work it out together. Is it time for us to stop getting involved in . . . well, you know what I'm saying?'

'I'd like to say, yes, but I don't have a crystal ball.'

Dan O'Reilly came back into the room without knocking. 'Sorry to interrupt.' He looked at the floor. 'Beverly, or Audra, told us she's sorry she saved you and she should have found a way to punish Lily for being ungrateful. Audra said she tried to do her best for both of you but you didn't understand that – or didn't want to understand it. She said you need to forget about her because she won't be any trouble to you again.'

Alex's eyes stung. 'OK,' she said quietly. 'That's probably for the best. You can't heal some things.'